Intrigue & Infamy

A Victorian Crime Thriller

Carol Hedges

Little G Books

This edition by Little G Books (September 2019)

For Avalyn & Edward

About the Author

Carol Hedges is the successful British author of 17 books for teenagers and adults. Her writing has received much critical acclaim, and her novel Jigsaw was shortlisted for the Angus Book Award and longlisted for the Carnegie Medal.

Carol was born in Hertfordshire, and after university, where she gained a BA (Hons.) in English Literature & Archaeology, she trained as a children's librarian. She worked for the London Borough of Camden for many years subsequently re-training as a secondary school teacher when her daughter was born.

The Victorian Detectives series

Diamonds & Dust
Honour & Obey
Death & Dominion
Rack & Ruin
Wonders & Wickedness
Fear & Phantoms

Acknowledgments

Many thanks to Gina Dickerson, of RoseWolf Design, for another superb cover, and to my two patient editors.

I also acknowledge my debt to all those amazing Victorian novelists for lighting the path through the fog with their genius. Unworthily, but optimistically, I follow in their footsteps.

Intrigue & Infamy

A Victorian Crime Thriller

'Midway upon the journey of my life
I found myself in a dark forest,
For the straight path had been lost.'
Dante, Inferno, Canto 1.

'Do not associate with the crowd of pimps, avoid dice
gambling, the theatre and the tavern, actors, jesters,
smooth-skinned lads, moors, flatterers, pretty-boys,
effeminates, paederasts, quacks, sorceresses, night-
wonderers, and magicians. If you do not want to dwell with
evil-livers, do not live in London.'
Richard of Devizes, C12th.

London, 1866. A balmy summer night in July and, on the surface, all seems well. The Season is coming to its climactic end, and across town, mamas and papas are breathing sighs of relief in the knowledge that their daughter has hooked an eligible beau, meaning that the vast sums of money expended in clothes, jewels, renting a property in the fashionable quarter and hiring a pretty little horse for her to ride through the Park has paid off.

Others are counting their profits also. Many small businesses have done well from supplying the necessary accoutrements needed for a successful Season: furniture makers, purveyors of fine victuals, carriage-makers, landlords and especially the numerous tailors and dressmakers, who have slaved away long into the night to provide the elegant gowns and suits worn by the glamorous elite, as they pursue their hedonistic few months of balls and partner-hunting.

None more deservedly so than the bespoke tailoring business of Solomon Halevi & Son, located in Soho, but known by reputation throughout the whole of the metropolis, for a Halevi suit is the unspoken mark of a man of means and exquisite taste.

Look more closely.

Here is the shop itself, shuttered up, though the small flickering light of a candle can be glimpsed blossoming somewhere deep in its recesses. Suddenly, there is the splintering sound of a door being kicked open, followed by a silence. A short while later, wisps of smoke begin curling out into the street. Then tongues of flames lick hungrily at the window frames. A few passing night idlers pause and stare curiously.

Finally, with a mighty roar, the conflagration takes hold. The window glass shatters, breaking the wooden shutters and giving a few bold opportunists the chance to grab the elegant suits displayed therein, and bear them off into the night. Someone with slightly more altruism goes to alert the fire service.

A night constable appears on the scene, blowing his whistle to summon aid. He tries to enter the shop but is beaten back by the flames. Meanwhile, a bucket chain has formed, made up of local residents and shop owners desperate to stop the conflagration from spreading to their properties.

As the cry of 'Fire! Fire!' echoes round the neighbourhood, the sound of space-devouring hooves and the rattle of wheels on cobbles presages the arrival of the fire engine. Scarlet and gold in the gaslight, burnished and glistening, it is greeted with cheers by the crowd of onlookers, who have emerged from a hundred foul lanes and festering tenements, to dance and gibber on the pavement in their excitement.

By the time Detective Sergeant Jack Cully of the Metropolitan Police (Detective Division) arrives upon the scene in the early hours of the morning, accompanied by a couple of Scotland Yard officers, the shop and the workrooms above it have been reduced to a scorched and blistering wreck. Acrid smoke fills the air, while heat still pulses from the ruined building.

A small group of concerned citizens still remains on the pavement, awaiting any interesting developments and the possible appearance of blanket-covered bodies. Another group of garment-workers stands slightly apart from the disaster tourists, exuding bewilderment. Two female piece-workers have put down their bundles of cuffs and collars and are openly sobbing.

"What is going on?" Cully asks the young constable on guard.

"Shop fire, sir. Couldn't say how it started, no actual witnesses." He pauses, then lowers his voice, "There is something else, sir. Can you follow me?"

Cully can tell by the young constable's face that he is not going to like what is coming next. He follows him down the side alley, picking his way cautiously over pieces of burned wood and shards of broken glass.

Reaching the rear of the shop, he sees the door is ajar. Cully peers cautiously into the small burnt-out back room. A charred body lies on the floor just by the open door.

"Ah," Cully says quietly. "Not just a shop fire, then. Do we know who it might be?"

"I haven't inquired, sir. I was waiting for you to arrive."

Jack Cully steps over the threshold and stares at the scene, trying to capture what is before him. First impressions were always important. A dead body was the end of a chain of events, frequently long and complicated. Sometimes it was possible to get an idea of that chain right from the start.

He takes out his notebook and writes swiftly, noting the time of day, the position and state of the body, and its surroundings. He notes that there is a safe in one corner of the room; it appears to be still closed. He observes that the body lies on its back, arms raised in a protective gesture. Hopefully the man died before the flames engulfed the building. Either way, he tries not to imagine what the final horrific moments must've been like.

After filling two pages with notes, he takes a careful look around, checking that he hasn't missed anything important, then closes his notebook. "Right. Let's talk to the workers. See if any of them can shed light on who this might be."

****

At about the same time as Detective Sergeant Cully is beginning his enquiries, a young man in a caped travelling cloak descends the gangplank of a cross-channel steamer, recently arrived in Dover Harbour on a full tide.

Shouldering his bag, he stands on the quay, looking curiously all around him. He breathes in the sharp sea air, listens to the slap of water against timbers, the cries of gulls wheeling in the sky above his head. He takes a few minutes to readjust to the daylight, so bright and shiny after the cabin light that shivered and shuddered at him all night.

His companion on the voyage, a middle-aged priest with a small bird in a small cage, now bids him adieu and strides off in the direction of a group of other priestly-clad men, who greet him with stiff bows and formal smiles, before conveying him swiftly away, presumably to some monastic enclave.

The young man's name is Angelo Giacomo Bellini, and he has come to England to find adventure and excitement. His past is ordinary; his future, he hopes, will be limitless. But until such time as his quest begins, he has two other important tasks to accomplish: first, he needs to source somewhere to breakfast, and then ascertain the time of the next London coach.

An hour later, replete with eggs, muffin, toast and preserves, the young man pays his fare and steps aboard the coach. Several passengers eye him askance: his travelling attire and accent mark him out as a foreigner, but he pretends not to notice.

The coachman climbs onto the box, gathers up the reins, and flicks his whip over the backs of the horses. The coach jolts and sways out of the inn yard. The young man sits back, a smile of satisfaction upon his face. Every step is taking him further away from his previous life and towards the new one.

Maybe the breakfast didn't live up to his expectations (which were pretty low, given what he'd been told about English cuisine), but he is sure that London, the greatest city on earth, will amply fulfil all his hopes and dreams, once he gets there.

****

Meanwhile, Detective Sergeant Jack Cully has commandeered an upstairs room at a local public house to use as a discreet place to interview Solomon Halevi's workers, who have arrived at their place of work to discover there was no work and no place. After a quick consultation with his men, it has been decided not to mention what lies in the back room until more is known of the circumstances surrounding the fire.

Cully begins with the two young female piece-workers, Miss Adelina Chiappa and Miss Florina Sabini, because they are the most visibly distressed. Questioning them first will allow them to be on their way soonest.

Cully motions them to a bench, where they sit huddled together like two orphan fledglings in a storm. Miss Sabini bites her lower lip and picks compulsively at her hands. Her companion stares straight ahead, her eyes wide with horror and dismay.

"Ladies, what can you tell me about working for Mr Halevi," Cully says gently.

There is a long pause. The two young women frown, shake their heads, start to speak, stop, sigh, start again. At last Miss Sabini ventures that they have only been sewing collars and cuffs for a couple of weeks, so they really can't say.

"We took on the extra sewing as we've been trying to save a little money for when winter comes and the big stores don't want piece-workers anymore. He was orlright. Paid us on delivery."

"But we ain't going to get paid now, are we?" Miss Chiappa murmurs sadly, indicating the baskets of sewing. "Two night's work, all for nothing."

Jack Cully, whose wife Emily once worked as a sweated seamstress for a big department store on long hours and minimum pay, sympathises with their plight. Both young women have the pale, unhealthy complexions and round shoulders that bespeak long hours stuck inside, sewing by candlelight.

"Where is Mr Halevi?" Miss Sabini asks. "Maybe we can get some of our money, at least."

Cully shakes his head. "We do not know where he is, at present."

But he is beginning to suspect that he does. There is a hideously burned body lying on the floor of a shop, and a suspicious absence of the shop owner. It does not take a genius to draw a link between the two.

****

The hopes and dreams of two distressed piece-workers couldn't be further from those of another young inhabitant of the great city, for whom such aspirations resemble brightly coloured bubbles floating down a sunlit stream. Her name is Miss Juliana Celestinia Rose Ferrers Silverton, only daughter of Mr Maldon Silverton, stockbroker, of Park Mansions, Park Lane.

Juliana has her own dear little phaeton with a pair of matching snow-white ponies. She has a generous allowance, which she spends mainly upon beads and bonbons, and ribbons for her small white lapdog Pootle. Her wardrobe shimmers with silk dresses, her dressing table is adorned with scent bottles and silver-backed brushes.

Juliana is seated at her dressing table. She wears a flattering rose-coloured peignoir that conveys a pleasing glow to her skin. At her elbow is a delicate porcelain cup of chocolate. Her personal maid Carruthers is brushing the blonde curls, teasing them into shape, while her mistress contemplates her smooth, clear-tinted porcelain complexion in the gilt mirror and practices lowering her beautiful long eyelashes in a suitably becoming fashion.

This is her world. It has been ever since she arrived back from the exclusive finishing establishment in Europe, where she acquired the *ton* and style that has enabled her to catch Harry Haddon, a man admired by every girl in London for his fine black horse, his refined figure, and his extravagant clothes.

And what a catch he is! Juliana sighs at her reflection. Six feet tall, with elegance imprinted on every lineament of his moustached face. He is young, handsome, with burnished boots, burnished spurs, burnished whiskers. He shines all over like a meteor, or a lobster that has been kept a little too long in a darkened room. And all this shiny magnificence is now hers to possess.

A light tap-tap on her bedroom door heralds the arrival of her mother, Mrs Doria Silverton. She glides silkily into the room, beaming with satisfaction.

"My darling girl! Last night was a complete triumph! And how cleverly you managed it!"

Juliana allows a brief smile to play at the corners of her rosebud lips. Truth be told, it took very little 'managing'. Men, she has discovered, are rather weak creatures, easily manipulated into doing what one requires of them. (She assumes that the same state of affairs will also apply once married.)

Her requirement was to be engaged by the end of the Season, for she had absolutely no intention of being touted desperately round the last few balls and parties like yesterday's cold mutton. Thus, she laid her plans carefully, wearing the most *killing* pale blue silk dress ~ a colour that only a fair-haired woman can really carry off, and the finest of her jewels.

She also made sure her nearest rival, Georgiana Worthington, was engaged in earnest conversation with one of her former beaux, leaving the field clear for her to inveigle the handsome young dandy into the conservatory on the pretext of desiring to see the orchids. The combination of a beautiful young woman, the heady scent of exotic blooms and several glasses of fine champagne did the rest.

"Your dear father is in his study, composing a suitable announcement for *The Times*, and for the various other newspapers, and periodicals," Juliana's Mama pauses. "Carruthers ~ you may go. Close the door on your way out."

The maid departs. Whereupon Doria Silverton pulls up one of the little gold painted chairs and places herself in it.

"Now, Juliana, I want you to tell me everything that passed between you both last night. Leave nothing out. It is a Mama's duty to make sure the proposal was done correctly. There must be no misunderstandings: we do not want a rerun of that unfortunate Rosamund Staines business, do we?"

A frisson of horror runs through Juliana's delicate frame. Rosamund had started the previous season as the universally acknowledged belle of her select group. Lively and vivacious, she had attracted many devoted gallants and suitors.

It was to one of them that she had plighted her troth ~ and then had to hastily un-plight it again when the truth emerged that he had a wife in Germany and was being sought by her family for desertion. As far as anyone knows, poor Rosamund is now a governess in some faraway barbaric location. Possibly Yorkshire.

So she takes a deep breath and relates, word for word, what took place in the conservatory with the young man, the moonlight and the orchids. When she has completed her narrative, her Mama smiles in a satisfied manner.

"Just as I hoped. Thank you, my dearest girl. I shall now go and instruct your father. Upon my return, we will begin to make plans. There is a great deal to do."

Juliana waits until her mama has left. Then she opens a drawer in her dressing table and pulls out some letter paper, an envelope, and the little tasselled gold pencil she used last night to fill in her dance card.

She writes at speed, signs the page with a flourish, and seals the envelope with her own personal seal. She will endeavour to slip the missive into a pillar box in the course of the day. Preferably when nobody is around to ask her what she is doing.

****

Meanwhile, Jack Cully dismisses the two young piece-workers, and moves on to the pattern cutters and pressers, who inform him that business had been hectic, but was beginning to tail off as the end of the London Season approached. They had all worked for the Halevis, father and son, for some time, moving from Moses & Sons, the famous rival.

From them Cully also learns that Mr Halevi lived above the shop, was unmarried, and came to London from Hamburg with his father, also a tailor. He had taken over the business recently, upon his father's sudden death from heart failure. Cully's suspicions about the identity of the blackened body are growing incrementally. Given that no incarnation of the owner has materialised.

His final interview is with a short middle-aged man with a swarthy complexion who identifies himself as the overseer of the sewing-room and general manager. His name, he tells the detective sergeant, is Oreste Idile, an Italian, and he has worked for Mr Halevi senior ever since he set up in business, first in the East End, then moving to this better location two years ago.

Father and son were fair men, Idile tells Cully. Neither tolerated shoddy workmanship, and soon sacked anybody whose quality of work fell below the high standards they demanded. Which was why any suit bearing the Halevi label carried such status, and could command top price in the clothing business. Even second-hand, a Halevi suit was still highly covetable.

"Did he have any enemies?" Cully asks, pencil poised over notebook.

His question provokes a long silence, during which Cully is treated to a searching stare that goes on slightly beyond the comfort zone.

"We are *foreigners*," the overseer says, spitting the word out as if it had a foul taste. "Moreover, we are also Jews. There are always enemies."

****

Detective Inspector Leo Stride sits behind his desk, stirring a cooling cup of bitter black coffee with a pencil. His thoughts are as dark as the brew set before him. Out there, in the real world, people are committing crimes and getting away with it.

They are lying, stealing, pickpocketing, cozening and cheating their fellow citizens. They are murdering them, and chopping them up, and throwing their bodies into the Thames.

And here he is, stuck behind a desk, unconnected to that world. Detective Inspector Stride is a long-standing officer, now reduced to an officer of long sitting. He was made for patrolling the highways and bye-ways of

London. He was made for proceeding, for pursuing the criminal fraternity (and occasional sorority) through the winding alleyways and tiny footstreets.

He was not made for dealing with mountains of paperwork. Yet that seems to be his role in life now. His desk is piled with reports, documents, folders and pieces of paper written in neat copperplate and headed: '*For your immediate attention*'.

Stride stares down at the green folder, that has once again found its way to the top of the pile. He has not seen it for a while, mainly because it had been deliberately placed at the bottom of the pile.

Yet miraculously, here it is once more. Stride views the folder rather like a guest who has not been invited to dinner, but turns up nevertheless, and then refuses to leave at the end of the evening. He has not invited the folder, it tells him nothing worth knowing, but now, he cannot think of a way of getting rid of it.

Wearily, he opens the folder, noting that yet another sheet of paper has been added. The folder originally described the theft of six pigs from a backyard. Over the course of the summer, the thefts of various other animals have also found their way into the folder, so that currently, it resembles a whole farmyard of pilfered livestock.

Stride checks the time. It is a long way from lunch. He places the green folder back at the bottom of the pile and picks up what is now the new top file. It is from one of the night constables, for whom spelling and punctuation are optional extras.

Pencil in hand, he skims through the hastily written, unparagraphed report, occasionally uttering mild expletives and circling bits that he cannot read or is unable to tolerate.

There is a knock at the door.

Stride glances up, relief plastered all over his face. Detective Inspector Lachlan Greig enters, looking thoughtful.

"I've just learned something rather unusual from one of my sources," he says.

"A reliable source?"

"He's never been wrong before." Greig gets out his notebook. "He tells me that there is a small group targeting the shops and businesses of foreigners living in the city. They want to get rid of all immigrants, whom they believe are driving down wages, occupying houses that should by rights be rented to native Londoners, and taking their jobs away."

Stride rolls his eyes ceiling-wards. "Oh, not this again? Surely you're not going to take it seriously? Some lunatic has got up a grievance and found a few misguided friends to share it with. We've passed this way before: remember the red paint outrages? The Bethel Brethren? It's a similar group."

A frown gathers between Lachlan Greig's eyebrows. "Mebbe I'd have agreed with you, but have you glanced at the newspapers recently?" he remarks in his lilting Scottish accent.

Stride gestures helplessly towards the over-flowing desk.

"You think I have time to waste reading their spewings?"

In response, Greig produces a list from his pocket. He unfolds it and reads: "This is from *The Inquirer* under a headline that says: **London Festers in the Fist of Anti-Foreign Feelings!** The article goes on to list examples: *July 2nd: the windows of a French confectioners are broken & the words 'filthy foreigners' is written on the door. July 9th: ditto a grocery specialising in foreign goods.* Now, I know these events could be seen as random acts of vandalism, or the effects of a hot summer, but put together with what my informant says, perhaps there is a link? Should we investigate d'you think?"

Stride shakes his head. "Lachlan, you have not been in this city as long as I have. Every summer we get this. Heat and alcohol – a deadly combination. Men get drunk; fights break out; windows get smashed. There are still some parts of the city where old wooden buildings exist, so …"

Greig holds up a hand. "The newspapers are beginning to put two and two together."

"And make of it five, I don't doubt," Stride scoffs.

"*The Inquirer* certainly thinks there is something in the wind."

Stride mutters something impolite about wind and Richard Dandy, *The Inquirer's* chief reporter, and his nemesis.

"Nevertheless …" Greig persists.

Stride waves him away.

"Has anybody died? No. It's just the overheated mind of the popular press trying to get sales. I do not intend to take this seriously. And nor should you. By the time we get the first autumn fog, it will all have faded away. You'll see. Now, if you would excuse me, I have paperwork to get on with. As usual."

Detective Inspector Stride starts digging around in one of the piles of reports, as if urgently seeking something. Greig observes him for a few seconds, then shrugs and walks away.

It is a pivotal moment. Though neither man realises it.

****

Jack Cully is returning to Scotland Yard, methodically processing what he has seen. A well-reputed businessman has his premises burned to the ground while he is still inside. The safe was not opened, so robbery could not be the primary purpose. What was the motive, then? The words of the overseer keep ringing in his ear. He wishes they didn't.

Cully knows very little about the Jews who inhabit the same city as his family, other than they prefer to keep themselves to themselves. Of course, he has encountered other members of the community in the course of his job, the men black-hatted and black gaberdine garbed, as they go quietly around plying their trade in second-hand clothes.

Once, in hot pursuit of a pickpocket, he had passed one of their synagogues and heard, drifting out on the summer air through an open window, a man's voice raised in melancholic chanting in a language that was totally alien. It had sent a shiver down his spine at the time.

As he returns to Scotland Yard, letting his feet do the walking, his mind is free to do the thinking. He remembers how, as he and the overseer watched two constables carefully lift the blackened corpse and place it on a stretcher, the overseer suddenly noticed a ring on one of the fingers, and was able to confirm Cully's suspicions that this was indeed the body of young Master Halevi.

Cully recalls following the constables as they carried the stretcher to the police van. The overseer and the staff had stood at the top of the alleyway, like a guard of honour silently waiting. As the body passed them, each man had grasped the edge of his collar and torn it. Before he left, he told the manager that the body would be taken to the police morgue for examination. He was informed, in return, that it must be returned as soon as possible, so that the appropriate mourning rituals could take place.

Cully has decided not to mention that, given the circumstances in which the body was discovered, there will have to be a coroner's inquest. He is going to push that one further up the food chain.

****

There is a certain house close by the River Thames. It is rich with old timbers, a gravelled walk, fruit trees and walls bordered with espaliers. There is a fishpond, great stacks of chimneys, mullioned windows of various sizes, and pointed gables.

The huge front door is carved from heavy oak and studded with square iron nails. It has an ornate lions-head knocker and a clanging bell. It is the sort of house that is crying out for the word 'Hall' to feature somewhere in its name ~ and indeed it does, being known in the neighbourhood as Haddon Hall, the familial seat of Sir Nicholas Haddon, former MP, now head of a large city finance and insurance company.

We join Sir Nicholas upon the terrace, overlooking the wide expanse of lawn leading down to the lake. He has finished his breakfast and is now enjoying a cigar. Seated opposite is his wife, Lady Marie Haddon, for much to the surprise of his contemporaries, Sir Nicholas, a grey-haired, chisel-chinned, good-looking widower in his early fifties, vigorous and in robust health, remarried a few years ago.

His wife is a much younger woman. Even more of a surprise (though it is not known to those in his intimate circle), Lady Marie Haddon was not born in this country. In fact, her birth and early life are a bit of a mystery. Also not known to those who encounter her socially, is that before marrying Sir Nicholas, she used to be a governess.

Such things happen in novels. They can also happen in real life. People meet in seemingly random ways. They fall in love. They marry. And here they both are, she toying with her coffee cup, he puffing smoke from behind a copy of the morning paper. Birds sing merrily in the shaded grove, and carp plash in the still water. A peacock calls stridently from somewhere in the distance.

Eventually, she breaks the silence. "About little Danny ..."

Sir Nicholas lowers the newspaper.

"The tutor will be herein a couple of days. Are his rooms prepared? Also, the schoolroom?"

She bends her graceful head. Her brown eyes, soulful and appealing, glance up at him through her thick lashes. "Our boy seems so young ..."

Sir Nicholas gives a bark of laughter. "Nonsense! I was three when my father hired a tutor. Could recite Ovid by four. Spoke fluent German by six. Daniel's a bright little chap. If we want to get him into a top public school, then Oxford and then the Law, it's high time he set his shoulder to the wheel."

After all, Sir Nicholas Haddon thinks (though he doesn't speak his thoughts aloud), he doesn't want him following the same path as his older stepbrother. Student *manqué*, army refusenik, wastrel, feckless and footloose, happy to lounge around the city, smoking Turkish cigars and drinking sherry-wine.

"I had thought," his wife ventures hesitantly, "that I might teach him myself. At least until Christmas. It is what I am trained to do."

Sir Nicholas' brows meet in a frown of disapproval. "That was before you married me, my dear. And you have only ever taught girls. I don't think embroidery and water-colours will suit. The education of a boy is an entirely different matter. It is a serious business, for he must be prepared to meet the world head-on. No, it won't do, I am afraid. Daniel shall have a man tutor, until he is ready to go to prep school. It is already arranged. He comes highly recommended."

"I'm sure you know best."

The words are spoken with an acquiescence belied by the fiercely clenched hands beneath the snowy tablecloth.

Sir Nicholas rises, tossing the newspaper carelessly onto the breakfast table.

"In this matter I do, my dear," he says, kissing the top of her head. "And now I must hasten away. The City waits for no one. I shall be back for dinner, as usual."

He goes in through the French windows, humming happily under his breath. He does not ask his wife what she has planned. Just as well, for she has nothing planned. Her old life is a foreign country, and in her new life, in another country just as foreign, she has made no friends.

Although her origins have been studiously kept secret, the women in her husband's circle seem to realise instinctively there is something not quite *comme il faut* about her. She isn't one of them. Nobody has said, but in this set, power comes in not saying, but knowing. And they know she is not top drawer, like themselves, and draw back from her.

This is the reason she is never solicited, in little notes scribbled on pressed paper, to *'run up to Town to do a bit of shopping, with tea and ices at Gunters.'* Her advice is not sought upon the trimming of a bonnet, the lunch menu, or the hiring of a lady's maid. Even when she presented Sir Nicholas with a son, the birth announcement was not followed by a tidal wave of congratulations and little smocked baby dresses.

Lady Marie sits on, hands folded in her lap, waiting for the housemaid to appear and clear away the breakfast things. She thinks about the small boy in his nursery,

17

eating his bowl of bread and milk. Soon he will come running to find her, and when he does, he will scramble onto her lap, wind his chubby arms around her neck and rumple her silk dress.

From tomorrow however, all this will cease. Her little son will no longer be hers to cuddle and spoil. He will be at the beck and call of a timetable. His life will be passed within the walls of the newly appointed schoolroom, with a stranger who will eventually gain more influence upon him than his own mother.

He will have gone from her loving womanly hands into the world of men. The future is a cage closing around him. Lady Marie Haddon reminds herself that she must keep up the appearance of being happy. She was happy once upon a time. Happy and in love. Before life, the great trap, snapped her in its jaws.

She rises. Her breath is a mere zephyr on the summer air. It is time to go to her dressing-room and prepare for the day. She enters the stately panelled garden room. Her eye no longer sees the two glorious Gainsboroughs, all pearly white and shimmering, that hang on the opposite wall.

Once, the fair clouded head of a girl by Romney, that hangs above the hearth, would have drawn her gaze (the pictures in the house are all famous). Some have been associated with the Haddon family for generations.

Now, she passes through the room with its ornate gilded furniture and Turkish carpets, the soft lamps, the bowls of sweet-scented flowers, as if it were all so much scenery. It no longer fills her with that sense of wonder.

The wretchedness of her thoughts has communicated itself to every object about her, and all outer things take their colour from that inner life that holds its slow course of secret anguish in her breast.

Yes, she is here, surrounded by these things. Surrounded by all that rank and wealth and fashion bestow. A fine house, equipage and expensive jewels. Yet she feels the draught bitter, even though the goblet that holds it is of gold.

The idea comes to her that she has escaped the dull slavery of the schoolroom for the equally dull slavery of a captive wife, albeit a rich one. Just as in the former case, there is nothing she can do but endure.

****

Time moves on. It knows no better. The noon bells of the City chime in loud dissonant chorus, waking the late risers from their slumbers. Here indeed is one such, who opens bleary eyes upon a world that seems vaguely and indefinably different to that of yesterday morning, though how and why, he can't decide as yet.

A quick sideways glance elicits that he slept alone. So that wasn't the problem, then. He sits up, yawns, stretches, and calls for his shaving water. A few seconds later his man appears, bearing clean towels, a bowl and his razor. He greets his master, receiving a grunted reply.

"May I be the first to congratulate you, sir," the servant says, placing the bowl on a stand and lathering up the shaving brush.

The young man waits patiently for outlying parts of his brain to call in with relevant information.

"Aww. Yers. Ah. 'member it now. How did you know?"

The manservant forebears to explain the speed whereby any private event becomes public knowledge amongst the servant community.

"I expect your father will be delighted, sir. She is, indeed, a charming young lady, if I may be so bold as to offer an opinion upon the matter."

"Offer away, old man," the engaged one says, yawning and lumbering out of bed. He seats himself in front of his dressing-mirror. While the valet applies lather, then razor and hot towels, Harry Haddon plays back such details as his hungover brain can recall.

There was champagne. And dancing and moonlight, and Juliana looked damn bewitching in that blue dress. So, he had finally done the deed! He has little recollection of the actual words, but it obviously worked.

Mind, he'd been thinking about it for a while. She was the prettiest girl he'd ever set eyes on. They'd shared some jolly times together over the past few months. Balls and parties and river picnics. And the Pater kept dropping hints about getting a job and settling down.

The Pater. Ah. Better jog on over to Lombard Street and 'fess up to the engagement. And he needed to ask the Pater for the family ring. Girls were fussy about that sort of thing. So, Harry runs a hand over his barbered face, splashes himself with cologne, and allows his servant to help him into freshly laundered linen.

Then, having drunk his morning coffee and consumed a fresh roll, he dons his coat, places his top hat at a jaunty angle and sets off. Swinging his cane, Harry strolls along the Strand, the independent heir, admiring his reflection in the plate-glass shop windows. He is wearing a new pair of yellow leather pigskin gloves that fit him perfectly and his pointed boots are highly polished.

He is the picture of a fashionable young buck about town. A *flâneur*. He is aware of the subtle sideways glances of passing women, but he tells himself he has no time for such fa-daddling now. He is an engaged man.

Reaching his father's place of business, Harry greets the doorman, ambles across the marbled foyer and hails one of the stooped clerks, who climbs reluctantly down from his high wooden stool and goes to fetch Sir Nicholas.

While he waits for his father to appear from the inner recesses, Harry lights up a cigar, and stares out of a window. He wonders how the clerks can bear to sit all day scratch-scratching away. It is not the sort of life he'd ever envisage for himself.

After a short interval, the door at the far end of the atrium opens, and Haddon senior emerges. The expression upon his face is weary, bordering upon exasperated. Harry ignores it, greeting him jovially.

"What ho, Pater!" he sings out, "Got a bit of good news for you: Engaged to a topping girl. Popped the old Q last night. Absolute stunner. You're going to love her."

Sir Nicholas eyes his son and heir bleakly.

"Really? I suppose congratulations are in order, then. Though some prior indication of your intentions would have been welcome, not to say appropriate. I assume I can therefore guess the reason you have honoured me with a visit?"

"Well, a girl expects a jolly old ring, Pater."

With a sigh, his father leads the way to his inner sanctum, where he takes a small brass key off his watch-chain and unlocks a drawer in his desk from which he takes out a rather battered maroon leather ring box.

He places it on the desk between them.

"Here it is then. The Haddon Diamond. Do you think you can be entrusted not to lose it in transit, I wonder?"

"Of course I won't, Pater. Family heirloom and all that."

Harry stubs out his cigar, removes his top hat and then twirls the brim between his hands, a gesture reminiscent of his time at Eton when he was up before the headmaster for some misdemeanour.

His father regards him warily. Behind his facial expression lurks the memory of other entanglements and less salubrious relationships from which he has had to extract Harry. Usually by paying the woman a considerable sum to keep her mouth shut.

"So, tell me about the young lady. What are her people?"

"Her name is Juliana Silverton and she is dashed pretty. Think her pa sells stocks and bonds," Harry says hesitantly, because if you are a young man in love, asking about the occupation of your beloved's father is not top of your to-do list.

"I see. And how exactly are you intending to live once you are married? I can't imagine your future wife will want to share bachelor quarters off the Strand. I expect she will desire to eat and have a proper roof over her head. Possibly a carriage.

"You will need to find an occupation of some sort, because if your allowance doesn't cover your lavish lifestyle now, it certainly won't cover your future expenses. Besides, you cannot idle away your time once you have marital obligations. It is not acceptable. You must find a job that pays a decent salary. Have you had any thoughts on the matter?"

Harry flinches. He hates it when the Pater uses that cold sarcastic voice; it makes something inside him fold up, like a damp umbrella.

"I … I … am giving it a lot of thought," he replies earnestly, twirling his hat even faster. "A lot," he repeats. "Maybe I could come and work here?"

The expression on his father's face is not that of someone who has unexpectedly been made an offer he can't refuse.

"Here? Oh no. I think not. What on earth would you DO?"

"Err … well, you know, Pater, whatever it is you do here. Dunno what it is, but damn me, I'm sure I could give it a go. What do you say?"

Sir Nicholas' mind drifts back to a certain summer day, a holiday by the Mediterranean Sea, and a small bold boy dressed in a sailor suit, with golden hair like liquid sunshine who scrambled over some rocks out of sheer bravado, and then lost his footing, falling into the sea below, from which his body was never recovered.

His tragic death left Harry, then barely a toddler, as sole son and heir. But now he has another son, he reminds himself. It is always good to have a spare. Especially when the current heir is as inadequate as Harry.

"Perhaps you could favour me with the address of your future father-in-law," he says wearily, closing his eyes to indicate that the conversation is now ended. "We have matters to discuss."

"Yes, rather, Pater. Got it right here … somewhere," Harry fumbles in a pocket of his gaudy silk waistcoat until he finds a small piece of crumpled paper upon which his beloved has carefully written the name and address of her father, being slightly more *au fait* with how these matters are managed than her affianced.

Sir Nicholas glances briefly at the name and address and nods curtly. He selects a quill from the pot on the desk, and draws a piece of paper towards him.

Harry watches him write. He heaves a sigh of relief. That went better than expected, given the level of his expectations was pretty low to begin with. At least he wasn't given a wigging. Eventually, Sir Nicholas glances up from the page.

"I am sorry ~ was there something else you wished to discuss with me?"

Harry takes the hint. Clapping his hat on, he shoves the ring box into an inner pocket and is shown out by an usher. Gaining the street, he hauls out his pocket watch. Time to meet up with some fellows at his club and break the happy news of his forthcoming nuptials.

With a bit of luck, they should stand him a few celebratory bumpers. Harry Haddon sets his hat at a jaunty angle, swings his silver-topped walking cane and ambles off.

****

There should be some formulaic language for this, Jack Cully thinks. A word that describes the smell of this white-tiled room: chemical and sharp, yet that fails to obliterate another more feral odour.

At least it is cooler in here than outside. He watches Robertson, the dour police mortuary surgeon, who is carefully probing the grisly remains of young Mr Halevi with a set of scalpels.

"Your presence is a little premature, detective sergeant, if I may remark. I have barely begun to examine the body. Why all the undue haste, may I enquire?"

Cully explains that the man was Jewish, and that his religion demands his body should be buried as quickly as possible in consecrated grounds, with the proper Jewish rites and observances.

"Ah yes, the funeral habits and customs of our foreign brethren," Robertson murmurs, his eyes gleaming. "Ever a source of interest. Did you know, for instance, that in Ancient Egypt, it was customary to extract the brain through the nasal cavities prior to embalming the body?"

Cully winces.

"I believe there are also some Hindoo sects in India whereby the widow of the deceased is actually burned alive on the funeral pyre that consumes the body of her husband. Not a practice we would like to encourage in this country, eh?"

Cully smiles cautiously. Robertson needs very little encouragement to share gruesome and obscure details about post and pre-mortem cases.

"And so, let us progress to our current body. Or what is left of it. Out of interest, did you know that the original Greek word *autopsy* means to see with one's own eyes?"

"I thought …"

The police surgeon raises a warning forefinger.

"I believe I am the expert here," he says. "Unless, of course, you have recently qualified as a surgeon? Yes? Ah, you have not? Then shall I continue?"

Cully clamps his lips together firmly.

The police surgeon rocks backwards and forwards on his heels a couple of times. He clears his throat. "Now, detective sergeant, this may be difficult for you to follow *verbatim*, as it were, but if, as you say, the body of this unfortunate man has to be released for religious reasons, I shall endeavour to present my assessment as precisely as I am able, given the limited time I have had to examine the body. I will favour you with a written report in due course. It is a shame that Detective Inspector Stride cannot be present. I know just how much he appreciates discussing the finer points of anatomy."

The police surgeon's eyes gleam with malice. As far as Robertson is concerned, Stride's squeamish reluctance to engage with any aspect of the grisly business of dissection is a constant source of amusement.

Cully used to be amused too, until Stride confided, in a moment of rare intimacy, that every time he visited the police mortuary he felt afraid, as if he was seeing his own death approaching, and the morgue had become a crypt. *Media vita in morte sumus*, as Robertson frequently remarked.

"In the absence of our colleague, let us explore the various scenarios," Robertson continues. "Do we have here, in the body of this unfortunate man, burning during life, or after death? Let us consider the alternatives. In the case of the former, I would expect to find evidence of vesications or signs of inflammatory reaction. So, I take my scalpel and I remove a layer of the cuticle … here … and lo, I perceive nothing. Therefore, upon an initial examination, I might conclude that the burns are *post-mortem*."

"His business premises were burned down. They found his body in the rear office close to the outer door."

"Quite so. Quite so. Now, if you will permit me, I have a few further tests and examinations to make before I can complete my observations."

"When can the Jews collect the body?"

The police surgeon's mouth is a lipless slit of disapproval.

"These Jews may have their own religious beliefs, which are all very well in their way, I'm sure, but this is England, and their beliefs must give way to ours. I shall notify you when I have finished, and whether I think there should be a coroner's inquest held. Is that clearly understood?"

Cully returns to the main police station, where he discovers a hubbub in the front entrance. Men wearing black hats and long black gaberdines are gesticulating and shouting at the desk constable in accented English or gesticulating and shouting at each other in some language Cully does not understand.

Their actions are being eagerly watched by a couple of members of the fourth estate, who lounge in the doorway, notebooks in hands, pencils poised.

"Wotcher Cully," one of them sings out. "Got some Hebrews in then, I see. What's afoot?"

"Twelve inches last time I checked," Cully replies tartly. "And it's Detective Sergeant Cully to you, Mr Dandy."

The chief reporter of *The Inquirer* takes a drag on his cigar and shrugs in a do-I-care way.

"Look, there's clearly been a frack-arse somewhere. Don't get Hebrews turning up on Scotland Yard's doorstep without cause. Care to give us a couple of words?"

"Go. Away. Is that sufficient?"

Cully signals to the desk constable.

"I'll deal with this, Constable Higgs. Meanwhile, can you escort these … gentlemen off the premises? They are blocking the doorway and stopping law abiding citizens who may wish to report a crime from gaining access."

Cully gives Dandy Dick a withering glance, then turns his back on Fleet Street's finest. He takes a deep breath, squares his shoulders and pushes his way through to the front of the small but vociferous crowd.

"Gentlemen, please!" he says, raising his voice to 'stop thief' level.

Instantly, silence falls. Every eye turns to Cully with a look of expectation. Hoping that he can pull out the correct words from somewhere, Cully starts to explain the various procedures that have to be gone through whenever a dead body is brought into Scotland Yard.

When he has finished, the silence continues for a further few minutes. Then, an elderly man with an unmistakable air of quiet authority, steps forward. His long grey hair flows down either side of his head, mingling with his beard. He carries a staff ~ it cannot, in all accuracy, be called a walking-stick.

He bows in a graceful manner.

"I thank you for your very clear explanation, detective inspector. I am Mr Halevi's rabbi. We understand that there are official things that must be done. But we also have important spiritual matters to deal with.

"The body of Mr Halevi must be cleansed, and the proper mourning rituals begun. We have to sit *Shiva* and mourn his departure from this world, as our religious custom dictates. We cannot do this until he is returned to us. I entreat you to do a good deed and allow us to take him with us now."

It pains Cully to refuse, and the hostile expressions and mutterings of discontent from the group of Jews does not improve the atmosphere. Eventually they agree to wait until the examination has finished and, after leaving the rabbi's details at the desk, they depart.

Their departure coincides with Stride's arrival.

"Ah Jack, there you are! Why on earth are there a group of Jews standing out in the street talking to that hack Dandy Dick and one of his penny-a-liner friends?"

Cully groans. He might have guessed that the polluters of public perception wouldn't give up on a possible scoop quite so easily.

"It's a long story," he says. "Where have you been?"

Stride brightens. "Early luncheon. Sally and I have been putting the world to rights. It's always good to get out of the office and commune with one of London's honest and upstanding citizens."

"I see," Cully says. He has communed with various members of it since early morning and is about to commune with them quite a bit more before the day ends. Luncheon is an event unlikely to happen.

Besides, Sally, eponymous owner of Sally's Chop House, *('Wholesome hot food from recognised animal species only')* used to be a member of the criminal fraternity before allegedly seeing the error of his ways and turning to the food and drink trade. Thus 'honest' and 'upstanding' are not concepts that come readily to Cully's mind.

Stride gestures towards the entrance door.

"Right. You'd better come straight to my office and tell me what that was all about. I don't want to be wrong-footed by the evening newspapers," he says.

****

While Jack Cully is enlightening his superior officer, enlightenment of a different kind is also taking place. Miss Juliana Celestinia Rose Ferrers Silverton, the only daughter of Mr Maldon Silverton, stockbroker, of Park Mansions, Park Lane is holding court at one of the tables in the elegant conservatory of the Pantheon Bazaar.

Cockatoos and macaws flutter amidst the luxuriant flowers and foliage. Goldfish swim lazily to and fro under the glass roof and azure sky above. It is the perfect location for a group of young ladies to take tea and gossip. And that is exactly what Juliana, Alicia Downe-Edwards, Charlotte Rockingham and Fiona Blythe are currently doing.

The three bosom companions of the engaged one have been summoned to celebrate Juliana's victory in hooking one of London's most handsome bachelors. There is also another reason, but like the good strategist that she is, it is not going to be revealed quite yet.

"So many, many congratulations, dearest Juliana," declares Alicia of the raven curls, leaning forward to pat the engaged one upon a silken knee. "And you managed it all by yourself!"

"Indeed I did," Juliana agrees. "Mama wasn't able to meet his mama and 'arrange matters' as it were, because his mama is dead, and his step-mama don't come up to Town."

"Oh my! A step-mamma. Do you suppose she is wicked as well?" Fiona exclaims opening wide her cat-like eyes.

"I have not met her, so I cannot say. I believe she has a small child; thus, her absence from London society."

"Sir Nicholas Haddon," Charlotte says dreamily. "How wonderful it sounds. And one day, you will be Lady Haddon, won't you? Shall we have to curtsey and be very humble in your presence?"

Juliana smiles indulgently. Charlotte's father is an MP. Her mother can trace her family back to the Angevins. Besides Charlotte is currently sporting a sapphire and diamond engagement ring, given to her by her besotted suitor, whose family heads up one of the best-known City banking houses.

"I shall expect nothing less, Charley. And of course, you must come and stay at Haddon Hall ~ all of you must come."

"Is that where you'll live, Jules? I thought you'd prefer a nice little flat in Knightsbridge, or Bayswater? So handy for the shops and galleries. Besides, doesn't Sir Nicholas Haddon live there?" Fiona asks, head cocked to one side.

Juliana's eyes gleam. "He does. With Harry's step-mother. She is very much younger than his father, and there is a mystery about her. Nobody knows where she came from, or who her people are. But there she is, rattling around that great place. Naturally, I intend to make it my business to unmask her."

The young women lean forward eagerly.

"A *mysterious* stepmother! How *very* exciting," Charlotte says.

"It's exactly like Lady Audley's Secret!" Alicia murmurs, naming the scandalous novel that they have all been forbidden to read, but have devoured cover to cover nevertheless. "Watch out Jules, she may push you down the well ~ if there is a well."

"Pooh, she doesn't frighten me! *Au contraire*, I look forward shortly to making her acquaintance and beginning my investigation."

"You will let us know how you get on, won't you, dearest one?" Alicia drawls. She is the only married member of the group, therefore regarded with respect as a consequence. Indeed, she has already been prevailed upon, privately, to advise the others upon certain intimate matters of concern that the group cannot possibly discuss with their Mamas.

"I shall indeed. But as there are many spare bedrooms, you will be expected to help me in my endeavours. All of you," Juliana smiles brightly. "For I intend to hold the best dances and the finest banquets and river picnics ever seen. But first, I shall secure you all invitations to my engagement dinner. It is to be in two weeks' time, on Saturday, so make sure you have no other engagements. One expects Mama is already choosing the table linen and planning the menu!"

Significant smiles are exchanged. Mamas are both a blessing and a curse in the airy world of these society belles. Acquiescing to their exacting demands, while at the same time evading their strictures, has been part and parcel of all their maturing lives.

"Ah, how lucky you are in Harry Haddon," Alicia sighs. "So handsome and more important: so very rich. There is something about ten thousand pounds a year that takes off the ennui of a dull companion."

Juliana smiles. "I agree. With five hundred pounds a year, he would probably be execrable."

Fiona opens her eyes wide at this.

"Well, I would never marry a man with ten thousand pounds a year whom I would not have with five hundred."

The others laugh at her.

"Marry for love? How droll. Nobody in their senses ever thinks of such stuff now. Marry for love ~ it is the next thing to being mad," Charlotte says.

A silence stretches out between them. Nobody wishes to point out Fiona's lack of any prospective marriage partner. Rich man, poor man, no man at all. Juliana consults a tiny gold wristwatch and sighs gently.

"So late? Sadly, I must go. There is much to prepare, for Harry is coming for supper tonight, and he will be bringing the ring."

A collective 'aaah' of satisfaction runs around the group. The giving of the ring marks that important moment when a girl passes over the Rubicon that divides hopeless spinster from potentially married woman.

After the ring, the announcement in the Morning Post and other fashionable weekly papers seal the deal, and make the transfer complete as far as public cynosure is concerned.

Juliana rises gracefully. She lays a slender gloved hand upon Fiona's gauzy sleeve. "Perhaps you might like to walk with me to the carriage, dearest?"

The two make their fond farewells to the others. Arm in arm, they descend the magnificent staircase and, ignoring the fancy stalls, make their way out to Marlborough Street where Juliana's carriage awaits.

They embrace fondly. Then, her tiny slippered foot resting upon the bottom step, Juliana turns, and leans forward until her lips are close to her friend's shell-like ear.

"You received my letter, did you not?" she murmurs. "We both remember our time at Madame Auvergne's finishing school. Let us be of one mind that we will forget certain people and incidents associated with that time."

Fiona Blythe's slanted cat-like eyes close slightly. She breathes in sharply.

"Oh, as to all *that*, I had quite forgotten about it already, I assure you. You did not need to write and remind me."

Juliana gives her friend a long searching look. She seems satisfied with what she sees reflected in Fiona's returned gaze, which radiates innocence and amnesia in equal amounts. She smiles, climbs into the carriage and is driven swiftly away.

If, however, Juliana could have read the thoughts rising in her friend's mind as Fiona walks off in the opposite direction, having no carriage (or fiancé), she might not have lounged quite so easily in the comfortable butter-soft leather seat.

For Fiona Blythe, the engagement of Juliana Silverton means that she alone of their little set is unmatched at the end of the Season. There is also another reason for her discontent, which she cannot divulge to anybody, as it consists of certain embarrassing incidents involving her attempts to attract the man who has now plighted his troth to Juliana.

Suffice it to say that a single woman in possession of a good grievance must be in want of a suitable outlet. Fiona Blythe might act sweetly compliant in public, but beneath the surface she is actually a seething mass of malice and malcontent.

****

It is a rough and jolting journey to London from the port of Dover via the coach, but such is the choice of those who cannot afford to travel any other way. It is a step up from the marrowbone stage, reflects Angelo Bellini, as he watches the English countryside lurching past him backwards. And a seat on top is welcome in the hot weather.

At midday, the coach reaches Canterbury, and stops at a Merrie Olde Coaching Inn, where all the passengers descend. After eating a flaccid ham sandwich and some unpleasantly warm ale consumed in a taproom redolent of stale tobacco and armpits, the young man hoists himself back aboard for the next leg (or wheel) of the journey.

Twenty-four hours later, as the sun starts to dip below the horizon, the coach enters the outskirts of London. It descends Shooters Hill, crosses Blackheath and traverses the Old Kent Road at speed. The young man feasts his eyes upon church spires, rows and rows of small mean brick houses, with here and there some shops, their plate-glass windows full of rather strange merchandise.

The air smells of dust and heat and drains ~ smells he is used to from his home city. The people scurry about like ants, though not nearly as well-dressed and elegant as the Italian ants he is used to seeing.

Finally, the coach sets him down. He stands at the kerb, his bag at his feet, waiting for the adventure to begin. After a few minutes, he is approached by a thin elderly man clad in a jacket that has seen better days, but only from the side-lines, and a soft-brimmed hat. His prominent cheekbones, unkempt hair and restless mournful dark eyes bespeak a man for whom hardship is a way of life.

The two eye each other speculatively. Eventually, the approacher speaks, his heavily accented voice marking him out instantly as of foreign extraction.

"You are the young man who is expected?"

The young man indicates that his presumption is correct.

"You follow me, if you please."

The young man shoulders his bag and trails after the elderly one, pausing every now and then to stare into a shop window, or eye a pretty girl in her summer bonnet. Eventually he finds himself outside a tall run-down lodging house in Exmouth Street. A sign in the cloudy window proclaims *'Rooms to let. No Irish.'* The man halts and gestures towards the front door.

"You are to knock," he says, and before the traveller can thank him, he is gone, melting away into the thronging crowd of pedestrians.

The youthful traveller knocks. There is a pause, then footsteps are heard shuffling along a corridor on the other side of the door. A key is turned, and the door opens a miniscule crack, to reveal another elderly man, his high domed forehead surrounded by wild wispy white hair. A pair of shrewd black eyes under thick beetle eyebrows regard the young man thoughtfully.

"You are late, young man."

The young man makes the universal gesture for maybe-you-are-right-but-what can-I-do-about-it? *"Mi scusi.* One of the coach horses shed a shoe. But I'm here now and I bring letters from home. And money and greetings from your many friends and admirers in Italy."

The man grunts. The door is opened wider, and the young man steps over the threshold, breathing in an aroma of Swiss cigars.

"Come. Supper is waiting in the back kitchen. A simple meal, I'm afraid. We do not live like kings and princes here in London. Tomorrow, you will set out for the place of employment I have secured for you. It is a good place and you will have many opportunities to learn all about the English and their ways."

The young man drops his bag in the hallway. In the kitchen he sees a platter of bread, sausage and olives set out on a wooden table, the table top much scored with knife marks. There is a small saucer of olive oil for dipping the bread. A squat elderly woman dressed in black, her hair hidden under an indoor cap with old-fashioned lappets, smiles a toothless greeting.

"*Veni, veni, signor. Mangere,*" she says, pulling out a chair.

"This is Ysabella. She looks after me. Her husband was one of the dear comrades who fought by my side in the revolution."

The old man sighs. He strokes his white beard, his expression clouding.

"It is my honour to serve such a great man," the old woman says, standing as tall as her shortness allows.

While the young traveller eats his supper (so much tastier than the insipid English fare he has sampled so far), his host outlines the arrangements.

"You are about to enter an English upper-class family as tutor to their young son. Your duties are not onerous and well within your intellectual capabilities. While you are there, you should take every opportunity to study the way of life of these people.

"Discover how they think; learn how they see the world. In particular, keep careful notes of who visits the house, and any conversations they have that might be useful to our cause. Your employer was once a member of the English parliament; he has many friends who are still members of parliament. Make notes."

"I understand you perfectly."

The old man's brows meet in a frown.

"Above all things: do not fall for the so-called 'charm' of these English. They are perfidious: they will smile to your face and shake a big stick behind your back. Remember you are an outsider, a foreigner. Because if you forget, they will remind you.

"You can never be one of them, so do not try. Keep your eyes on the ground and your ears open. See them as specimens in a laboratory, to be studied with a detached interest. Probe them, dissect them, but do not attempt to join them."

The young man scrapes up the last delicious drop of olive oil with the remnant of his bread.

"I shall bear everything you have said in mind."

"See that you do. I shall expect regular reports. Make sure you send your letters on certain specified days only. I have a suspicion that the Post Office is opening and inspecting my correspondence."

The older man rises and ushers the young man into a small dismal parlour crammed floor to ceiling with piles of books and manuscripts.

"Tonight, you sleep on the floor here. Tomorrow, you will no doubt find a softer pillow to lay your head. I shall leave you to unpack and settle yourself. Good night, grandson. We are all expecting great things of you. Do not disappoint us."

****

There is no disappointment expected or felt in the elegantly furnished bedroom of Miss Juliana Celestinia Rose Ferrers Silverton. Absolutely none. Quite the contrary, in fact.

The fair Juliana is at her evening toilette, patting her creamy skin with rose water while her maid unpins and brushes out her hair. On the dressing table, within easy reach of her rosy fingertips, is a rather battered ring box. Inside the ring box is the Haddon Diamond.

Juliana exhales the gentlest zephyr of a sigh, and a few tiny worry lines surface upon her alabaster brow. Truth be told, she does not *like* the old-fashioned cut of the stone at all. And the ring is too large and too heavy for her slender white finger.

But Harry gave it to her so sweetly, looking so handsome as he stammered out his request that she accept it as a token of his undying love, and she knows it is extremely priceless, and has been in his family for ever, so it possesses great sentimental value.

Also, in wearing it, she will be the envy of all her unmarried friends. Well, one unmarried friend. And for that last reason alone, she is prepared to put up with the ugly old thing. For now.

More importantly, Harry has spoken to her Papa, and the union has been sanctioned. Finer details, such as the various settlements, are to be discussed next week. Meanwhile, on Sunday, she and her Mama are attending an 'at home' where her status will be publicly recognised, leading swiftly to a personal invitation to spend some time at Haddon Hall. She has bought a pretty little notebook in which she intends to write up her thoughts and experiences about that visit. Yes, indeed.

Juliana allows the rhythm of the maid's brushing to soothe her. One hundred strokes, twice a day. That is why she has such lustrous hair. She thinks about Fiona Blythe's hair, which is distinctly lustreless, and the colour of wet mud.

Of course, one's hair is not the only thing to attract the eye of an eligible bachelor, but it certainly helps. Dainty fair curls peeping out of a summer bonnet adorned with cherries … oh yes, that was what she wore for the river picnic when she first noticed Harry's gaze fixed upon her. She remembers it clearly.

The door to her room opens gently to admit her Mama.

"Well, I think that all went off extremely well, do you not?" she murmurs, gliding across the room. "I always say that a light supper with cold pressed tongue, ham and salads is just the thing for a hot summer day. Your father and I are most impressed with Harry. Such lovely manners.

"He understands exactly what might be said and what might not. He carries himself so well. And his linen was exquisite ~ I noticed it at once. And so deferential to your dear Papa. We couldn't wish for a more suitable future son-in-law."

Her eyes light greedily upon the little ring box.

"May I?"

"But of course you may, Mama," Juliana nods.

Her mother opens the lid, breathing a quiet 'Ah' of approval as the big diamond catches the evening sunlight, throwing rainbows onto the walls.

"The famous Haddon Diamond. How lovely. And what a lucky girl you are!"

And she is a lucky girl. A very lucky girl indeed. Especially given certain events that happened in the past. But the past is just that: past and gone. Far enough away to be just a fading memory. Unlikely ever to return to stain the present or jeopardise the future.

So, Juliana lets the Haddon Diamond wink and glint in the dying light, and imagines her life as the wife of handsome Harry Haddon and, in time, the mistress of Haddon Hall, and she smiles at her rosy reflection in the oval looking-glass. Her course is set fair, with no sign of squall or tempest to shipwreck the little barque that carries her hopes and dreams bravely into the future.

****

London at night. The bewitchment of a great city, a domain of darkness lit by gas-lamps and inhabited by the ghosts and phantasmagoria of previous existences, who co-mingle with the outcasts of the present.

London at night is a pantomime and a masquerade. Dark space and light space are polarised. The garish lights of gin palaces and music halls give way to the pitch black of unlit courts and fetid alleyways.

Look more closely.

Here are Constables Flawn and Clyde on night patrol. They are young. They are keen as mustard. They have whistles and night sticks and a promotion ladder they are eager to climb as quickly as possible. They are out looking for miscreants. And it seems they have found one.

Leaning against a tavern wall is a slouchy unattractive youth with a spotty face and a greasy cap. He is eying up the passing revellers in a considering sort of way. The two officers exchange a look, then draw alongside.

The youth immediately plasters on an incredibly innocent expression, and attempts to saunter off. Alas, he finds he is unexpectedly unable to enact this manoeuvre, as he is pinned to the wall by the two constables.

"Oi ~ wotchoo doin'? You lemme go ~ I ain't done nuffink," he protests.

"Good evening, young Bolder. That's a *very* smart jacket you're wearing," Constable Flawn remarks. "Not your usual style at all. May I inquire where you purchased it?"

"Got it off one of them Jew merchants," the youth says, making enough unblinking eye contact to suggest that this might not be exactly so.

Constable Flawn, who, at five-foot-ten is an impressive figure of a man, transfers his grip to the jacket collar and tugs it upwards sharply, which in turn causes the whole jacket to slide off the youth's bony shoulders.

"Well now, would you look at that!" he exclaims. "Brand new, never been worn. And here is the name of the tailor who made this jacket, stitched for all to see. Funny that. Just a short while after his shop was burned down, and all the stock gone missing, here you are in a jacket that'd cost me a year's wages, at least. I'd say this looks suspicious. What would you say, Constable Clyde?"

"Oh, I'd say it looks very suspicious."

"Dunno anyfink about that," the unfortunate youth says sulkily. "Wasn't there. Like I said, I bought it off of some old Jew and that's the God's own truth."

Constable Clyde pulls out his notebook.

"Name of old Jew?"

"How'd I know? Black coat. Skull cap. Beard. They all look the same, dun't they?"

"Time and place of purchase?"

The youth screws up his face in a concentrated manner. The two constables wait. All of a sudden, he tries to make a break for the street, but is brought down by Constable Flawn who extends a leg, sending him sprawling into the gutter.

"Oi, that was assault, that was! Bloody ecipol! I'll have the law on you!"

Constable Clyde hauls the unfortunate youth to his feet.

"Round here, we are the law, my lad. And right now, we, the law, are not happy, are we, Constable Flawn?"

"We are not. I am particularly unhappy, Constable Clyde, owing to the lack of truth what I am hearing from this young man." The constable sticks his face half an inch from the miscreant's face. "*We* are now taking you in for questioning by one of the detectives. So quick march, m'lad, coz it's a tidy step to Scotland Yard and the nice cell we have waiting for you."

$$****$$

Detective Inspector Stride is walking to work on a bright, sunny Saturday morning that chimes ill with his current state of mind, which is anything but bright and sunny. He has spent the past couple of days moving reports and documents from one part of his desk to another, occasionally transferring them to the floor, which has now become incorporated into his filing system.

Once upon a time, he reflects bitterly, he knew every street in the city, every dubious tavern, every highway and byway where crime lurked. Once upon the same time, he was a real policeman in the actual and literal sense of the word, he reminds himself, as he barrels through the door to Scotland Yard, mutters something indistinct to the desk officer, and goes to find somebody to complain to.

Eventually, he does.

"How did your meeting go yesterday?" Cully asks, glancing up from the report he is writing in one of the quieter back rooms of the police station.

Stride rolls his eyes. "This Jewish business … the commissioner wants all the stops pulling out."

"Oh?" Cully's eyebrows shoot up. "Seems a trifle excessive."

"Apparently he and the Home Secretary both have their suits made by Halevi & Son. Several MPs also have their suits made by Halevi & Son. They have taken the news of the fire very badly, and as a result, we are to leave no stone unturned. Have we released the body?"

Cully confirms that the body has been finally released. Also, that he has written up all his interview notes, and by the way, there is a man in the cells who was plucked off the streets last night by the night constables and might be able to shed some light on the actual conflagration.

"Then I suggest we interview him forthwith and see what he has to say."

The youth Bolder is sent for and eventually arrives, accompanied by the two constables who arrested him.

He is shifty, unshaved and truculent, He eyes the two detectives with small suspicious eyes.

"Oi, I ain't had any brekfist," he says. "I know my rights. You has to feed me regular. And you has to charge me wiv a crime or else you has to let me go."

Stride waves him wearily to a chair. The two constables retreat to the door, where they hover expectantly. An interview conducted by DI Stride is always a learning experience in police procedure. Interesting words of a vernacular nature get uttered. Constable Clyde retrieves his notebook in anticipation.

"Now then, Mr … Bolder," Stride says silkily, consulting the arrest sheet. "I see you are accused of loitering in a suspicious manner whilst wearing an item of very stolen apparel, viz and to wit: an expensive Harris tweed jacket made by an exclusive West End tailor. The former may be par for the course. Young men frequently loiter, do they not? The latter, however, associates you directly with robbery, arson and a very nasty death."

Stride slowly raises his head from the sheet of paper and smiles in a crocodilian fashion at the unfortunate Bolder, who gawps back at him, mouth opening and closing like a stranded guppy.

"I am waiting for your explanation, Mr Bolder," Stride says quietly, though with menace hovering in the background, cracking its knuckles. "In your own time. Please feel free to enlighten me."

Bolder turns his cap inside out a couple of times. Stares at the floor, the far corner, the ceiling. Meanwhile Stride sits silently, tapping the end of a pencil on the side of the desk.

"Look, it was like this, see," the youth finally ventures, "I 'appened to be in the neighbourhood like, just minding me own business, an' then this man, see, he ran past with all these clothes in his arms and the jacket

… fell outer his grasp. I picked it up and I shouted, *Oi mate, you dropped something*, but he was long gone. So I fort well, finders keepers as they say and that's God's honest troof."

"So not 'some Jew', then?"

Bolder concedes the possibility of non-Hebraic connection.

"This man? Can you describe him?"

Bolder swallows. Bites his thumb. Stares at a pimple on the end of his nose in an unappealingly cross-eyed manner.

"Couldn't say," he ventures finally.

"Couldn't or won't?" Stride's words crack the silence like a whip.

Bolder flinches, as if his skin has actually been flayed by the words.

"Look mister, give me a break. It was dark. He was running. He dropped the jacket. I picked it up. I don't know nuffink else, so it ain't no good asking me, coz I told you everythink wot I know. Honest."

Stride stares at him for a long time. Then he glances sideways at Cully.

"Your opinion, detective sergeant. Do you think this 'honest' young man is telling us everything he knows? Or should we pursue the matter further ~ maybe in front of a judge and jury?"

There is a swift indrawing of breath from the honest one.

"Wilf Harbinger," he squeaks. "You ask him about it."

"Ah. Not a name that rings any bells. You ever come across him, detective sergeant?"

Cully shakes his head.

"So where might we find this Wilf Harbinger?"

Bolder mutters words to the effect that a visit paid to the Rat and Bottle public house might elicit further information, and that's all he has to say on the matter.

Stride makes a careful note of the information. After which he informs the honest Bolder that though he is technically free to depart, his movements will be the subject of scrutiny, and if he is discovered to have tipped off Wilf Harbinger about the police's interest in him, there is a nice cell waiting. Understood?

Bolder nods.

"And now get out!" Stride orders. "And think yourself lucky: if I ever come across you again, it'll be the worse for you."

Bolder gets out. With alacrity.

Stride waits until the door closes behind him. He gestures at the pages of notes he has taken. "Bloody paperwork. Wherever I go, it follows me. Do you know the actual meaning of the word *policeman,* Jack?"

Actually, Cully does; Stride enlightens him at least every other week, but he dutifully shakes his head.

"It comes from the ancient Greek: *Polis* means city … we are men of the city. Not men of the paperwork. We should be out there, on the streets, catching criminals. Ah well. The Rat and Bottle, eh? See if you can run this Wilf Harbinger to earth. And take one of the constables with you: it doesn't sound like the sort of place you'd want to drink in alone."

The Rat & Bottle is the sort of low dive that gives low dives a bad name. Located off a side street, down a dark alley, round a blind corner and behind a derelict tenement, it fails every year to make *Bradshaw's Handbook to London and its Environs*. If ever it did, the entry would probably be accompanied by the advice: Best avoided like the plague.

It is the sort of pub where nobody will know your name because frankly, they can't be bothered to ask it.

Detective Sergeant Cully, accompanied by a fellow officer, lifts the rusty door latch, crosses a floor that crunches suspiciously underfoot, and approaches the bar, where a grubby-capped barmaid is moving stale spilled beer from one end of the counter to the other with a torn rag.

The lunchtime patrons stop talking, eye the two men suspiciously, then develop a sudden interest in the whorls and striations of their wooden tables.

"He ain't here," the barmaid says without looking up.

"Who isn't here?" Cully inquires innocently.

"Whoever you're looking for. Mr P'licemen."

"How do you know we're police?" Cully inquires. Both men are deliberately not wearing uniform.

The barmaid points at the constable. "Recognise him. Seen him about. B'sides, you ain't regulars, and nobody but regulars drinks here. In't that right?" she says, addressing the wider room, who mumble agreement into their pots of ale, still keeping their heads down but not missing a single word.

"We're looking for Wilf Harbinger," Cully says, raising his voice so that the drinkers in the far corner can hear him clearly. "Anyone know where we might find him?"

There is a communal shaking of heads. A muttered chorus of 'never heard of him'. The constable and Cully stand their ground, arms folded. They wait. Suddenly, a man rises swiftly from one of the benches and makes a dash for the door. The constable grabs him by his coat sleeve.

"Not so fast. Mr Harbinger ~ I presume?" Cully says.

"Never heard of him," the failed escapologist says.

"Oi Wilf, you left your cap behind," one of the drinkers calls out, waving aloft a soft cloth cap.

Harbinger swears under his breath. He glares at the helpful customer, who grins back unabashed. Harbinger is one of the regulars, but as he has the reputation of a man who does not stand his round, thus he is owed no loyalty whatsoever.

The constable catches the cap, passes it to his victim, then hauls him out of the Rat & Bottle by his coat collar. Cully follows. The drinkers bury their noses in their pint pots. Crisis over. Wasn't them.

Wilf Harbinger is a lanky man with an unshaven chin, droopy moustache and the resigned air of one who has been unjustly treated by life.

"I had a pint in there wot I nivver finished drinking," he complains, as the constable steers him towards the nearest wall and props him up against it.

"And as soon as you answer our questions, you can go back to it," Cully says. "First question: why did you try to make a run for it just now?"

"Wasn't what you thought. I had to see a business colleague. Important meeting. Didn't realise the time. Gonna be late now, thanks to you two."

"But I thought you just said you hadn't finished your drink?" Cully remarks innocently.

There is a brief pause. A variety of expressions flit across Harbinger's face. None of them chooses to settle.

"Question two," Cully continues. "What do you know about the fire at Halevi & Son's tailoring shop?"

"Never heard of him. Never heard of it."

"And yet you were seen running away from the shop on the night it burned to the ground, carrying an armful of expensive handmade items. Can you explain that?"

"Who says I was?"

"We have it on good authority. A witness saw you, and has now handed in an item that you dropped in the street as you ran."

Harbinger's face radiates 'cornered rat', but his brain and mouth have not quite caught up and decide to continue digging a verbal hole.

"I never took nothing," he protests. "Coz I wasn't there, was I? Must've mistook me for someone else."

"Really? He might be prepared to swear to it in court," Cully says obliquely. "Deliberately obstructing a police inquiry by withholding information is a criminal offence. Dealing in stolen goods is a criminal offence. Refusing to answer my questions is a criminal offence. If you know anything or saw anything, you need to make a clean breast of it. For your own sake."

Harbinger looks from one unsympathetic face to the other and finds no hope. He shrugs resignedly.

"Orlright, maybe I was … passing by, like."

Cully and the constable exchange a triumphant look over the top of the miscreant's head. Then Cully takes a notebook from his pocket and flips it open.

"Suppose you tell us everything you saw, right from the beginning," he says, pencil poised.

****

Cully runs across Detective Inspector Stride as the latter is returning to Scotland Yard after luncheon. The two detectives head for Stride's office, where, after moving several bundles of paper from the visitor's chair to the floor, Cully sits down and debriefs Stride about his encounter with Harbinger.

"We are chasing the minnows," Cully says. "These men are just the lower end of the chain. The final recipients of whatever leftovers remain. The big fish, according to our informant, have a far greater target than merely pilfering stock from a burning business."

Stride cups his chin in his hands. "Go on, enlighten me, do. What are these big fish up to?"

"There seems to be a lot of anti-foreigner hatred abroad at the moment, which is resulting in property and shops being targeted. Many foreign-owned businesses in the city have recently started paying gangs of private individuals to patrol their areas at night to protect their premises."

Stride raises his eyebrows in shocked surprise.

"Isn't that our job?"

"The business owners in question do not think that they, as foreigners, are being treated with the same care and concern that the owners of English businesses are. In fact, they are positive they are not, and that if there is a choice between solving a crime committed against an immigrant or a British citizen, it is the immigrant who will be given the short straw. This is what I was told by Mr Harbinger."

"Vigilantes? WE are the Metropolitan Police. WE keep the peace in this city!" Stride cries, bringing a fist down upon his desk, causing a pile of reports to slide onto the floor. "Anyway, I thought you told me a moment ago that this man was seen running away from the Halevi shop carrying a pile of clothes?"

"His story is that he was rescuing the items from the flames," Cully says. "He swears that he handed them all over."

"And you believe him?"

Cully spreads his hands deprecatingly.

"I can't see how we would go about proving otherwise. I tried to get a name and a description. Mr Harbinger was merely able to supply me with the information that it was 'some Jew'. I considered applying to the Jews for the name and address of the recipient, but as it is clear that neither of the two men we've spoken to committed the arson attack, and it is this that we are investigating, not the theft of the merchandise, I thought it best to discuss it with you before proceeding any further."

"Astonishing," Stride murmurs. "Truly astonishing. I've never come across anything like this since the police force was started. People taking the law into their own hands ~ it's a recipe for anarchy, Jack. Out and out anarchy. The Home Secretary will be outraged. You were quite right to bring this straight back to Scotland Yard. It must be nipped in the bud before the idea reaches wider members of the public. Next thing, we'll have armed bands roaming the street, and civil war breaking out amongst the populace!"

Cully doubts this. Stride is well known for his propensity to over-think situations. Especially after a morning drinking strong black coffee and dealing with paperwork, and there are three empty white china mugs and a pile of folders on his desk. He recognises the green one sitting atop the pile.

"These vigilantes ~ was your man able to supply you with any names?"

Cully shakes his head.

"The exact question I put to him. He could not tell me. These people patrol under strict anonymity, constantly changing personnel. But he was quite sure that there was a specific group of individuals targeting foreigners."

Stride pulls a face. "Lachlan came to me with some tale about a group. Of course, as it was only a rumour, and sounded rather implausible, I advised him to forget about it."

"And now?"

"I'd still say the same thing. It's been a long hot summer. People start imagining all sorts of terrors: Giant pigs living in the sewers, people with scales coming out of the river at night, wolves running wild on Hampstead Heath. You know how it is."

"It might be worth following up though," Cully says thoughtfully. "We have got deliberate arson and a suspicious death on our hands after all."

Stride grimaces. "It's up to you. But if you want my opinion, you will be wasting your time going down that road. You should be questioning his clients, and the owners of rival firms. Moses & Sons. That's the road I'd be heading for. There's a high probability it was either a customer with a grudge because his suit didn't fit, or one of his competitors."

Jack Cully disagrees. But he has learned over the years to disagree without actually looking as if he does. So, he merely nods, while mentally resolving to seek out Lachlan Greig and compare notes.

****

Sunday morning in London. The shops are shut, the streets are almost deserted. The whole aspect of the great city is that of an immense and well-ordered cemetery. Those coming from one of the numerous places of worship have the air of uneasy spirits who have risen from their graves and find their current locus changed beyond all recognition.

The men in suits and top hats who occupy the weekday streets are replaced by women in aprons and caps. They walk carefully from numerous cookshops, carrying the basins and baskets that contain the family's precious Sunday dinner. For man must rest, while woman must work. The god of Mammon gives way to the lord of the roast.

Look more closely. Here is our youthful traveller and his bag. He crosses Hammersmith Bridge, pausing to peer down at the water below, then sets his face towards Richmond, leaving behind him the smoke and grime of the city.

The day is fine, the air is clear, and the walk along the side of the river is beautiful, with leafy lanes, grassy meadows, and green willows bending down to dip their fronds into the water. This is exactly how he imagined the English countryside.

A few oarsmen scull along. An attractive young woman and her less attractive female companion pass him. He raises his summer straw hat. They lower their eyes demurely. A heron stands motionless, poised in the shallows, like a grey stone statue.

He is tempted to break into song. Some joyous ditty from his homeland, involving fair damsels, sunshine and abundant wine, but recalling the words of his grandfather about not drawing attention to himself unnecessarily, he contents himself with whistling a merry tune instead.

Eventually, after stopping to consume the tasty bread and cheese lunch packed for him by his grandfather's faithful housekeeper Ysabella, he reaches the small back lane that leads to the rear entrance of Haddon Hall.

The young man unlatches the ornate iron gate and steps inside. Ahead of him stretches a smooth manicured lawn with, in the distance, the barley-sugar brick chimneys of the house. He strikes out in its direction.

As he approaches a kind of shrubbery, he sees a woman walking along the path. What a graceful figure she has, he thinks to himself. She comes towards him. She is very young, he thinks. She approaches even nearer. She is not a beauty is his next thought: her cheekbones are too evident, her chin and mouth too strong. She stops in front of him. And she is unhappy, is his final thought.

"Young man, you are trespassing. Who are you? And what are you doing here?" she demands sharply.

He sweeps off his hat and makes her a low bow.

"*Scusi signorina, scusi.* Allow me to introduce myself: my name is Angelo Bellini. I am the new tutor," he says.

Immediately, her expression changes. Her shoulders stiffen; her mouth tightens; she stares at him intently. He reads and interprets both stance and expression. *Yes, sad lady, you were not expecting a foreigner. But here I am.*

"I see. My husband did not tell me you would be arriving today," she says slowly.

"Ah … it is *signora*," he corrects himself, "I am delighted to make your acquaintance. I have brought with me letters of recommendation from Milan, where I obtained my degree, and Paris, where I taught for some years. It will be my delight to instruct your children in all branches of knowledge."

"One child," she says on the back of a sigh. "My son. His name is Daniel. He is only four years old."

His expression does not change.

"Then Daniel and I shall become the best of friends, I am sure."

There is a swift pattering of feet and a small boy in a white sailor suit hurtles around the corner, his cheeks red with the exertion, curly locks flying. Seeing his Mama in conversation with a stranger, he stops, his eyes growing round like saucers.

The tutor puts a finger to his lips in a conspiratorial gesture. He bends and opens his bag, taking out three brightly coloured balls. He tosses one into the air. As it reaches the apex of its flight, he tosses another, then the third, deftly catching each one and sending it skywards once more. The small boy laughs and claps his hands with delight.

"Mama! Look, look!"

The tutor palms the balls and puts them back in the bag.

"How would you like to learn to juggle, young master?"

"Could I?" The small boy shoots a questing glance at his mother, who has watched the little performance in silence.

"Danny, this is Mr Bellini, your new tutor. Your father has hired him to prepare you for school, where you will learn everything that you will need to make your way in the world of men. I am not sure juggling is part of the curriculum."

The tutor flashes her a charming smile.

"In life, everything is part of the curriculum, *signora*. In my country, there are little boys the same age as this one who can juggle, do somersaults and sing and dance. For what is life without amusement, eh?"

He picks up his travelling bag.

"May I be shown to my room? I must unpack my bag and prepare lessons for this little one. The sooner we begin upon the long road to Parnassus the better."

****

It is a warm Sunday evening, and in Bruton Street, many of the house windows are open. Soft light spills onto the pavement. Outside number 4, a line of carriages is gathering, for Lady Grantley, elderly, widowed, crippled with rheumatoid arthritis but still a fully participating member of London society, is 'at home' to her particular friends and select acquaintances.

Let us mount the black and white tiled steps and enter the spacious hallway. Our coats and hats are taken by a housemaid, who bobs a curtsey as we follow a stiff-backed footman up the richly carpeted stairs.

Lady Grantley's 'at homes' are not the usual Mayfair crush, for M'lady believes that the chief object of a house is to keep the vulgar mob out, rather than entice it in. The house has been prepared with her customary meticulous eye for detail.

There are fresh flowers in tall vases, the chairs are arranged as M'lady likes them, the parquet floor shines, and the classical paintings look down from the walls with an air of eager expectancy.

And here she is, the hostess herself, her thick white hair confined by a large evening cap, her dark birdlike eyes sharp and piercing above the lined, raddled face, which still bears witness to the exquisite young woman she once was, even though late hours, bad temper and rouge have done much to impair her youthful beauty.

We are not announced, as we are not part of the inner circle of high-ranking politicians, members of society's elite or young people of a lively and irrepressible disposition, for M'lady likes to surround herself with the *jeunesse doree* of the metropolis, as if she hoped that some of their golden youth might fall upon and rejuvenate her.

Therefore, as we are unnoticed, let us fill our plates with tea-cake, and take ourselves over to a seat in the alcove, where we may observe proceedings without being observed in return.

Lady Grantley, resplendent in sparkling jewels and pearl-grey silk, accepts a cup of tea from the hand of a tall broad-shouldered, handsome young man, upon whom she bestows an indulgent smile.

"So, my dearest boy, I do not see her. Has she arrived yet?" she asks.

"Not yet, aunt Eliza," Harry Haddon replies. "But Gad, I am sure she won't be long. Then you'll see what a stunner she is."

And even as he speaks, there is a flurry of activity by the entrance, and the footman steps into the room and announces: "Mrs Doria Silverton and her daughter, Miss Juliana Silverton."

A hush descends. Every eye is transfixed upon mother and daughter, for although there has been much speculative discussion in the social marketplace, this is the first time the young couple have appeared together in public as an engaged pair.

Juliana is dressed, as becomes a future bride, in white. Diamonds sparkle at her throat. Her rosy lips and delicate nose, the profusion of ringlets that dance around her fresh face all contribute to the effect of her charm. Tonight, she is young and fresh. She is a sylph, a wingless white angel. She reminds the onlooker of sunshine and gladness. Tonight, Juliana is absolutely and quite deliberately irresistible.

Handsome Harry steps forward, holding out his hand. Juliana extends her tiny gloved fingers and, followed by her Mama, she glides on her embroidered satin slippers to the high-backed armchair where Lady Grantley sits and holds court.

Introductions are made. The young lady drops a pretty curtsey, charming the old woman with its effortless execution. The mother smiles. Social pleasantries are exchanged. The correct conventions are observed. The older women size each other up, the young people eye each other and look pleased with themselves, as well they might, knowing they are the belle and beau of the Season.

The guests look on fondly, because young love, even if it has been planned and carried out like a military manoeuvre, is still delightful to witness. Doria Silverton clasps her hands dramatically to her bosom and declares in hushed tones to her hostess,

"Have you ever seen such a handsome pair?"

Lady Grantley sips her tea and watches as Harry takes Juliana to visit each person in the room. Eventually, she breaks her silence.

"Indeed, they make a charming couple. You know, of course, that I have a special regard for my nephew. Ever since his older brother fell to his death, I have made it my business to look out for Harry. He was merely a baby when Bertie died, and away at boarding school when his mother passed away, and I believe the two terrible losses have left their mark upon his character.

"It has not been easy for him growing up. His father, my brother, has been preoccupied with his grief, then his business and now, the new wife and the child. I make no criticism; I merely state the facts, as I always do in every situation."

She pauses. Doria Silverton nods in what she hopes is a sympathetic and understanding manner. She is aware that she is being told important matters, relevant to the future of her daughter. She mentally makes notes.

"I have several properties in London that I have inherited from my late husband," the old woman continues, folding her twisted fingers in her lap. "One of them is a cottage in Chelsea that I think would be most suitable for Harry and his bride to begin their married life together. It only has four bedrooms, and there are no stables or a carriage house, but with a cook and a couple of servants, it will do for their needs. Of course, when I die, Harry will get this house and the other Grantley houses ~ I have made provision for that in my Will."

"You are most generous," Doria Silverton murmurs.

"Nothing of the kind!" Lady Grantley retorts, somewhat sharply. "I won't have my husband's estate being passed to some by-blow of my brother."

Doria Silverton's eyes widen. Of course, she has heard whispered tales of Sir Nicholas' sudden marriage, the difference in age between him and the new wife, the unknown provenance of the latter … who in society has not? But what has she now learned? That the small boy currently enjoying the Haddon money, rank and name is actually *de la main gauche?*

This would explain the reluctance of society to embrace Harry's new stepmother. It also explains why she is not here tonight to help welcome the newly betrothed couple ... but she must not draw conclusions, Doria Silverton tells herself hastily. Nor make any kind of response, until she knows the lie of the land better. This is not her 'set'. Thus, she keeps her features neutral, and merely murmurs something appropriately vague, while mentally filing the juicy titbit away for future exploration.

The evening progresses. Tea is drunk, sparkling conversations are had, until, at the appropriate time, Doria Silverton signals to Juliana with a slight lift of her eyebrows that it is time to depart. Farewells are said, another pretty curtsey offered, and Harry walks them downstairs to the waiting carriage.

On the return journey, mother and daughter discuss how elegant Harry looked in his well-cut evening clothes, and how many flattering and admiring looks the young couple received from Lady Grantley's guests.

They remark upon the beautiful rooms, the varied and brilliant company. They do not discuss the interesting situation of Harry's new step-mama. Doria Silverton has decided *that* little piece of information is best kept for her own friends to pick over.

Her dear innocent daughter must be kept far from anything so unsavoury. It is her duty as a mother to protect her from the smarts and *mésalliances* of the world. She will find them out for herself soon enough.

****

Breakfast at Haddon Hall is a lavish affair. Silver-domed dishes contain scrambled eggs, kedgeree, bacon and other meats. There are racks of toast, starched white table napkins. Servants bustle to and fro, setting the fragrant coffee pot in front of the lady of the house, ready to be dispensed.

Since his recent elevation to the ranks of the formally educated, Master Daniel is now allowed to take his breakfast downstairs, seated at the far end of the long dining table, with his tutor and one of the nursery maids in attendance.

Lady Marie watches his progress with pride. He scoops up bread and milk, stuffing his small cheeks. The maid mops up the milky dribble on his chin. Meanwhile, his father turns the pages of *The Times* with a preoccupied air, occasionally muttering something incomprehensible from behind its pages. Every time this happens, the gathered breakfasters freeze.

Eventually Haddon folds back one of the pages and passes it to his wife with a grunt and the stab of a finger.

She reads: *Mr and Mrs Maldon Silverton of Park Lane Mansions are delighted to announce the engagement of their only daughter Juliana Celestinia Rose Ferrers to Harold Ingram Haddon, son of Sir Nicholas and Lady Haddon of Haddon Hall, Richmond upon Thames.*

The article goes on to describe, in gushing terms, the devotion of the bridegroom, the affection of his fiancée, how they are rarely seen apart from each other. Mention is also made of the wealth of the young lady, and the numerous properties and estates of her intended's family.

"It is nicely done, do you not think?" she ventures, having little idea whether her assumption is correct, but feeling some sort of comment is required.

"Humph. Eliza writes that the girl made a pretty show of herself at her latest 'at home'. The mother was in attendance too. She describes both as *interesting and agreeable creatures*. High praise for my sister."

"You must be proud of your son. It sounds as if he has found an ideal partner in life," Lady Marie murmurs, casting a covert and loving look towards the diminutive figure now dipping his toast soldiers into his lightly boiled egg. She mentally crosses her fingers that her praise will be accepted; frequently, the subject of his eldest son reduces Sir Nicholas Haddon to apoplectic rage.

As expected, her husband regards her quizzically, as if she is some exotic object.

"Well, the gal must have some spunk about her to cast her lot in with him," he declares. "Only hope is that once married, he'll settle down. A friend offers a post in the colonial service. India. It will do. The sooner Harry starts making his way in the world the better."

"Would it be appropriate to invite the young lady and her Mama to take tea one afternoon?" Lady Marie asks cautiously.

"Do whatever you wish, my dear. Only don't expect me to put in an appearance. These tea-drinking events are of little interest to me, but if it gives you pleasure, go ahead. I have to meet with the girl's father in the next few days to arrange the final marriage settlements and other transactions. *L'homme propose et Papa dispose*, eh?" he says, giving a short bark of laughter at his joke.

The tutor raises his head from his plate and subjects Sir Nicholas to a long level glance. Lady Marie sees it. Briefly, their eyes meet, then the tutor lowers his gaze and focuses upon his coffee cup.

The servants glide from sideboard to table, replenishing toast racks, filling milk jugs. The small boy suddenly burps loudly, giggles, and is hushed by the nursery maid. His father lowers the paper and gives him an indulgent nod, "Better out than in, eh, Danny my boy?"

He gets to his feet, dropping the newspaper onto the table.

"Don't wait dinner for me ~ there is a late meeting with the shareholders, and Montmorency is speaking in the House, so I'll get a bite to eat at the club."

He strides across the room, pausing by the tutor's chair. The young man raises his eyes and glances impassively into his employer's face. Haddon says something to him in Latin. He waits. There is a micro-second pause, then the tutor replies, also in Latin.

Haddon laughs appreciatively. Then, patting his son on his curly head, he leaves the dining-room, ignoring the little boy's plaintive cry: "When will you play with me like you promised, Papa?"

The nursemaid wipes egg from Haddon junior's face and bustles him out of the room. His mother watches his departure with longing hungry eyes. The tutor stares at his plate, an enigmatic smile upon his face. Last night he wrote a long letter to his grandfather in which he painted a vivid picture of the marriage and the character of his employer. In Italian. It could probably be summed up in one word: bad!

The sense of lingering awkwardness between Lady Marie and the young man is as long as the mahogany dining table. After a few minutes, he wipes his mouth on the cream linen napkin, rises, bows, and walks out of the room.

Lady Marie is left alone. If one can be said to be alone, with two footmen, a housemaid and an under-housemaid in attendance. She moves her toast crumbs around her plate with her index finger. He has only been here a short while, but already her husband prefers the company of the tutor.

Thus, he dines at their table. The two men bandy classical quotes, talk about authors they have read. The tutor asks pertinent questions about how things are in England, a topic he is extremely interested in. Her husband explains constitutional matters, drawing upon his time in Parliament, and upon the experiences of his friends who are still there.

Sir Nicholas describes his travels abroad. He does not mention that he met, courted and married his wife while he was pursuing these travels. She has been excised from his narrative, like a page cut from a book.

How can she compete with this? Her knowledge stretches to a little mathematics, history, needlework, the Bible, French verbs, globes, watercolour painting, and what to do in the case of a thunderstorm at night. That was all she had been taught, and all her subsequent employers required of her.

The girls in her charge were expected to dress finely and show off their rag-tag accomplishments only as far as they served to attract a husband. She recalled their father telling them constantly that the Latin for woman was *mulieris*, which meant soft-minded. Their entire purpose was to marry wealth, run their own households and procreate.

Had she not caught the eye of Sir Nicholas, visiting the house with a letter of introduction from a family friend, who knew what would have become of her? The girls were on the point of leaving. Her position was coming to an end. There were no other suitable families in the area to whom she could apply for a governess post.

The prospect of unemployment, of eking out her days and squandering what was left of her youth in some lonely English attic, sewing shirts for pennies, was intolerable. The thought of the other alternative of making a living was enough to make her contemplate ending her life. She was fortunate in the extreme to have found a man willing to marry her.

A clatter of cutlery wakes her from her reverie. The housemaid has dropped the basket of silverware. Lady Marie rises and glides from the room. At the foot of the stairs, she pauses, daring herself to go into the schoolroom and demand to participate in her son's lessons.

But at her back, she hears her husband's voice chiding her. Forbidding her the sweet joys she once enjoyed. With a heavy sigh, she climbs the stairs to her own chamber, where her writing desk awaits her attention.

Lady Marie Haddon finds a sheet of pale pink pressed paper. She composes a polite letter to the mother of her stepson's future bride. When she has written it, she reads it through slowly and carefully, before blotting her words and consigning the invitation to an envelope.

And such is the miracle of the Victorian postal service, that a short while later the letter lands on the Silverton mat, where it is picked up by a maid, and brought straight to the mistress of the house, who reads it, nodding her head a couple of times in a satisfied manner.

Having perused the letter, Doria Silverton hurries upstairs to her daughter's sitting room, where she finds Juliana busily going through her wardrobe, for it is the end of the Season, and all the beautiful gauzy butterfly dresses that enchanted and dazzled must now be cast aside.

Next Season, she will be a married woman, and therefore not expected to display her charms quite so lavishly. As her mother enters, Juliana is contemplating a straw-yellow silk dress, very low cut and embellished with tiny glass beads. It was her favourite outfit and caused many a male heart to flutter apace.

"Oh Mama, can we not arrange for some sort of trimming to be sewn to this?" she asks. "It seems such a shame to let it go."

Doria Silverton smiles indulgently. "I will ask Mrs Butler what she suggests," she says, naming the dressmaker responsible for the lovely ballgown. "I gather sleeves are completely changed now, so we must do something with it, whatever we decide."

She shows Juliana the letter. "This has just come by post. It is an invitation from Harry's stepmother, Lady Marie Haddon, to take tea with her tomorrow afternoon. Should you like to go?"

Juliana's eyes sparkle with keen interest. "Oh, I should indeed! I am wild to see the house where Harry grew up. Please accept, Mama; write at once!"

Doria Silverton smiles at her daughter's eager face. How lovely she is. How fortunate that she has a daughter whose looks have secured her a good match. She allows her thoughts to dwell briefly upon the daughter of a very good friend.

Thin, flat chested and raw-complexioned, poor Grizzy has ended yet another season without an offer and will now spend the winter enviously eyeing the good fortune of her younger rivals before embarking upon a future as a lady's companion.

No dull routine and stifling boredom for Juliana, though. For Doria Silverton is sure the young couple are well suited, in looks and temperament. After speaking with his aunt Lady Grantley, and learning of the old woman's intentions, she is even more satisfied.

Juliana will live in luxury. She will have everything she could possibly desire to make her thoroughly happy. What more could a Mama ask?

"I shall reply at once, my pet," she smiles. "And then we must start making guest lists and think about ordering the wedding stationery. There is such a lot to do before your wedding day arrives."

Juliana waits until her mama has closed the door. She sits on for a while, hands clasped in her lap, eyes dancing with excitement. The more she has tried to find out about Lady Marie Haddon since her engagement to Harry, the more frustrated she has become.

Nobody knows anything about her. Nobody has encountered her socially. But tomorrow, Juliana will meet her elusive future mother-in-law for the first time. Tomorrow, all will be revealed. She has a notebook, a little pencil with a gold tassel and a lively imagination. She can hardly wait.

****

Meanwhile, the object of Juliana's devotion and hope of her future happiness is refreshing himself with a tasty hot luncheon at his club, because it is hard work living up to everybody's expectations, though admittedly, the expectations of his father are so low he probably couldn't even crawl under them, let alone live up to them.

Harry is eventually joined at table by three male friends. They are also young, privileged individuals. They too have allowances, or inheritances, which means they can be scrupulously indolent, on the understanding that should they ever decide to apply a well-tailored shoulder to a wheel, they have fathers happy to buy them commissions in the army or use their influence to obtain them good positions in the city.

Harry regards them now as his best friends in the whole world; he has known them ever since they were at Eton together ~ though in those days, the friendship was of a less amicable and more hierarchical nature, inasmuch as he was frequently to be found in their company inverted with his head down a latrine.

But time heals most things, and memory fades the rest into almost oblivion, and now here he is, happily sharing a meal with Anthony Rice, Giles Cooper and David 'Duke' Stuchberry as equals, in the knowledge that all Season, he alone has been the *nulli secundus* in the eyes of the reigning beauties.

The usual joshing about cravat pins, waistcoats, pointed boots and cuff studs being done, the four get down to the serious business of life: putting away as much roast beef, potato and claret as they can take on board.

While they eat, Anthony Rice holds forth upon the group's current favourite topic: the general degradation of London life. He is the group's acknowledged leader: a tall, stick-thin young man with dark floppy hair, a hawk-like nose and long angular face. His top hat is always a fraction taller than anybody else's, and his impeccably tailored black suits give off the impression that he belongs to the undertaking profession.

"I took a walk down Bond Street this morning," he says, in his affected drawl. "Might as well have been walking in the wilderness. Or some great desert. Everywhere, the shops are shut. Even my hatter has closed up and left town ~ gone off to the Isle of Thanet with Mrs Hatter and the little Hatlings."

He gives an affected laugh at his joke.

"I tell you, London at the close of the summer is like some primitive place. You could stand day and night in Bloomsbury with your tongue out, but you won't find a doctor to look at it for love nor money. All departed for the seaside or some other place of plebeian recreation."

"How about your servant Beasley?" Giles Cooper says.

Rice rolls his eyes to the ceiling.

"Beastly Beasley has abandoned me for other climes ~ he's gone to get the family place ready for the hunting crowd. But I do not consider Beasley a source of entertainment. Anyone who has not been to a good public school is a pot plant. Their conversational range is so limitedly banal, that dammit, it is barely worth one's while exchanging the time of day."

Harry remembers that Rice was an Oppidans, and such was the awe in which he was held, that his dame allowed him many freedoms denied to lesser mortals such as himself. It was considered a privilege to do his *rips* for him. Not that Harry was ever asked: his academic record was pretty dire, though offset by his skill on the sporting field, a place Rice detested and never frequented.

"Life as we know it is fleeing the capital," Rice continues, his deep-set dark eyes glowing with an inner ire. "Our places of entertainment are ungarlanded and the lights are gone out. You can't get your boots cleaned or your shirt collars mended.

"Even the sixteen-shilling trousers man who haunts my neighbourhood like a turtle between two boards, has gone. The only people you meet nowadays are Jews, Italian knife grinders and filthy foreign penny ice sellers, and I refuse to acknowledge their greasy blandishments."

He pauses to cut a piece of beef and convey it to his mouth in a gesture reminiscent of posting a letter. Harry has always found Rice's views on the lower classes and immigrants slightly distasteful, the public expression of them rather embarrassing.

However, Giles laughs uproariously, so he joins in. Just a second too late. Rice spots his reluctance and focuses in on him with keen intent.

"So, Haddon, how is the lovely Juliana? Found out what she's worth? I hear on the jolly old grapevine that her father is loaded. You should be in for a tidy little sum once you tie the matrimonial gallows knot, eh?"

Harry shifts uncomfortably in his seat. There is something about the venal expression on Rice's aquiline features that makes him squirm. He stutters out a halting reply.

"Don't know about all that. Leaving it up to the Pater to arrange."

"Best way, old man. And I'd not rush into an early wedding. Maybe hang out for a year or two. Make her wait. Women should learn their place."

Rice's views upon the female sex are well known amongst his particular set. He openly despises them. He has never been seen in the company of a woman, (apart from his venerable Nurse, upon whom he dotes) nor expressed any interest in squiring one to the numerous parties and balls.

"I'm not such a fool as to ever tie myself down to matrimony," Rice continues. "Footloose and fancy-free, eh Cooper? Can't have our lives run by the damned petticoats, it's not manly."

Cooper sniggers. The two eye each other knowingly, as if sharing a secret joke. Each word, each laugh is a barb to Harry's heart, as he knows it is meant to be. He tries so hard to fit in with these men, he has always tried since they were schoolboys together, but at some point, he is excluded. The door is closed, and he is on the outside. So it was then, so it is now.

A sudden vision rises in his mind: a small boy in tailcoats writing letter after letter, pleading with his father to let him leave the prestigious public school where he was bullied and so unhappy, promising to be a good boy if he could only come home.

His father never replied.

He comes to with a start. Rice, Stuchberry and Cooper are staring at him. He coughs, wipes his eyes with a handkerchief, mutters something about a piece of gristle stuck in his throat. They shrug. His temporary discomfort is of no concern to them whatsoever.

The conversation passes on to more important matters: where the three young men will dine later and what entertainments will be enhanced by their presence. They do not invite Harry to join them.

Rice pushes his half-eaten plate of food away. "You'll pick up the bill, eh, Haddon? I believe it is your turn to pay, you stingy dog."

Cooper laughs. Stuchberry smirks. Harry always foots the bill; it is the price for being allowed to be in their company. Harry knows it. Rice knows it too. But, ever compliant as always, Harry swallows the insult and smiles weakly as Rice whistles up his hat and stick from a servant and beckons his two boon companions to follow him.

Harry is left to contemplate the greasy plates and spilled drink. All things considered though, a luncheon for four is a small price to pay. He reminds himself that at least he is not going to spend the rest of the afternoon tied to his bed, locked in a boot cupboard, or with his head stuck down some stinking latrine.

****

Night-time in the city. It is 2 a.m. with a full moon sailing in a clear star-studded sky, and something like a deep sleep has fallen across London. Not that the city is hushed and silent; it never is. Night prowlers are afoot. Evening revellers are abroad.

The city at night occupies that interval between the death of the previous day and the birth of the next. It is in an intermediate state, almost an undead one. This is another place, more necropolis than metropolis, somewhere alienated and strange.

Homeless wretches huddle in doorways; furtive crime stalks about seeking victims to devour. Gas-lamps flicker like corpse candles, and distant screams from some profligate course up and down the streets in shuddering echoes.

Look more closely. Here is a group of men walking down a West End street. They are trying to look inconspicuous. They are failing badly. Something about their furtive manner, their air of wary vigilance, coupled with the hour they are out and about, immediately starts warning bells ringing in the minds of two night-constables smoking peacefully in a doorway as the men creep silently past.

Earlier, the constables have read a briefing from Scotland Yard, circulated to all police offices. As a result, they have been on high alert from the beginning of their shift. The alert level may have dropped slightly overnight, but the sight of the little group causes it to rocket up the scale until it reaches the red zone.

They step out, one blowing his whistle to summon aid, the other racing ahead of the group, before turning to bar their way with outstretched arms. The men come to an uneasy and straggly halt.

"Now, gents, I am going to ask you a simple question, to which I require a simple answer," the constable says, "What are you all a-doing out of your beds at this time of night?"

The group goes into a huddle and confers in a language that is foreign to the constable. He is joined by his companion, who jerks a thumb towards the men.

"Suspicious."

His colleague agrees.

"Very. Foreigners. Talking in jibber-jabber. Must be them. Stands to reason. See that one," he points. "What's he got under his jacket, eh?"

Upon examination, what he has proves to be a stout wooden stick. More sticks and a couple of kitchen knives are also discovered, along with a small box of lucifer matches. The group falls silent as the seriousness of their position becomes apparent. They shuffle closer together, staring at the two constables in baffled alarm.

There is the sound of pounding feet. Two more officers appear on the scene, summoned by the whistle. They make a rapid assessment of the situation. They examine the confiscated weaponry. They get out their handcuffs.

"Right," one of them says briskly, "We'll take the lot of them down to Marylebone. They can explain themselves to Inspector Jasperson. *If* they can. Good work constables, it looks like you've caught that gang of criminals who've been smashing up and setting fire to people's property. Might be a commendation in it for you both."

The little gang are marched away. One tries to protest, but is smacked around the ear by the officer. The two night-constables resume their rounds, progressing at the slow even speed universally known to all beat constables as 'proceeding'.

Silence falls. Briefly.

Then, in the distance, comes the unmistakable sound of breaking glass, followed, a second or two later, by the *whooomp* of flames taking hold.

****

There is nothing more guaranteed to put a dampener on the day of Scotland Yard's detective division than the sight of a vociferous crowd gathered outside the building. So, when Detective Inspector Stride turns the corner and sees not one, but two vociferous crowds, he feels an immense weariness stealing over him ~ though it could also be attributed to new boots.

He recognises one of the crowds: it contains the usual mix of London citizenry, who emerge from various holes and corners whenever the word gets around that 'something interesting' is happening.

Stride has never fully understood how they find out, but they are always present, as they are now. He notes that a couple of fruit sellers and a small matchgirl are already plying their trade hopefully at the back.

This crowd also contains various members of the fourth estate, amongst them, the louche individual known as Dandy Dick, chief reporter on *The Inquirer*, and one of the few individuals who can reduce Stride to frothing fury by his mere presence.

Stride is just contemplating his next move, which will involve making for the back of the building, head down, when his name is called out by someone in Crowd Two. At first, he does not recognise the owner of the voice, but then, as the person steps forward, he sees that it belongs to Mrs Lilith Marks, owner of the Lily Lounge Tea-room, and several other restaurants and tea-rooms scattered throughout London.

Accompanying her is a striking dark-haired young woman, whom he also recognises as her daughter Essie. Stride hasn't seen Essie for a while. She has altered much since he last encountered her. Her face has softened, losing its former sharpness of expression, and her dark eyes have lost the haunted look of someone trapped in a nightmare from which she could not escape.

"Good morning Mrs Marks, Miss Marks; what brings you both here?" he asks.

Lilith's mouth is set in a firm line. "Good morning, Detective Inspector Stride. We have come to complain about the way our shops and businesses are being made the subject of a campaign of deliberate attack," she says. "Last night, another business ~ my daughter Essie's shop ~ was destroyed in a fire. It was pure chance that she was not on the premises.

"We believe that we are being selected because we are not seen as members of British society, and whoever is at the back of it wants to drive us out of London, maybe out of the very country we have chosen to make our home."

The second crowd, having discovered it now has a spokesperson, forms up behind her and begins to air its grievances.

"They smashed my shop windows," a man says, his accent showing him to be a Frenchman. "And they wrote words on the wall. Vile words that I would not utter in the presence of these ladies."

The ladies in the first crowd look disappointed.

"My bookshop was a-set on fire," adds a swarthy bearded man wearing a long coat tipped with fur. "Many of the books, and the icons I brought over from my native country, went up in smoke. They pinned a note to the door telling me to Go Home."

Meanwhile, the first crowd, who have so far been acting as passive onlookers, decide it is time to step into the fray as active participants.

"The man's right. We ain't safe in our beds no longer," booms a large ample-bosomed woman in a dilapidated bonnet.

"I am sure that isn't the case, Mrs Comfort," Stride snaps at her.

"Well, where was yore p'licemen when everything woz goin' up in flames then? Coz I nivver saw hide nor hair of one!" interjects a small wizened man with a large cap and a loud voice.

The crowd agrees with his assessment. Other incidents of police negligence are discovered and aired. Crowd Two, seeing they now have supporters, proceeds to list their experiences, in a variety of musical foreign accents. Crowd One takes them on board, adding their own running commentary.

Stride holds up his hand for silence. To no avail. To make matters worse, he catches the edge of Dandy Dick's gleeful expression. He is just contemplating his next move, and lining up who to shout at first, when a police constable appears in the doorway.

"Message from Marylebone, sir. Inspector Jasperson would like a word. Got some men in the cells he thinks you ought to interview. As soon as, he said."

The two crowds pause, grievances temporarily put aside in the face of something new and possibly even more exciting. Stride seizes the opportunity to barge a way through the massed ranks, beckoning Lilith Marks and Essie to follow him.

Once inside the building, he motions them both towards the Anxious Bench.

"I'll see if Detective Sergeant Cully is in. You can tell him what has happened."

Stride locates Jack Cully, who is patiently explaining the finer points of apostrophes and full stops to one of the new recruits. Briefly, he outlines what is going on and to whom. Cully immediately grabs a pencil and a piece of paper and follows him back to the foyer.

"I'll now leave you in DS Cully's capable hands," Stride says.

He pushes his way through the massed crowds again. They are now busily bonding over their mutual complaints, so ignore him. Stride whistles up a cab. A morning that promised nothing but trouble and paperwork has just brightened up considerably.

****

Meanwhile Jack Cully conducts Lilith and Essie Marks to one of the interview rooms. The two women are seated, refreshments are offered and declined. Then Cully places the piece of blank paper squarely in front of him and looks at them enquiringly.

Lilith nudges Essie. "It is your business, my dear. You must speak."

Essie stares straight ahead, her dark eyes remote and wary, and for a moment, Cully remembers their first encounter: an empty theatre, with crimson velvet seats stretching away into unlit blackness, and a young woman dressed in white, her raven-black hair coiled snakelike around her head.

Miss Sybella Wynward. Or, as she was known in the theatrical profession, Mimi Casabianca, the Masked Medium ~ now reborn as Essie Marks, long-lost daughter of Lilith Marks. It was Cully who went in search of her; Cully who identified her and then persuaded her to return to London, to be reunited with her real mother.

The link between them has never been snapped: every month, a cake is delivered to the Cully household, baked by Lilith in gratitude for what he did. Now, Cully waits patiently for the young woman to speak.

"After you reunited me with my beloved mother, Mr Cully, I spent some time learning about the life I never lived. Part of that education involved getting in touch with my Jewish heritage ~ I wrote to my grandparents, who had never recovered from my mother leaving the community. They are old and frail now, but they welcomed me with open arms.

"It was my grandfather's suggestion that I used my designing and sewing talents to set up in business, so last year, I started Nathan & Marks. We make and supply costumes and outfits. My cousin Benjamin Nathan is my partner, and our families have funded us until we get on our feet.

"We rent the ground floor in a terrace off Leicester Square. We sell to the theatre and opera houses, and we were building up an exclusive client list of members of society who wanted bespoke costumes for parties and balls.

"It has been an exhausting six months, and since Easter, I have been sleeping overnight at the shop, as we have had to fulfil so many orders for the Season. It was pure luck that I decided to go home last night, or I wouldn't be here to tell you what happened."

Essie pauses, her eyes wide with horror. "Last night, someone broke the shutters, smashed the window, and threw a lighted torch into the shop, which went up in flames.

"This morning I arrived to discover all our remaining stock, our trimmings, our machines, our patterns and sketches had gone. But there is worse," she opens her bag and takes out a torn smoke-blackened piece of paper. "This piece of paper was pinned to the door. As you can see, what we went through was no chance accident. It was deliberate and it was planned."

Cully takes the paper from her. He breathes in sharply as he reads the hateful words.

"The people who did this must've known I was living there," Essie says bitterly. "But they did not care. My life meant nothing to them. Because, you see, I am just a *'filthy foreign Jew'* as far as they are concerned."

Lilith puts out a hand and grips Essie's hand tightly.

"No! Never! You are as precious to me as life itself," she exclaims. "Detective, we are at your disposal. Anything we can do to help in this matter, we will do. Just say the word."

"Where is your cousin?" Cully asks Essie.

"He is in Venice, buying beads and trimmings. He is not due back in England for a couple of weeks. Should I write to tell him what has happened?"

"Maybe wait a few days, just until we have investigated further. It could be that someone saw what occurred. I shall send a couple of men to make house to house inquiries. The main thing is that you are unharmed. I am indeed very sorry for the loss of your stock, but beads and feathers can be replaced. Daughters cannot."

Lilith wipes away a tear. "That is exactly what I said, Mr Cully. My sweet girl ~ to lose her again: it hardly bears thinking about."

"Then do not think about it," Cully advises. "Go home, make some tea and wait for us to get in touch with you. Detective Inspector Stride has been summoned to Marylebone Police Station ~ I gather a group of men were detained last night. Let us see what he has to say when he gets back to Scotland Yard. I will keep you informed of any developments."

Cully rises and accompanies the two women to the foyer, where he shows them out into the bright busy street. Then he returns to his room to write up everything they have told him. First Mr Halevi, now Essie Marks. Is the nightmare expanding?

Meanwhile Lilith and Essie head towards the West End, where Lilith owns the restaurant concession in one of the big department stores that line Oxford Street like predatory behemoths, their windows full of enticing goods that the passing public never knew they needed before seeing them temptingly displayed behind plate-glass.

"He is a good man," Lilith says. "He will do his utmost best to find the people who did this. We can trust him."

Essie stares straight ahead, oblivious to the admiring stares of young bucks swinging past them. In her mind's eye, she is seeing the blackened, gutted building, imagining the trays of beads melted and fused into treacle by the heat of the flames, the grotesque twisted shape of the sewing machine ~ her pride and joy, upon which she had created theatrical costumes fine enough to rival any of the long-established businesses. Her precious business, destroyed in a single night at the hands of a group of men who hated her because of who she was.

And now?

To start from scratch all over again was like contemplating climbing a mountain in bare feet. Essie heaves a sigh. Lilith squeezes her arm.

"We will rebuild again. Have no fear on that score. I shall call in every favour owing me."

"But it is so *unfair*! Why should you have to ~ you have suffered so much in your life," Essie exclaims.

"Yes, that is true, but it is also the more reason to persist. I have suffered, and so have you, but we have survived. And we will survive this setback. We have a roof over our heads, food on our table, and your life has been spared ~ that is the most important thing."

They reach John Gould & Company, and are shown inside by a liveried doorman. They shake their umbrellas, leave them in the umbrella stand by the door and make their way up to the restaurant. Over tea and cakes, mother and daughter consider their options.

"I shall write at once to cousin Benjamin and advise him what has happened," Essie says, ignoring Cully's advice. "We will need far more beads and trimming than we agreed. Soon it will be the pantomime season and then the Christmas costume balls. Oh Mama, where are we going to make all our clothes? The workroom is utterly destroyed! Customers won't know where to find us! Why did this have to happen? What did I do to deserve it?"

Essie's handsome face is a picture of despair.

Lilith reaches across the table and places her hand on her daughter's arm.

"My credit at the bank is good: you can borrow money in my name until you are back on your feet once more. After we have refreshed ourselves, let us visit Petticoat Lane and see what we can find. Dresses can be unpicked and remade, so can laces and embroidered ribbons. As for your clients, I suggest we have new business cards made, with my address on them. You can work in the kitchen in 'temporary premises' until you find somewhere more suitable."

Essie's eyes fill with tears. "You do not have to do all this for me. It is too good of you."

"I do not have to, but I want to," Lilith replies firmly. "You were absent from my life for so many years. I owe you everything that I could not give you then."

Essie's face clears, like sunshine returning after a rainstorm. "Then I accept. I will work every hour Almighty G*d sends, and I will make you proud of me, Mama."

"I am already proud of you," Lilith smiles.

They finish their cakes and drink their tea. Then arm in arm, they set out to replenish Essie's lost stock as far as they can. Lilith maintains an upbeat attitude, urging Essie to see the setback as an opportunity, encouraging her not to dwell upon the sudden change in her fortunes, to put the disaster into the past and move on.

Yet later, in the quietness of their shared bedroom, Lilith will lie awake long into the night, as events from her own past come flooding back out of the darkness, hitting her with full force. As she listens to Essie's gentle breathing, she will recall the agony over the baby daughter she was told had died. Her desertion by the man she thought was her husband. The gradual descent into poverty and degradation.

Most of all, she will remember a particular winter's night, standing on a bridge over the river, with swirling grey water below, and trying to pluck up the courage to hurl herself in, ending what seemed to be a life of pain and futility.

And she will weep, silently, so as not to wake her daughter sleeping peacefully beside her, as she acknowledges that she can never escape from her past, for the heart is a prison, and memories are the bars.

****

Meanwhile another mother and daughter are attending an important tea-party. They alight from their carriage outside the front entrance to Haddon Hall, where a Haddon footman conducts them up the tiled steps, through the ornate front door and into the entrance hall. Their outdoor coats are then spirited away by a parlour maid in a spotless apron and a smart little afternoon cap.

Doria Silverton and Juliana follow a second maid, who conducts them to the panelled drawing room, papered in wine-red figured damask, with a black marble fireplace and dark mahogany furniture that brings to Juliana's fertile mind some of the more lurid settings of Young Lothair's Secret Bride ~ another of the forbidden texts much circulated in her not-so-distant youth.

They are announced. Lady Marie rises, extends the requisite two fingers, indicates the chairs placed around the small rosewood tea-table. The guests sit. Juliana finds herself covertly glancing around the heavily draped interior, trying to work out which of the panelled walls might contain the secret entrance to the basement torture chamber, or which of the pictures, in their heavy gold frames, hides the locked safe containing the incriminating letters, the lock of hair and the faded photograph.

While Juliana is mentally filling the pages of her investigatory notebook with lurid imaginings, her mother is working her way through the customary social niceties that must be undertaken on an occasion like this.

Lady Marie, in a plain dove-grey silk dress, returns the comments in a slightly artificial tone, as if she has learned them by rote from some etiquette manual (which she has). After a few stilted exchanges, she indicates to the hovering staff that they may now serve her guests with tea.

Delicate porcelain cups receive the fragrant amber liquid. Plates of tiny crustless sandwiches, little iced and plain cakes and fruit tarts are offered. Plates are filled. Neither guest, of course, will actually eat any of the tempting goodies. One does not stuff oneself with food upon these formal occasions. Such vulgarity is for the lower orders.

Thus, Juliana politely crumbles buttery pastry while she listens to Lady Marie and her mother. It is like observing a fencing match: thrust and parry, thrust and parry. Her mother frames innocuous but probing questions, Lady Marie skilfully evades them.

From under her long eye-lashes, Juliana peers at her hostess, mentally pricing her dress. The silk is good, the trimmings obviously hand-made, but the wearer seems ill at ease, as if she has put on someone else's attire for the occasion.

She also notices that Lady Marie keeps plucking the back of one hand in a nervous gesture, while superficially listening attentively to Doria, who has now moved on to a detailed account of their evening at Lady Grantley's 'at home', reeling off the names of the guests like a shopping list. Juliana suspects it is all their hostess can do not to yawn.

Half an hour passes by. An elegant sufficiency of nothing has been consumed, and no interesting, personal or controversial topic has been discussed. A classic text-book visit. Then, a divergence from the script: Lady Marie glances at her silver wrist-watch.

"My little boy will be finishing his lessons shortly. Would you like to meet him?" she asks.

The two guests exchange a quick horrified glance, its content encompassing small boys, dirty boots, sticky faces and grubby hands.

"Oh well, of course we both *adore* small children, who does not?" Doria Silverton coos, "but alas, we must now take our leave. A delightful visit. *So* kind of you to show an interest in my dear girl. Another time, perhaps …?"

The three women rise. Cordial handshakes are exchanged. False friendly smiles are offered. The maid shows the two visitors out into the hall, where their coats attend them. As soon as she hears the front door close, Lady Marie sinks back onto the sofa, relief plastered all over her face.

Her ordeal is over. Now she will only have to take tea at the Silvertons, and then hopefully, her societal duties will be done and dusted until the actual wedding itself. How the mother talked and talked though, her voice so unctuous and grating.

And the young woman, her stepson's fiancée ~ so beautiful and poised, in her gauzy azure dress and cream shawl. But how she stared, as if she was looking at some creature from another land. Suddenly, Lady Marie grabs the plate of untouched sandwiches and gulps them down ravenously.

Meanwhile, mother and daughter trip-trap down the front steps to the carriage. As she waits for the footman to hand her into its comfortably padded interior, Juliana glances back at the house. Her gaze travels upwards. Somebody stands at a first-floor window. A young man. Their eyes meet, locking together for a few brief seconds. Then Juliana gets into the coach and is driven off.

All the way home, Doria Silverton keeps up a bright flow of chatter, commenting upon the house, remarking on the food, the servants and most of all, the hostess, about whom she has a great deal to say. This is probably why she does not seem to notice that her normally lively daughter is maintaining an unusual silence.

As for the young man whose gaze so disconcerted the fair Juliana, he remains at his post at the window, watching until the carriage is a mere dust-cloud on the horizon. Then he stands for a while longer, deep in cogitation.

Eventually, he straightens his cravat and descends the staircase, entering the drawing-room, where he finds his small charge greedily stuffing himself with cake. His mother watches him with anxious adoration.

"I do hope he won't be sick," she murmurs, as the tutor enters. "My husband is very strict about giving him sweet stuff."

"*Signora*, the little one has worked hard all day. Now he deserves a reward."

And so do I, he adds silently, waiting for her to instruct a servant to pour him some tea and offer him a plate of cake. Alas, Lady Marie ignores him. She only has eyes for her son. The rest of the world is mere scenery. A few seconds pass. The tutor stands by the table, watching her fierce maternal devotion to the boy, whose face is becoming encrumbed with sweet cake.

"I would have sent him to you earlier, but I gather you had visitors," he says, casually.

Now she tears her gaze away and looks at him.

"Oh. Yes. It was my step-son's fiancée and her mother. But they have gone back to London now."

Aha. The *fidenzata*. So that is who she was. He has heard all about her. And about the son, who is such a bitter disappointment to his father. His employer has confided, perhaps unwisely, in the young stranger who has entered his house.

He gathers that Harry, the heir, has an inheritance but no settled employment. To the annoyance of his father, he just 'loafs around' ~ an interesting expression that he had to look up. It has nothing to do with bread.

Ah, these upper-class English, he thinks. So cold, so angry, so disloyal. It must be something to do with their climate, the filthy air they breathe, the solid, heavy tasteless food they consume. He has yet to come to terms with gravy. What is the point of it?

But of course, these are private thoughts, to be kept to himself. So he smiles, compliments Lady Marie on the engagement, and politely requests the rest of the day off. He has realised that when she is absorbed in worshipping her boy, she is pretty immune to anything else, and is open to granting favours.

Sure enough, without even looking at him, she accedes to his request. The tutor hurries away to change his clothes and make preparations. He has received an urgent summons, by letter, from his grandfather. There have been unfortunate developments. His presence and advice are sought.

As he sets out on his walk, he resolutely focuses upon what lies ahead of him, banishing from his mind the image of a fair-haired young woman with a porcelain complexion, wearing an elegant bonnet and a becoming cream silk shawl. There will be time enough to revisit it.

The tutor boards an omnibus, whistling a merry ditty from his homeland. As each mile takes him further away from Haddon Hall, he casts off the big, formal English house, with its mirrors, chandeliers, fine furniture and paintings, its feeling of frigidity and stasis.

Money is wasted on the rich, he has always thought this, just as, conversely, poverty is wasted on the poor. Reaching his grandfather's shabby lodgings in Exmouth Street, he raps smartly on the door in the pre-arranged manner.

The door is instantly opened by Ysabella, whose wrinkled face lights up in a smile at the sight of him.

"*Entrare*," she says. "They are waiting for you. Come."

The young tutor follows her squat black-clad figure as she waddles along the shabby hallway, struggles down the uncarpeted stairs, and goes into the dark basement kitchen, where a single candle burns on the table, which also contains the usual basket of bread, a saucer of greenish-gold olive oil, and a blue pottery bowl of black olives.

The old man sits at the head of the table. He has been joined by four other men, younger, but clearly Italian in their dress and demeanour. The grandfather rises, embraces him warmly, kissing him on both cheeks. Then motions him towards the vacant chair at the foot of the table.

The young man sits. For the first time, he notices the condition of the four strangers. One has a bandage round his head. Another man's arm is in a sling. A third has a black eye and a purple bruise on his cheek. He turns to his grandfather, his eyes questioning.

"What has happened to your friends, *Nonno*?"

"They were beaten up by members of the police force ~ yes, I see the horrified expression on your face, but it is true. My friends and comrades were out on the streets after dark, as we were given a tip-off that some businesses were going to be attacked."

"There is a war being waged against all foreigners," one of the men says grimly. "It has been going on since the summer. They want to drive us away because it is their country, they say and we have no place in it. They write letters to the newspapers saying we are anarchists, only here to take their jobs and houses and lower wages."

"If I speak Italian in the street, I am stared at," a second man says. "The other day, a man came up to my son and asked him when he was going back to his own country. He was born here!"

"It used to be mainly the Jews. Then the Irish. Now it is anybody who looks or sounds foreign," Giovanni Bellini says disgustedly. "Even I, an infirm old man, was pushed in the street recently by a gang of boys. They threw my hat into the gutter and told me to get out of London before worse happened. Where do they learn such behaviour?"

"And the policemen do nothing?" the tutor frowns.

"The policemen do not care," the first man says. "That is why we decided to act, and this is how we were treated. We are not criminals, but we are treated as if we are criminals. We have made a complaint, but what good will it do?"

"What do you advise, grandson? You may be young, but you have a wise head on your shoulders."

The men lean forward, their expressions anxious but hopeful. The tutor purses his lips. Silence descends.

"Maybe you should play them at their own game," he says at length. Then, seeing their puzzled looks, he continues, "Go to the newspapers and tell them your side. Let them see your cuts and bruises. Write letters pointing out all the wonderful things we contribute to London life. Counter the bad stories with good ones."

"And the gangs of Englishmen? How do we stop them destroying our shops and businesses now we have been told we cannot protect them ourselves?" the old man inquires.

The tutor shakes his head.

"I do not know the answer to that, *Nonno*. But one thing I do know: these people will be caught eventually, because they will grow over-confident, and that'll be their undoing. In the meantime, my advice is to be vigilant.

"Whenever you are out in the streets, particularly after dark, stop and look back over your shoulder. Please take care of yourself, *Nonno*, I don't want you to put yourself into danger."

****

Let us move location from a run-down lodging house to a slightly more salubrious area of the city. A row of small brick-built terrace houses, their steps, once clean, now soot-smutted from the day's accumulated chimney smoke. There are geraniums in pots on window sills, silver metal milk-cans hang from area railings.

It is a respectable neighbourhood. Curtains are clean, door knockers bright. Small children play hopscotch, tipcat and bowl hoops in the gathering twilight, waiting for the summons to come inside to supper.

A man in a well-brushed suit and a bowler hat walks around the corner, and is immediately hailed by a small girl, who, forsaking her playmates, shouts a greeting before launching herself at him with such force that he is nearly overset.

"Now, young Violet! Now! Steady on," the man says, holding her by both small shoulders. "You'll have me flat on my back in the gutter if you're not careful!"

The small girl laughs joyously.

Jack Cully hoists his daughter onto his shoulders and carries her, shrieking with delight, into the small back kitchen, where Emily, his wife, is stirring a pot of stew. The baby lies cooing in her crib, waving her small pink feet in the air.

Cully surveys the domestic scene, feeling the cares of the day slip from his shoulders as he lowers young Violet onto the rag rug by the fire.

"Supper is almost ready, Jack," Emily smiles by way of greeting. She hands Violet the cutlery, and the girl carries it carefully it to the scrubbed table.

"Busy today?" Emily asks, as she ladles stew into three bowls, and then cuts bread from the loaf on the dresser.

"No more than usual," Cully replies, taking Violet to wash her hands under the scullery tap.

The family sit down to their evening meal. Violet chatters about her day, the people she saw (mainly princesses of startling beauty), the number of dragons slayed. Emily keeps an eye on the baby, who gradually falls asleep.

When the stew has all gone, she collects the bowls and takes them to the scullery, returning with the kettle. Emily fills the fat brown teapot, then places it and the cups on the table. Violet takes this as a sign that she can get down, and goes to find her rag doll.

"No cake with your tea tonight, Jack," Emily says, sugaring his cup. "Violet had the last slice for her lunch."

"I doubt we'll be getting any more cakes for a while," Cully replies. Then, in response to Emily's quizzical glance, he tells her about Lilith and Essie Marks' visit.

Emily listens attentively, her eyes growing round in horror as the events are related. For a few seconds after he is done, she remains silent, deep in thought. Then she sits upright, straightening her shoulders determinedly.

"We must help that poor young woman, Jack. And I think I know how: Sarah, one of my outworkers has a sewing machine she no longer uses. It was my first one; I loaned it to her when she began working for me.

"She has moved on to a big department store and does not need it. Indeed, she wrote to me only last week asking what she should do about the sewing machine. I was going to write back and tell her to sell it, but now, I shall write to her and ask for it to be taken round to Mrs Marks' house as soon as possible. It will be quite good enough for Essie to use, and it means she won't have to buy a new machine. What do you think?"

"I think you are a marvel, Em. But then, I always think that," Cully smiles.

"There are many who might be glad of extra work," Emily continues. "Since the baby arrived, I haven't been able to take in nearly as many orders, and with Christmas coming up soon, I know women in need of a little more money. I shall give Essie some names ~ it will be up to her whether she writes to them, but I can vouch for them. When times are hard, we must pull together."

Emily rises, smoothing her apron.

"Let me feed the baby and put Violet to bed," she says. "Then I shall write to Essie and Sarah. Might you slip out and post the letters for me? I should very much like them to be delivered tomorrow morning early."

"I will do it, Em. And while you are busy with the girls, I shall wash the pots! Now, how is that for a modern man?"

Emily Cully gives him the indulgent look known to all wives. She scoops up the sleepy baby and signals to Violet to come with her. At the door, she turns.

"Why is the world full of such hatred, Jack? What difference does it make whether you are a Jew or a Christian? Whether your skin is fair or dark? Whether you speak one language or another? Underneath, we are all human beings, aren't we?"

Later, Jack Cully leaves the house, Emily's letters in his jacket pocket. It is a clear night, the vast scoop of velvet black sky full of pin-bright stars. The air smells of damp, and soot and horse shit, the familiar London smells.

Cully walks the silent streets in search of the nearest post box, while the Sleeping Beauty city murmurs and shifts, mutters and groans, waiting for the rough kiss of dawn to wake her, and the jingling clattering morning carts to fill her streets once more.

****

"*Police brutality?*" Detective Inspector Stride brings his clenched fist down upon his office desk with such force that the contents rise, briefly, before descending into their former chaotic piles.

"How DARE he!" he continues glaring at the front page of *The Inquirer,* whose lead story bears the headline: **Innocent Foreigners Beaten to a Pulp by Brutal Police Officers**. Underneath, in slightly smaller letters is the equally astonishing sub-heading: **A Member of Scotland Yard's Detective Division looks on in Approval.**

"I take it they are referring to your visit to Marylebone Police Office yesterday," Cully says. He gestures towards the dramatic illustration that accompanies the article.

The picture shows two half-naked men, their eyes wide with horror, being belaboured around the head and body by four uniformed officers with sticks. Blood streams from various wounds and orifices, while in a corner, Stride, admittedly a crude rendition, but easily recognisable to friends, colleagues and miscreants, is laughing and egging them on.

"It's a pack of lies. There was no brutality involved," Stride declares.

Cully picks up and peruses the offending article.

"Two of the men have complained that they were struck about the head by the arresting officers. One has a sprained wrist."

"I'm sure it was an accident. These things happen, especially if it is a dark night."

Cully makes a mouth. Marylebone constables have a reputation. It is not a pleasant one. He reads on:

"They also complain about being kept overnight in a cell with no toilet facilities and without being charged with any offence, when they had done nothing more than walk about the city trying to make sure their businesses and those of their friends and neighbours were safe."

"And that's the thing I MOST object to," Stride exclaims. "They are trying to do our job for us ~ and while doing it, they are preventing our street constables from doing theirs."

"Didn't the attack on Miss Marks' workshop take place on the same night as these men were arrested?" Cully askes innocently.

Stride glowers.

"So you are saying that it would not have happened if the constables had allowed a gang of men ~ armed with sticks and matches, remember, to patrol the streets without let or hindrance?"

"I'm merely commenting," Cully says equably.

Stride gestures angrily towards the offending picture.

"He's done this deliberately. It's an act of spite and revenge. I've a good mind to go round to *The Inquirer's* office and have it out with that miserable excuse of an editor. Indeed, I think that is exactly what I will do. This picture is nothing short of libellous!"

"You could do that, I agree," Cully nods. "But might it not just provoke a further article, naming you specifically and making fun of you? Today's news is tomorrow's fried fish wrapping. By Wednesday, nobody will either remember or care."

Stride's face goes through a series of contortions that, in a different context, say a circus tent, might have been considered amusing. Cully waits. He knows Stride's arc of irritability generally bends towards common sense in the end.

While he is waiting for the trajectory to hit ground normal, the door opens and Detective Inspector Lachlan Greig enters. He also carries a copy of a newspaper ~ this time a well-known and respected one.

"Ah, gentlemen, I thought I might find you here," he says. "Now, this might interest you both. I have been reading the correspondence in *The Times* newspaper for a while. At about the time Mr Halevi's shop was destroyed, someone styling himself *Paterfamilias* wrote a fiery letter advising people not to shop at what he calls *'un-British establishments'* because it will only encourage the spread of what he chooses to call *'the current migrant plague'*.

"Strong words indeed, but they now seem to have found a sympathetic echo amongst other readers of the newspaper," Greig allows himself a wry smile. "As a 'foreigner' myself, I have been following the arguments with interest. I have the latest instalment here, if you would care to hear it."

Greig opens the newspaper and turns to the correspondence page.

"Ah. Here we are. A letter by 'M' ~ a loyal Englishman, who refers to *'swarms of Germans, Frenchmen and Hindoos invading our great city'*. An odd combination! But he contends that no decent woman is now safe walking the city streets."

"Balderdash!" Stride exclaims.

"Indeed, so you might think. But here is 'Puella' who complains of being stared at by *'swarthy Hebrews in filthy black garments'* every time she goes for an innocent walk through the streets of London. Worse, her perambulations are constantly interrupted by *'dirty little foreign boys with barrel-organs and flea-ridden monkeys'* or, heaven forbid: *'ragged Italians selling unwholesome ice-cream from barrows'*."

"I have seen similar letters in other newspapers and weekly magazines," Cully agrees. "There appears to be a concerted campaign against immigrants at the moment. At the far end, we have the destruction of businesses. The letters may seem a different thing, but I fear they will inspire those who hate these people to go out and take the law into their own hands."

"You have got no further in your inquiries about Mr Halevi, then?" Greig asks.

"We have questioned the Jewish community, as well as everybody we could think of connected with him and his business. I believe that he either died trying to defend his business, or trying to escape the flames. The fact that his body was found lying close to the door of the back room seems to confirm it."

"I thought we'd consigned this sort of thing to history," Stride says disgustedly.

"Ah well, maybe history isn't just something that is behind us; it also follows us," Greig says thoughtfully. "The Halevi family left their own country and came here to make a better life for themselves. The son was murdered trying to defend that life. And until we catch the men who did this, they will do it again. And again."

"So, what do you suggest?" Stride says impatiently. "Should we enrol every foreign man over the age of twenty in the police force and arm him with a night-stick?"

"Nothing quite so drastic," Greig counters. "But I think we should try to collaborate with these people, rather than treat them as criminals. These men know their neighbourhoods, and the people who live and work in them. It'd be a bit like using informers, only on a larger scale.

"What harm would it do to speak to them? It'd prevent us locking up the wrong individuals while the real criminals got away scot free. And it'd show we were sympathetic to their plight. We cannot be in every street, or on every corner. We need more eyes and ears on the ground."

"Neighbourhood watchers. It's certainly an idea worth considering. What do you think?" Cully says, turning to Stride.

"WE are the forces of law and order," Stride repeats stubbornly. "That is how it works in this city. In every city. Without one official police force, we descend into mere anarchy."

"Maybe it is time to try something new," Grieg suggests. "For we are dealing with a group of people who are prepared to go to any lengths to drive people out of the city. They have succeeded in creating a climate of hostility in both press and public. How long before another innocent foreigner is killed? Or another Essie Marks manages to escape by pure chance?"

Stride looks from one to the other. Then he raises his hands in a gesture of defeat.

"I see I am outnumbered. Do what you want. Set up your neighbourhood watchers. Only I warn you, if it all goes horribly wrong, I won't be held accountable."

****

Unaware that she is helping to shape police policy, Essie Marks stands in front of her ruined premises. The heat from the fire has been damped down. Now, for the first time since the blaze, she is able to step over the threshold and make an assessment of what exactly might be salvageable, and what she has lost for ever.

Carefully avoiding fallen masonry and smashed fragments of tiles, she enters, wrinkling her face as the acrid smell invades her nostrils. She looks around, searching for something to reclaim from disaster.

There is nothing left. Just ash and charred wood, smoke blackened walls, piles of burned rubbish that once were hats, feathers, costumes, spools of lace, fancy masks. Essie stifles a sob.

Here, amidst the wreckage and debris, it is hardly possible to believe that, only a few days ago, she was sitting at her worktable, sunshine streaming through the window, humming a tune as she sketched the design for a Venetian noblewoman's ballgown, a commission for a new client.

As if to taunt her, the clouds part, and bright sunshine unexpectedly floods the ruined interior with light. Dust motes dance mockingly. Essie's eye is caught by a flash of something shiny. She walks over to the window and reaches out her hand.

It is a brass button, attached to a piece of ripped black woollen cloth. Even though it is a warm day, Essie feels a sudden cold shiver go through her. She stares down at what she holds in the palm of her hand. The brass button winks slyly up at her.

The button must've come from the coat of one of the men who set fire to her shop. Essie closes her eyes, as she used to do when she was Mimi Casabianca, the Mystic Medium. Rocking to and fro, she allows herself to enter a state of trance.

The pictures rise up in her head.

He comes along the street. She sees him, in outline. He wears black, and is with a group of other men. They stop outside the workshop. They smash the window; he lights a match from the box he is carrying. The torch is lit. Leaning in, he throws it through the window.

And as he withdraws his arm, quickly now, his coat sleeve catches on the nail she kept meaning to bang into the window frame. He doesn't realise, eager to run off with his friends, before the building catches, and people notice and come out of their houses and rush to put out the flames.

He is not of her class. She has been in the business long enough to recognise that the cloth is top quality, and the button has some sort of family crest on it, indicating that it has been handmade specifically for its owner. This is somebody who can afford bespoke suits. Somebody who can afford to have his family crest stamped onto his suit buttons. Somebody who can afford to hate and destroy at will.

As if she has suddenly come back from a long distance and found herself here, Essie opens her eyes and stares fixedly at the shiny button, letting her gaze grow wide and unfocussed, until her pupils expand like black holes that reach down into her soul. Her lips move in a silent litany.

Then she takes a deep shuddering breath, before tucking the button safely into an inner pocket. Wherever this man is, whoever he is, she will find him. She has placed a curse upon him, a summoning curse. It will draw him to her. All she has to do is be patient and wait.

Essie remembers reading somewhere that Death is supposed to be a tailor, measuring people for their final suit invisibly and in silence. In tailoring terms, then, she has now opened her sewing case, and taken out her tape-measure.

She takes a long final look around her ruined premises, silently bidding farewell to the place where everything that was and might have been, is now no more. Then she steps through the door and walks away.

****

While Essie Marks is making her way home through the dusty streets, mourning the loss of her livelihood,

Juliana Silverton sits in the rose-papered parlour of the family mansion, pensively chewing her thumb.

So far, life has always been kind to the fair Juliana. No bumps and hiccups for her. No boulders strewn in her way. No dangers or difficulties to navigate. Her path to young womanhood has been smooth and problem-free.

But now, all of a sudden, it isn't.

Ever since that fateful day when the family carriage transported her back through the ornate wrought-iron gates of Haddon Hall, Juliana's world has been turned upside down. If only she hadn't glanced up. If only she hadn't seen the young man standing at the window. If only their eyes had not met.

She feels like Bluebeard's wife … she has unlocked the door to the secret room and revealed … well, what has she revealed? Aye, that is the rub. The more she thinks back to that fleeting glance, the more confused and terrified she has become.

For fair Juliana has 'a past'. It has been hinted at already. A past that she does not want anybody, especially Harry, to whom she is about to be married, to know about. And maybe the young man she saw was a big part of that past. Or possibly he wasn't. One young man at a window might look like any other, after all.

Only. Only. The way her heart started pounding, the way the colour rose to her face, the intensity of his gaze … how could it not be him? But what is he doing in England? Surely, oh, please no, he has not come seeking her?

Juliana moves from her thumb to her pretty paisley shawl. She twists the long, fringed ends round her slender white fingers, pulling the threads so tightly that she feels the fingers going numb. She is used to being in control of her life. Now, suddenly, that control has been wrested from her grasp.

What to do? Oh, what to do? She cannot tell Mama. That is out of the question. She dares not mention it to Harry, who would probably slap the young man round the face with his riding glove and challenge him to a dual, (her extensive novel-reading habit has given her great insights upon how young men behave when their honour is challenged).

And of course, once the story became public knowledge, it would be the end of her engagement, the end of her social standing, the end of everything in life that she holds dear. She would be shunned. She would have to leave London. For ever.

Such is her distress that, early in the morning, while the whole household was sleeping, Juliana had got up in the tightly-packed darkness, lit a candle and written a desperate letter pleading for advice and counsel to the only person in whom she had any confidence.

Now, she is waiting with barely contained impatience for her adviser and confidante to arrive. Which she is about to do. For there is a discreet knock at the door, which opens to reveal the trim parlour maid, and at her back, Fiona Blythe, best friend and keeper of secrets, who advances into the room, her expression solicitous, but her eyes bright with anticipation.

"Darling Jules ~ what on earth has happened? I have been quite *wild* with worry ever since I read your letter," she says, seating herself on the sofa beside Juliana, and taking a trembling hand in hers.

"Oh Fee, it is absolutely the worst thing ever," Juliana cries. "HE is here. Romeo. Remember him? He is in England. I saw him the other day."

"Ah," Fiona breathes. "Yes. Romeo. I do remember him. And here? Really? No, it cannot be! Where, exactly did you see him?"

"That is the worst of it ~ he is at Haddon Hall, Harry's ancestral home. He has been engaged to tutor his small brother. Oh, what a calamity! What am I going to do?"

Pat, pat, goes the comforting hand.

"But are you sure it is him? Absolutely and positively sure? After all, one foreign young man might look very like another. It could be a complete stranger, and you are fretting yourself for nothing."

Juliana withdraws her hand and gropes for her tiny lace-edged handkerchief.

"Oh, I have tried to think it, Fee. But it cannot be done. As soon as his eyes met mine, I knew. And I am sure he knew too. That's why I wrote to you. You are the only one who knows about … and so I need to ask you to help me. You will help me, won't you, Fee? For the sake of our friendship?"

The fair one fixes pleading, terrified eyes, tears fringing the long eyelashes, upon her friend's face, which, truth to tell, gives off very little in return, though beneath the surface, cogs and wheels are turning at an alarming rate, as Fiona Blythe processes what she has been told, and calculates how she can turn her friend's disaster into some benefit to herself.

"But, what is it that I can do?" she asks.

"Oh, your presence has already given me such hope," Juliana sighs. "We shall take tea, and discuss ideas how to stop him from talking about me. To anybody. Ever."

"Why should he?"

"Oh, because, you know, he might. I never wrote to him to explain why I had to leave so suddenly. So he might tell Harry, just to spite me. And once he found out about him, Harry would have to break off our engagement, wouldn't he?"

"I see. Yes, I expect he would in the circumstances. But what if Romeo refuses to do what you ask?"

"Oh, I am sure he will not. After all, I could get him dismissed … a single word from me in Harry's ear hinting that he was disrespectful when I visited Haddon Hall, and that would be the end of him."

Privately, Fiona doubts this very much. Juliana, as usual, overestimates her powers of persuasion. That 'single word' would open up a Pandora's Box of scandal, leading to the public revelation of the affair, and the lie told to cover it up. However, she mentally files it away under: to be considered as an option.

The parlour maid enters, carrying a tray of tea-things. Juliana tells her that she may leave the tray on the rosewood side table, and then go. There is a pause in the conversation while her white fingers flash hither and thither amongst the tea things, the heavy diamond ring sparkling as she bends her fair head over the Indian sandalwood and silver tea caddy.

"Mama is out shopping with some of her friends, thank goodness. I do not want her to see me in such a state ~ my nerves are such a jangle and I am sure I look a perfect fright, do I not?" she sighs, passing her friend a delicate porcelain cup.

Fiona sips her tea and smiles in a weary 'no-of-course-you-look-completely-fine' sort of way. She has spent so much of their friendship propping up Juliana's many *faux crises* about her appearance. She is fed up of it. Enough is enough.

"What are your thoughts so far" she asks, straight-facedly. "Have you discovered whether Haddon Hall contains an abandoned well or deep lake you could push him into?"

To her shocked surprise, she sees from her friend's expression, that Juliana has indeed considered this option.

"Oh, that would be the best solution, wouldn't it? But it is too risky. We know that the murderers always get exposed in the end ~ even if it is only in novels."

"You could just do nothing. After all, you might be mistaken."

A frown gathers upon the fair one's alabaster brow and two spots of angry colour rise into each cheek.

"But I am NOT mistaken! I told you I recognised him! And he recognised me. To do nothing runs the risk that he might decide to confide in Harry's father, or God forbid, that boring little step-mother. I worked very hard for this ring, and I am not going to allow Harry to slip through my fingers."

Fiona tightens her lips and says nothing. She understands her position now. She is not here to suggest anything, merely to agree with whatever plan Juliana has already decided upon.

"I think that a carefully written letter, where I explain the consequences of revisiting the past, might be the best thing to do," Juliana continues.

"I agree," Fiona says, a little too quickly.

"I am so glad. And of course, should he decide to renew the relationship, after having seen me again, you will be there by my side when I reject his unwonted advances, won't you?"

Fiona blinks. Once again, Juliana over-estimates her charms. It is doubtful that the young man would wish to renew the acquaintance, after all this time and in the current circumstances.

"I? Oh, I don't think …"

"Oh, but you MUST. You are the only person who knows what happened. I cannot possibly face him! Besides, to see an unmarried young man, and a foreign one to boot, on my own, wouldn't be proper! I must have a chaperone, and who else, in the circumstances, could possibly do it but you?"

Juliana lifts her left hand wearily to her forehead. The diamond engagement ring winks.

Fiona sits in silence, her lips folded primly, her hands clasped in her lap. She has never heard such stupidity in her life, outwith the pages of some sensational novel.

"So, what do you think?" Juliana asks eagerly, peering into her friend's face.

Fiona blinks her cat-shaped eyes. What she is actually thinking is: if you are blonde, rich and rose-complexioned with large liquid-blue eyes, a tiny waist and a pushy Mama, the world is yours for the taking.

If, on the other hand, your face and figure does not quite fit into the current fashion, and if you cannot simper and blush to order, and if your parents do not see the need to indulge your every fashion whim, you end up with no sparkly ring on your finger and are treated to tight-lipped looks over the familial breakfast table.

But these are private thoughts, of course, not thoughts to be shared. Especially in the current situation. So she bites down on what she is thinking and tunes her face to solicitously helpful and kindly friend instead.

"If that is what you want to do, then of course I shall be happy to help you in any way that I can," she murmurs, and is immediately enveloped into a fond rose-scented embrace, with a second later, the embracer laying her head upon her shoulder and bursting into tumultuous sobs.

Fiona gently extracts herself. Salt water plays havoc with silk.

"I knew you would! Oh Fee, I have cried myself to sleep since I saw him. But now, after our little conversation, I feel so much better."

"Write your letter. Then let me know how he responds."

The two dear friends embrace. Then Juliana rings for the parlour maid, and Fiona trips out of the room, waving her finger tips, while Juliana sinks back into the sofa, relief plastered all over her fair features.

On the other side of the door, Fiona Blythe stands in front of the big gilt-edged mirror, tying her bonnet strings. Stripped of the sympathetic veneer, her small pointed face shows just what she really thinks.

Fiona knows she is the 'ugly duckling' of the group. Her role has always been to throw Juliana's beauty into even higher relief by comparison. And now, fate suddenly offers her a chance for payback. Should she seize the opportunity to avail herself of it, though?

She reminds herself once again that no appropriate or inappropriate man has ever paid court to her. Foreign or otherwise. She has no fiancé, no ring, no admirers, secret or public. No happily married future awaits her. Just a deep burning sense of injustice.

Fiona Blythe stares at her reflection, her eyes hardening into feral points. Malice through the looking-glass. Then she barrels through the front door, already plotting her next move as she goes.

Meanwhile, Juliana hurries upstairs to her writing desk to begin her letter to the young man she saw at the window. Her Romeo. For that was what she called him during the hot sultry summer in Mentone, when she and Fiona were sixteen, and attending Madame Auvergne's Select Finishing School for High Class Young English Girls, both of them a long way from home and their Mamas' vigilant eyes.

He was her Romeo, from the moment she saw him strolling along the boulevard at Mentone, the bright Mediterranean sunlight glinting off the sea, and the smell of fruit trees in the air.

And of course, by the same token, she was his Juliet. The affair had lasted as long and burned as brightly as the summer sunshine. Stolen kisses, fond caresses, and whispered promises of forever under a blue, blue sky.

That was all it was. But. But. Juliana couldn't help herself. She had boasted to Fiona, of the relationship, revelling in the fact that she had managed to secure the devotion of a handsome young foreign man.

Suddenly, another bear-trap opens its jaws: hadn't she, in the course of some whispered midnight conversation, hinted that she and he had been more to each other? That the innocent flirtation had progressed far further than it actually had, and certain familiarities had taken place?

She tries to think back and remember. But her words are lost in the mists of time. Oh, the shame! She only hopes Fiona has forgotten. Yes, she must have, Juliana reassures herself, for she did not mention it.

The little flirtation had bobbed along happily for a few weeks. Then, unexpectedly, Juliana had received a letter from home requesting her immediate return to England. Her Mama was gravely ill.

All else forgotten, Juliana had packed her trunk and caught the first steamer. No time to tell Romeo of her change of plans. Or that she would not be coming back. Ever. Ah, the recklessness of youth. Leading to the regret-fullness of slightly older youth.

Inspired, her pen flies across the virgin page.

****

Meanwhile, the two *innamorati,* unaware that their joint futures lie in the hands of a pair of scheming females, are engaged in the very male business of earning a living. In the case of one, this involves dinning Latin and Mathematics into the head of a small boy.

In the case of the other, it involves a deal of trauma and suffering. For handsome Harry Haddon is discovering that hard work does not agree with him. Indeed, the whole getting up in the morning and sitting at a desk malarkey has far too much resonance of his schooldays.

For finally, with extreme reluctance on both sides, his father has found him a job at his place of business. It offers few opportunities to show off his fine black horse, his elegant figure, and his extravagant clothes, and many opportunities to stare out of the window and yawn.

Harry's days of idleness and fine tailoring seem like a beautiful dream now. His office, if you can call the glorified cupboard that he now inhabits an office, has a desk, a blotter, some empty shelves, a paper weight, and a set of pens and other writing materials.

Every day, at 9.30am, he enters his office. At 9.35 some grey little clerk, whose name he can't remember, brings him a pile of documents to read and sign. Sometimes he reads one. Mostly he just signs them or doodles in the margins.

At 12.30, he briefly escapes his prison cell ~ sorry, office, for lunch, from which he is expected to return by 1.30 for more of the reading and signing palaver until 4.30, when he is released into the world once more.

Harry hates his job. He does not want his job. *Dammit*, he does not even need it ~ he has his inheritance, and his doting elderly aunt to sub his lavish lifestyle and tip him the odd guinea in return for a charming smile and a compliment upon her appearance.

But this is the first time in living memory that the Pater has shown any interest in him, beyond the usual eye-roll, sigh and head-shake of their relationship, and Harry desperately wants to prove that he is not the complete waste of space that his father thinks he is.

As it is now 4.30, Harry Haddon signs his name on the last document in the pile of documents he hasn't read. He blots the signature, then waits for the small grey clerk, (is his name Simpson, or Sampson?) to knock at the door.

Once he has handed over the various papers and folders, he is a free man. Tonight, he is going to pitch up at his club, then meet with his friends for a roistering night on the town. They will drink in a series of taverns, possibly visit the music hall, or one of the more rakish gambling dens, where his handsome face and broad shoulders will attract the usual admiring glances.

With a bit of luck, he won't be home before dawn's early light. Sadly, unaccompanied. It has been dinned into him that any misdemeanours or indiscretions might jeopardise not only his forthcoming marriage to the fair and well-dowried Juliana, but lead to his office being relocated elsewhere. Possibly out of the country.

Swinging his walking cane jauntily, Harry heads home to his bachelor apartments to change from man about business to man about town. Then, metamorphosis complete, he sallies forth, in search of supper and boon companions.

All are to be found at Granthams Club, off Bow Street, a fashionable gentlemen's establishment that caters exclusively for the sort of swaggering rakish young swells, whose loud presence would never be allowed within the hallowed portals of the Athenaeum or the Garrick for fear of scaring their erudite members into early graves.

Granthams started out as a respectable public house with a debating club upstairs, but has long fallen out of respectability. Once, writers and dramatists met for literary soirées. The snug was a place for patrons of the arts and literary men to foregather.

Now, a mulberry velveteen coat lined with watered silk, irreproachable boots and a successful moustache are what marks out a member of Granthams Club, and town gossip, intrigue and quarrels have replaced the former discussions on Homer and Shakespeare and the latest Royal Academy show.

Harry Haddon loves Granthams. He eats his dinners off Granthams' china and swears that no dinners are as good as club dinners. He reads the newspapers he finds in the club newspaper-room, writes his letters on club paper and dispatches them by club messenger. If there were a club uniform, he would willingly wear it.

Here he is now, napkin tucked under chin, scraping up the last of the rich gravy from his plate of roast beef and potato. His glass of port is half-empty. His life is half-full. All it needs for fulfilment is the presence of his friends.

And as if the thought is father to the deed, they arrive, preceded, as usual, by their voices. Anthony Rice and Giles Cooper stroll into the dining-room. Two elegant-looking young men in well-tailored evening dress, exuding an imperceptible air of class and hauteur, and behind them, the aristocratic Stainforth twins, whose brushy dark red hair and freckles always give the impression that somewhere in their ancestral line a giraffe had been introduced, and pudgy Percy Alphege Mountjoy minor (Harry still thinks of some of his chums in public school terms). It is clear they have all been drinking and are well into their cups.

"Ah Haddon, we find you still at table," Rice drawls, clapping him affably on the back. "Eat up, man. We're off to the Cremorne. I have a private box reserved by the dancing platform, and a little bird tells me the lovely Dolly and her equally lovely friend Liza will be joining us. Not to mention a certain little buxom redhead that I know you had your eye on a couple of months ago, eh, you dog. Got your shilling ready?"

Harry conjures up a weak smile. His heart sinks. This is exactly the scenario he has been dreading: an intimate evening with three young women so far from respectability that they'd need a map and compass to find it.

He attempts to stutter out a reply, but is hauled to his feet by a laughing Giles. His hat is whistled up by Anthony and clapped firmly on his head. Then he is escorted out of Granthams to the tune of one of the Cremorne's more salacious ditties, bellowed out at full volume, and to the applause of the other diners who appreciate a buccaneering exit when they witness it.

The group pile into Rice's carriage and are driven off smartly in the direction of Chelsea and the glittering attractions of the Cremorne Gardens, where pleasure is carried on as a regular business and in regular business fashion. At some point in the journey, a couple of bottles of claret are produced and handed round. Fortification for the night ahead.

Arriving at the gate, they alight and get ready to enter the dazzlement of gaslight and cut-glass. After Harry has paid for the whole party, they make their way along the lantern-lit avenues of trees and gaslit groves to the wooden dancing platform with the brightly-lit fretted pagoda at its centre.

The dancefloor is full of couples, for the orchestra is playing a merry polka. The men and women twirl and circle like figures on a giant music-box, or marionettes in a show. Well aware of the effect a group of young bucks in the gorgeous array of evening dress has, Rice saunters round the dancing platform, occasionally stopping to clap a fellow diner or lounger upon the back. His companions follow, hands in pockets, drawling unintelligible comments as they go, with Harry Haddon bringing up the rear.

They arrive at Anthony Rice's private supper box (the equivalent of the Parisian *cabernet*). Rice swings open the door to reveal champagne in a silver bucket and a bevy of brightly-dressed painted ladies awaiting their attention.

"Oysters!" Cooper shouts at a passing waiter, who hurries off to fulfil the order.

Meanwhile the young men, with a certain amount of jostling and shoving, insert themselves into the booth, an operation that involves a certain amount of waist-squeezing and shrill shrieks of faked horror from the squeezed ones.

Harry is the last to enter, but by the time he steps through the door, the booth is completely full up. No space for him anywhere. He stands on the threshold, regarding the tangle of arms, the heaving white bosoms and the low, crude murmured endearments.

"Oh dear, it appears there is no more room at the inn, Haddon," Rice jeers. "Think you'd better jog along, old chap. Thanks for subbing us in. I'll send the bill for tonight's little caper to your rooms. Now then, off you toddle."

The others wave at him, laughing coarsely. The women regard him with indifferent painted eyes. Suddenly, Harry is fourteen again and back at Eton. He has failed to complete some task set by his tormentor, and knows he is going to be punished cruelly.

He turns and stumbles away, pushing through the revellers gathered round the dance-floor. The hectic air of carnival suddenly sickens him, the screech-owl women revolt him. Even the coloured cut-glass lamps with their enchanted fairyland appeal no longer fill him with that anticipated frisson of excited pleasure as they did of yore.

Harry quits the Cremorne and walks off into the night. His path takes him past doorways where huddled wretches stare at him, dull-eyed with misery. He keeps walking, passing lonely graveyards where the ghosts of former citizens lie in unquiet sleep.

Every now and then, church bells chime and a watchman calls the hour. Things scuffle down pitch-black alleyways. The world is on the move in the shadows around him. He wonders whether he is going mad in the loneliness of the night.

He pushes on, solitary, his feet his only guide. At one point, his footsteps direct him towards an unlit bridge, where he stops for a while, listening to the water flowing beneath him. There is a man walking a dog. It feels like meeting a ship with no lights far out on a black sea.

Only when the first streaks of dawn break in the eastern sky, does Harry finally hail a hansom at the corner of Farringdon Street, and is rattled away through a labyrinth of dingy streets until he reaches his rooms, where he clambers into bed, instantly falling into a sleep that is like plunging down an endless cliff-face into an eternity of nothing.

****

London begins the day early. Four a.m. and Billingsgate Market is already life and activity and bustle. Ships arrive at the wharf to land their catches. Boats from the North Sea bring lobsters; Dutch boats glide in full of eels; boats from Gravesend, Harwich and Grimsby and ports all around the country tie up and wait for the licensed porters to descend.

Sole, haddock, skate, cod, ling, sprats, fresh herrings are unloaded ready to be sold. So many fish suppers and club dinners and grand banquets are auctioned off and carried away in boxes and buckets, in carts and hands, ready to be cooked for the delectation of Londoners, leaving shiny-scaled relics of their presence for the scrawny battle-scarred dockside cats to fight over.

An hour later, Fleet Street wakes, for the newspapers have all been 'put to bed' the night before, and now it is time to begin again by assembling the last report from the late debate in the Commons, along with the more important sporting news, police reports, foreign news, theatre reviews, prices of stocks and shares at the close of business, births, deaths, marriages and mysterious advertisements of dubious provenance.

In various large bare rooms, resembling the receiving ward of a hospital, the first morning editions are spread out on deal tables, where they are assembled and folded with origamic dexterity by legions of porters, who carry the finished product to the door, where cabs and carts wait, ready to convey the bundles of twine-tied newspapers to the various railway stations.

Six o'clock. And here comes someone we have met before. He wears a frock coat, a top hat of impeccable origins, and is walking briskly in the direction of University College Hospital, where he is one of the surgeons.

Mr Lawton is coming into work early, having been summoned by an urgent note from his senior surgical nurse. Her name is Miss Sarah Lunt. As he peruses her note once more to remind himself of the details, Lawton smiles wryly, recalling the horror expressed by his male colleagues when he announced that she had been appointed to his surgical team. A *woman*! In a senior position in one of the most prestigious hospitals in London!

But Sarah Lunt has been working by his side for over a year, and the sky has not fallen in, nor has the hospital collapsed. She has quickly become a second right-hand. Lawton values her calm demeanour and pragmatic approach to the various traumas and tragedies they see enacted in front of them every day.

Now he enters the portals of the hospital, nodding to Featherstone, the hospital porter, a man for whom the expression 'a right little jobsworth' could have been invented. Since her arrival, he has ignored surgical nurse Lunt with studious determination.

Lawton hurries to the surgical ward. Sarah Lunt is waiting by the swing doors. She conducts him to a side room, where something that resembles an Egyptian mummy lies upon a bed.

"This elderly gentleman was brought in by two men who found him in the street in the early hours," she tells the surgeon. "He has suffered a vicious and sustained attack. His skull is fractured in several places and there is a deal of swelling. He also appears to have been kicked in the back and beaten with a stick. His left arm is broken, and his lower jaw has been dislocated. He has severe bruising. I have not seen the severity of it before. I have cleaned him and bandaged him to the best of my abilities."

Lawton winces as he views the motionless figure. Of all the suffering he sees, that of the very old and the very young moves him most.

"Do we have any indication who he is, or where he comes from?"

Sarah Lunt shakes her head. "His clothes are worn, but they are clean and well mended, so perhaps he has a wife or a maidservant at home who looks after him. I'm afraid, apart from a few muttered words, he has not spoken. I wanted to ask you whether, in your opinion, given the severity of his injuries and their probable cause, we should report the matter to the police?"

Lawton nods. "We should indeed. This is more than just a street mugging. I suggest we send a porter with a letter to Scotland Yard. I recommend it is addressed to Inspector Lachlan Greig. I have had dealings with him in the past, and found him to be a quick study."

"Then I shall write the letter at once, sir," Sarah says.

"You mentioned that the patient spoke some words ~ could they hold any clue as to his identity?"

She shakes her head. "I don't think so, sir. It was something to do with angels. He seemed very agitated about them."

****

When he looks back upon the week that is about to begin, the young tutor will think of it as the worse week of his life. It begins innocently enough, though. He wakes in the bright airy second-floor room that has been his ever since he arrived at Haddon Hall.

The sun is making the best of a bad job, and the appetising smell of bacon floats up from below. The tutor rises, stretches, goes to the window and looks down. Far below, the top-hatted, red-coated figure of the postman can be seen walking away from the house.

The tutor shaves, dresses, tying his cravat with care, then descends to the dining room to have his breakfast before beginning the teaching day. He nods at the parlour maid and wishes her a cheery '*Buon giorno,*' and she blushes becomingly because she is young and he is good looking (though a foreigner).

The tutor helps himself to bacon, toast and coffee and takes his food to the far end of the table, where a place is set for him. His employer has breakfasted and gone, leaving a copy of the morning paper folded neatly by his empty plate. The tutor eyes it, but does not pick it up. It is not his place to help himself to such things. Food, yes.

He sits down, noting that he breakfasts alone this morning. Lady Marie is nowhere to be seen. His small charge will be getting dressed for his day, supervised by one of the nursery maids.

Today, the tutor is going to try to explain the stars and planets. He has saved some different sized fruit, an orange, a lemon, some apples, plums and some grapes to use as examples. The child learns better when he can see and handle things. And he can eat the examples when the lesson is over.

As he butters his toast, Lady Marie Haddon enters the breakfast room. Once again, Bellini is struck by her pallid lacklustre demeanour. Her face barely registers any expression. Yet he has seen it light up when in the presence of the boy.

He half-rises, adopting a suitable servant-like expression. She motions him back to his seat.

"Please do not let me spoil your breakfast, Mr Bellini. I merely wished to inquire what lessons you are planning to teach Danny today."

The tutor smiles. This questioning is now a daily ritual. He enlightens her. Lady Marie listens, nods, approves. Almost smiles. Later, she will use the information to engage her husband in dinner conversation. He has listened to their stilted exchanges from the far end of the table.

The young man often tries to picture what is going on in Lady Marie's head, but she is so cold, so *English*, that it is impossible to penetrate the veneer of politeness. Only with the little boy does she show any animation.

Lady Marie prepares to leave. Then she pauses, reaches into her pocket and produces a letter. "I am sorry, a letter was delivered for you this morning. I almost forgot."

She glides out. The susurration of her dress is the only sound. He turns the letter over, reads his name in an unknown hand. He takes the butter-knife and slits it open. A single sheet of paper. A woman's hand. He reads.

A short while later, Bellini checks the time, and gets hurriedly to his feet. He crumples his napkin, drops it casually on the table and goes to find his small pupil. The letter now lies hidden under the napkin.

His exit is followed a few seconds later by the re-entry of Lady Marie. She has come to supervise the latest maid of all work, who is new and clumsy, and has already chipped a side-plate and the lid of a tureen. Sir Nicholas is displeased. The service belonged to his grandmother.

She watches the girl clatter the dishes onto a tray. Reaching the tutor's place, the maid gestures towards the letter.

"What shall I do about this letter, Madam? The tutor 'as left it by his plate."

Madam sighs. She picks up the letter.

"I shall return it to Master Bellini. Get on with clearing the table, Eliza."

Lady Marie goes into the conservatory, where there are plants to snip and water. She takes the letter with her. Of course, she has no intention of reading someone else's private correspondence. That would be quite wrong.

But, like cats and Bluebeard's wife, she is curious. So she does. And after reading the letter, she realises that she must now take swift remedial action to conceal what she has done, on a *sauve qui peut* basis.

Two hours later, the tutor enters the breakfast room in search of his missing missive. It has taken him a while to realise it is no longer in his possession. The table is laid for a light luncheon for one, but he spies a letter on the floor by his chair. It must have fallen from the table earlier.

With a sigh of relief, he picks up the communication and pockets it. He has not made a decision how he will respond. If he decides that he will respond. Which he also has not decided. Meanwhile, he would not like the contents to be read by anybody else in the house. It is, after all, a rather delicate matter.

****

Detective Inspector Lachlan Greig approaches Scotland Yard. He is whistling the Bluebells of Scotland (out of tune). Greig's world is currently a fine place. He has good colleagues, an interesting investigation, a recent promotion to detective inspector, and the love of a fine woman, Miss Josephine King.

This latter has taken some time to establish. Miss King is a business-woman and her time for serious relationships with men is limited by the hours she must put in. Greig has admired her from afar for several years. Only her commitment to her work, and his memory of a previous love affair that ended in heartbreak, has kept him from acting upon his feelings.

But acting has finally been done, and now he is even getting teased by junior officers about 'courting'. He finds he does not mind it a bit. So far advanced is the relationship, that plans are being made to introduce her to his sister Jeannie, the only family member he has in the world. It is a significant step and must be planned with caution. A great deal of future hangs in the balance.

Greig swings through the entrance to Scotland Yard, utters a cheery greeting to the duty officer and glances at the 'Anxious Bench' recently re-nicknamed the Bench of Disappointed Women, given how often it is occupied by members of the fair sex inquiring about the location of their men.

The bench is currently occupied by an elderly foreign looking female dressed head to toe in fustian black. At his glance she rises to her feet and totters over to him, plucking at his sleeve. She launches into an urgent monologue in a language he does not understand. But her distress and the tears that pour down the wrinkled channels of her face speak the translation.

Greig steers the distraught woman back to the bench. Then he signals for a glass of water to be brought. Over the next half an hour, a story emerges, in broken English punctuated by sobs.

Her master is missing. He went out last night (Greig notes that she does not say where). This morning she took him up his shaving water, but his bed had not been slept in.

He is a frail elderly man. 'They' (again unspecified) do not like him. He is being watched. So, clearly, something *male* has happened to him. At this point in the explanation, she wrings her hands and lapses back into the foreign tongue.

Greig, who has been taking notes, places his hand upon her black-gloved one. The old woman lifts her eyes to his face. She reads something there that gives her hope, for uttering a great shuddering sigh, she lapses into silence.

Knowing the value of silence, Greig lets it stretch out between them for a while. Then he gently elicits her name, address, and the name of her missing master. He promises to stay in touch with her, and encourages her to return home where, who knows ~ she might even find that her master has returned.

The old woman heaves herself to her feet, thanking him profusely in her language and totters out, uttering what Greig assumes to be some sort of blessing upon him as she goes. At least it isn't a curse, he thinks, as he heads for his small allocated desk.

There, he is going to find a letter marked 'Urgent' on the top of the pile of paperwork awaiting his attention. It is written by a Miss Sarah Lunt, a senior surgical nurse at University College Hospital. Greig will read it, join up the dots, and be on his way at once.

****

Meanwhile, another desk is also the focus of attention. An empty one this time, for Harry Haddon, scion of Sir Nicholas Haddon and employee in his father's business, has failed to arrive for work. His father is most displeased. A clerk has been dispatched to ascertain his whereabouts.

After hammering upon his door, the clerk is greeted by a red-eyed, unshaven figure in a silk dressing gown, who stares at him in bewilderment, as if he is a visitor from another world.

On being informed that his father is 'concerned' (a polite clerkish euphemism) about his health, as he has not attended his place of work today, the young man stammers out an apology, the suggestion that he thought it was Saturday, and a promise that he will be at his desk as fast as he can get a shave and a clean shirt.

Nothing is currently looking good for Harry Haddon. The strings that tied him to his old schoolfriends and to his former life are unravelling fast. Now, he is in danger of losing the hard-won respect of his father, such as it was. And possibly his job. The only lodestar in his miserable life is the lovely Juliana Silverton.

As he scrambles into his clothes, Harry reflects upon his situation. He decides he will keep his head down, work hard to make up for lost time, avoid the company of Anthony Rice and his friends and write a letter to his beloved.

He conjures up an image of her sweet face, her eyes, so pure and trusting. His Juliana. For her dear sake, he will bear the slings and arrows of outrageous circumstance. He will rise triumphantly above them. Once they are married, his life's path will be much better. He will be better.

Harry flings on his topcoat and hat, grabs his walking cane and erupts from the building like a well-dressed hurricane. He whistles for a cab and braces himself to enter the brave new life of Harry Haddon, reformed and reliable character.

****

A new life starts. An old life fades. Sarah Lunt sits on a wooden chair by the bed of the unknown elderly man, listening to his tortured breathing. Once again, she is reminded how fragile life is. How reliant upon such small things: a breath, a heartbeat.

The door opens and the surgeon enters, followed by a tall man with chestnut hair and a determined expression. She rises.

"This is Detective Inspector Greig, Sarah. And he brings news. He knows the patient's name, and where he lives."

Sarah's eyes brighten. So the old man will not have to be buried in a pauper's grave, or on the parish with no headstone and nobody to follow his coffin and mourn his passing.

"Tell me his name," she says. "Sometimes patients respond to hearing their names repeated."

"His name is Signor Giovanni Bellini. He is an Italian citizen who has been living in London for the past eight years. He has a housekeeper, who reported him missing a few hours ago. And a grandson, who is working as a tutor."

"Then he must be told what has happened at once," Sarah says. "The next couple of days will be critical, but given his age and the extent of his injuries, I am not sure his survival can be guaranteed," she pauses, catching the look that passes between the two men. "What is it?"

"We do not know where the young man is at the moment. The housekeeper could only tell us that he came over to England recently, and that his grandfather found him a post with a good family."

Sarah screws up her face in frustration. "No! That cannot be! We must find him! How can we trace him?"

"We shall do all in our power, Miss Lunt," Greig says calmly. "Let us, for a start, bring in his housekeeper and see what she can tell us. Please do not worry. We will find young Angelo, I am sure."

Ah – the name. Now the words the old man muttered before he lapsed into unconsciousness make sense to the surgical nurse. It was not angels he was calling for, but his grandson.

"Naturally I trust your decision, inspector," she replies stiffly. "But I have to stress that it is a race against time. The poor gentleman is fading fast. His injuries are truly horrific. Even a much younger man would struggle to survive what he has endured. The end cannot be far off."

****

Meanwhile, Harry Haddon is sitting at his desk in the small room that used to be a cupboard. He has meekly endured a scolding from the Pater, gone without his usual heavy luncheon, and managed to fill in a whole page of his black-bound ledger.

Now Harry is composing a letter to Juliana. It is the sort of letter a chap ought to write to the woman he is about to marry, although it is causing him much head-scratching and quill-chewing.

The girls Harry used to keep company with never required two pages of eloquent penmanship, being content with him leaving the money on the night-stand. Thus, he is having to dig deep to come up with something original and meaningful.

Notwithstanding his best efforts, Harry is struggling. He is mining every poem, every play, every bit of Ovid that he can recall. The resulting epistle is a stitchery of literary scraps, a thing of rags and patches, which he finally signs off with a flourish.

Having spent the best part of the afternoon upon his letter, Harry prepares to leave the office. He places the ledger on a shelf, puts a cover over his desk and places the letter to Juliana in his topcoat pocket.

The street outside is filling with pale stoop-shouldered clerks, all set upon one destination: home. Harry Haddon betakes himself to the nearest hostelry for a hot pie and a refresher. Normally, he would dine at his club, but as he is avoiding Cooper, Rice and the other chaps, it is not currently a place he wishes to visit.

After dining, Harry returns to his bachelor apartment, posting his letter to the fair Juliana on the way. When he gets in, he will find two letters on the hallstand awaiting his attention. One is from the management of the Cremorne and contains the bill for a lavish supper for eight, with champagne and other wines, plus breakages.

Harry will deal with this by readdressing the envelope to Anthony Rice, with an angry note saying that, as he considers their friendship at an end, he feels under no obligation to foot the bill for an entertainment that he did not attend. He will ring for his man, and instructs him to take the letter straight round to Rice's address, but not to stay for a reply.

The other letter, to which he will turn his attention once the man has left, is from his aunt Lady Grantley, proposing an evening supper and ball to be held to celebrate his engagement. This letter will also inform Harry that invitations have been sent to his dear schoolfriends Anthony Rice, Giles Cooper and David Stuchberry.

Harry Haddon will end the first day of his reformed life with his face in his hands and a looming sense of approaching crisis.

****

There is nothing like watching at a deathbed to remind one of the slender threads that joins us to this mortal world. As Sarah Lunt enters the small side room where the old man is fighting his last battle ~ one whose outcome is already predetermined, she wonders yet again at the tenacity with which the human spirit clings on to life.

Sarah carries a jug of water and a sponge, which are taken out of her hand by the elderly housekeeper, who has not left her master's side since entering his room. Muttering *grazie* she dips the sponge into the water before moistening the old man's lips.

While the housekeeper intones words of encouragement, Sarah lifts the etiolated wrist and checks his pulse. It is faint, fainter than yesterday, but still beating. She makes a note on the chart at the end of his bed.

Looking up, she sees the old woman's eyes fixed intently on her face in a mute plea. Sarah sighs. This is the hardest part of her job. We all avoid the thought of death, especially that of a dear friend or relative, she thinks. Nevertheless, death is an inescapable part of life.

"I do not believe he is in any pain," she says gently. "We have given him medicine to alleviate it. Hopefully he will just drift away peacefully when it is his time."

"He will not die until he has seen Angelo," the other says, her mouth set in a determined line.

"The authorities are doing their best to find him," Sarah says soothingly.

The old woman makes a dismissive sound. Then she hauls herself to her feet.

"I go make some good Italian soup for when he wakes," she says and stomps out of the room.

Sarah listens to her heavy footsteps echoing down the long corridor. Then she turns to the figure on the bed. *Who are you*, she thinks. What brought you to this country? She sends up a silent prayer that somebody from his community will talk to the police and help them to find the grandson before it is too late. The clock is ticking.

****

Meanwhile, unaware that his grandfather lies close to death in a hospital bed, the young tutor Angelo Bellini has finished teaching lessons for the day, and is taking a stroll in the grounds of Haddon Hall.

In his pocket is the letter he received from 'Juliet'. He is trying to decide the best course of action to pursue. The sun glimmers redly upon the old brickwork. The fading light flickers upon the leaves of the lime trees in the long avenue, changing the fishpond into a sheet of burnished copper.

All this natural beauty is not lost on the young man, who absorbs it all as if it were the good red wine of his native land. But all the picturesque setting in the world cannot detract from the problem he is now facing.

Truth to tell, he had, over the years, quite forgotten Juliana Silverton and their brief dalliance. It was of its time ~ he was young and had just graduated *summa cum laude* from his university. Life stretched before him, holding endless possibilities.

A pretty young English girl crossed his path, smiled at him, showed an interest in him. It was a summer romance, nothing more. One day, she was no longer sitting outside the pavement café, under the striped awning, twirling her peach sunshade. The next day, the same. By the third day, it was clear she had gone.

He had felt some disappointment, but it was soon shrugged off. Friends from his university had arrived, and in their boisterous company, all thoughts of the fair English girl were completely driven from his mind.

And now?

Now he curses that younger self for unwittingly embroiling him in this embarrassing situation. For what is he supposed to do? Until he received her letter, he hadn't given her a single thought ~ indeed, he had not even recognised her as she got into her carriage.

But she recognised him. *Oh Dio*! What a mess! Say he responds to her request never to speak of the past, nor to tell anyone they were acquainted (a strange English word for what they once were), will that be sufficient? It would break his grandfather's heart if he was dismissed for a youthful misdemeanour.

The tutor leaves the gravel walk and crosses the thick grass that leads to the wild area at the end of the grounds. Here, all is still. Only the song of a blackbird breaks the silence. He pauses, leaning against the trunk of an old oak tree, his brow furrowed.

For many minutes, the tutor stands motionless in silent contemplation. Then he reaches a decision: He will write to his grandfather, confess his past folly, beg forgiveness and seek his advice.

His grandfather might be an old man now, but once he was young and lusty, according to the stories bandied about his youth. And he knows the ways of these strange, cold English people. Yes, he must confide all to *Nonno*; that is the best thing to do.

Meanwhile he will not actually reply to the letter until he has received advice. After all, it is his future at stake also. He came here to find adventure and experience. He does not want to relinquish that quest before it has even begun.

****

Detective Inspector Stride eyes his colleague thoughtfully over the mountain of paperwork on his desk.

"I have called you in to discuss an extremely serious matter," he says, picking up a letter from the summit of the pile.

From where he is standing, Detective Inspector Greig can see the distinctive Home Office heading and the familiar spidery writing and black-inked signature of the Home Secretary.

"I gather there has been an attack on Mr Bellini," Stride continues. "You are aware of the circumstances surrounding his presence in London?"

Greig shakes his head. Stride waves him to a chair, then sits back, steepling his fingers. It is not often he gets the chance to enlighten his colleagues. Usually it is the other way around. When Robertson, the dour police surgeon, is doing the enlightenment, it comes with a side-order of sarcasm. He is going to enjoy his brief moment of superiority.

"Mr Giovanni Bellini is not merely an elderly Italian foreigner residing in our city. He is a fugitive from justice. He is wanted in his home country by the Italian police. In fact, so serious are the charges against him, that he has been sentenced to death *in absentio*. He has been living in exile in London for the past eight years."

Greig stares at him.

"Really? What on earth did he do?"

"Mr Bellini was the founder of a radical movement that tried to overturn the Italian government. His fellow conspirators were all rounded up, arrested and tortured.

Many were executed. He escaped by the skin of his teeth ~ disguised as a woman, the story goes, and fled over to England.

"Apparently the Home Office has been keeping a watchful eye on him. They intercept his correspondence, watch his coming and going, that sort of thing. Even though he is now an old man, there are many in his own land who believe in his cause, and want to restart his movement, in Italy or here. He is a very dangerous figure, and the outcome of the attack: his survival or death, is being anxiously awaited by the sort of people we might lock up if we ever caught them."

Greig tries to make the mental jump from the heavily-bandaged old man lying close to death in a hospital bed to the ardent and dangerous revolutionary being described.

Stride continues: "On the other hand, there are people in the Italian government who would be very happy to see an end of him. Indeed, they may well have been behind the attack upon him. The Home Secretary writes that we cannot permit foreign assassins free rein on our streets."

He pushes the letter across the desk.

"Read it for yourself, Lachlan. Your task is to discover as quickly as possible who attacked Bellini, and apprehend them, and for all our sakes, we'd better hope it was just some random thugs. It must all be done with the utmost discretion. I cannot emphasize that enough. Because if the newspapers get a whiff of this, they'll be crying revolution and anarchy and we'll have riots and civil disorder the like of which we haven't seen since the 1830s."

Greig reads, marks and inwardly digests the contents, noting the references in passing to the Prime Minister, the Queen and the preservation of the whole realm. The Home Secretary pens a fine, if slightly hyperbolic letter.

"Ah. I see. Perhaps I'd better send a couple of constables over to the hospital to guard the sickroom, d'you think?" he suggests.

"Do it at once," Stride says. "But tell them as little as possible. The hacks are bound to come sniffing eventually. The less they know, the less they can tattle."

"I shall accompany them in person. The nursing staff will also need an explanation for their presence."

"The nursing staff should be sworn to secrecy too. Not a word must escape the hospital confines."

Greig thinks about senior surgical nurse Sarah Lunt. Her steady gaze and calm unflappable manner.

"I am sure we can rely upon their utmost discretion," he says.

A few hours later, having settled his constables outside the dying man's door and briefed the nursing staff as best he feels able to, Detective Inspector Greig leaves University College Hospital by the rear entrance.

It is twilight and the lamplighter has begun to make his rounds. The warmth of summer is ceding to the mists and chill of Autumn. Greig settles his hat more firmly upon his head and strides out in the direction of home, and the supper that awaits him.

He has not gone far when he becomes aware that he is being followed. Greig has been a police officer long enough to tell the difference between an ordinary passer-by and a pursuer. He stops. The footsteps stop. He continues. The steps continue.

He reaches a corner, slips round it and ducks into a darkened doorway. Two men, broad-shouldered, muffled by scarves, with hats pulled down low over their faces walk quickly past his hiding place. Seeing nobody ahead of them, they halt, glance all around.

They backtrack. Walk around the corner. Greig waits a couple of minutes, then steps out of the doorway. He is just setting foot to footway when he feels a heavy hand descend onto his shoulder. Another hand bends his arm up smartly behind his back, holding it in place firmly.

Pinned between his two assailants, Detective Inspector Greig can do nothing but stand where he is. A finger is placed against his mouth. The message clear. The two men mutter instructions to each other in a foreign language. Then, taking an arm each, they walk him swiftly away.

****

Inspector Lachlan Greig's captors escort him through a bewildering series of small streets, and back alleys, sometimes doubling back on their tracks, until they reach their destination.

The men, who have remained silent throughout, finally come to a halt outside a small shop selling macaroni, bowls of beans, olives and peppers, sausages of various kinds and skins, and great wax-stopped bottles of green, yellow and purple liquids.

Despite the late hour, the shop is doing a roaring trade. Greig sees squat, black-cowled women carrying baskets containing half-yard lengths of crusty bread; olive-skinned children are wheedling scraps and several brigandish-looking men with black beards and clay-pipes lounge in adjacent doorways eyeing the passing trade speculatively.

The air smells hot and oily. The two men enter the shop, mutter a greeting at the owner, then convey the inspector through to the back, where a table laid for supper awaits. They motion Greig to a chair, then remove their outdoor clothing.

An old woman enters. Greig recognises her as Bellini's housekeeper. She greets the visitors, then places a plate in front of Greig. The basket of bread is pushed towards him, and a platter containing sliced cold meats and cheeses is offered. A bottle of wine is uncorked.

"We apologise for bringing you here in such a fashion," says one of the men, now revealed as middle-aged with dark eyes and a well-barbered beard. "It was necessary, you must believe us. You recognise Ysabella, so you can guess why we wish to talk to you."

Greig nods. He had actually worked it out from the moment he heard the muttered conversation, picked up the name of the old man, and realised that he was not in any danger. The second man is much younger. He has a black eye, and a bruised, swollen right cheek. He now pours the wine.

"How is Signor Bellini? We tried entering the *ospidale*, but we were told we cannot visit him anymore."

Greig sucks in his breath, bites his lower lip. They know the state of the old man all too well. He sees it in their concerned expressions.

"My master will not die until he has given his blessing to Angelo," the old woman says obstinately. She edges the platter nearer to Greig. "Please, *ispettore*, eat, drink. We will talk."

Greig breaks off a piece of bread and forks some of the tasty looking sausage onto his plate.

"Do any of you know where this Angelo may be found?"

The men purse their lips, shake their heads.

"It is a secret. Only he knew. You see, *ispettore*, you may not be aware of who the signor is. In our country, he is a wanted man. Or a national hero, depending upon where you stand."

Greig informs them that he knows the old man's history.

"Then you will understand why we all have to keep ourselves low and out of the public eye."

"Do you know what happened that night he was attacked?"

"We know everything," comes the astonishing reply. "We were there. We also suffered ~ you see my friend's face? He was beaten up, though not as brutally as our beloved leader."

"I am indeed sorry to hear that … Mr …?"

"No names, *ispettore*," the first man cuts in quickly. "Just the truth about what happened. We had been at the Italian Workers Club, where we'd gone to drink wine, read the *Gazetta* and discuss the future of our beloved country. Of course, we continued our discussion on the way back. We were speaking our native tongue, when we were passed by a group of men. They began to taunt us. At first, it was just calling names, mocking the way we spoke.

"We ignored them. This sort of thing happens all the time. But they stopped and linked arms, barring our way. Then they attacked us. They punched us, beat us with their walking sticks, called us every foul name under the sun, shouted we should speak English, that we were filthy foreigners with no right to be here."

"I tried to protect Signor Bellini, but he fell," the bearded man said. "He fell on the ground. I shall hear the crack of his dear head on the hard, cold pavement as long as I live. And the coward who struck him down kicked him over and over again, until I shouted for the police to come. Then the men ran off. We picked up our beloved leader and carried him straight to the *ospidale*."

Greig looks from one to the other. He prides himself on his ability to spot a liar, but he reads nothing but complete truth in their expressions.

"You did not happen to recognise any of the men who attacked you?"

The older man shakes his head.

"I did not. It all happened so fast, *ispettore*. One minute they were behind us, then they were in front of us, then they were upon us, then they had run off, like the cowards they were."

Greig runs a finger thoughtfully round the rim of his glass. "But you are sure the men who attacked you were English?"

Both men nod emphatically.

"Thank you, gentlemen. You have answered an important question. On behalf of the Metropolitan Police, I am grateful. I will convey all this information to Scotland Yard."

He rises to leave. The younger man raises his hand.

"Not so fast, *ispettore*. My friend tells you the truth: he did not see the faces of the men, but I did. While I was bending over our leader, trying to shield him from the blows. I looked up into the face of the man who struck him down. *Ispettore, com'e vero Dio*, I would know that man again. If we ever met, on the street, or in Heaven or in Hell, I will never ever forget his face."

He crosses the room to a shelf and reaches down a sketchbook.

"In my country, I am a trained painter. Here in your city, I am a mere jobbing street artist. I make a living from sketching people who pass by and selling them their portrait. See here ~ this is the drawing I made of that man as soon as I got back."

He folds back the sketchbook. Greig studies the face depicted in charcoal on the creamy paper. A top hat hides the upper part of the man's features. Nevertheless, there is enough here to identify him.

Greig knows there is a fashionable theory called phrenology, that helps scientists and members of the police work out if a man has criminal tendencies. It does this by measuring and observing the shape of a man's skull, the set of the eyes, the arrangement of the features.

In a cupboard in Scotland Yard is a pair of brand-new brass callipers, used by some of the younger arresting officers to measure the prisoners' heads (and occasionally, the heads of their own colleagues).

He has never used them, preferring gut instinct to new-fangled science. Greig can tell a wrong'un when he runs across one. But the face that stares back up at him fits none of the criminal profiles that he has seen.

He reminds himself that there is no 'murder type'; most murders are committed by perfectly ordinary individuals who just happen to have killed somebody. And yet. The artist has caught a glint of something at the back of the eyes, like a door that isn't properly closed. And something dark and deeply unpleasant lurks at the corners of the thin upturned mouth. The face of a smiling beast of prey.

"May I take this?"

The artist tears out the page. Greig rolls it up carefully, is given some string to tie it and bids the trio farewell. The artist accompanies him as far as the street, and gives the tall inspector instructions to the nearest cab stand.

All the way back, Detective Inspector Greig plots his next move. If the image in his pocket is a member of the gang that has been causing so much chaos, then he has reason enough to circulate his face on a 'Wanted' poster as 'a person of interest'.

The cab drops him at Scotland Yard. Greig knows there will be officers still working shifts. By tomorrow morning, the drawing he has been given will be copied, circulated, and pinned on every police office noticeboard throughout the City of London.

****

Here is a table, laid for breakfast. There are boiled eggs, scrambled eggs, bacon and eggs, chops, racks of toast, pats of fresh butter, and fruit preserves of several kinds. There is a bowl of ripe pears and some hothouse grapes. There is coffee, tea, sugar, cream and milk in abundance.

A Park Mansions breakfast, fit for a princess. But this particular 'princess' is not partaking of the good things set before her. Instead, Miss Juliana Celestinia Rose Ferrers Silverton is glumly staring at a plateful of cold scrambled egg.

She has been thus engaged for the past five minutes, occasionally poking the unappetising pale-yellow mess with her fork. Meanwhile her Papa and Mama are making a hearty breakfast, as befits two individuals about to engage with the forces of business (the City) and commerce (the shops).

The conversation round the table ebbs and flows, but like the breakfast, Juliana is not participating. Yet in her pocket is the latest letter from Harry Haddon, full of elaborate and pilfered expressions of adoration. On her fourth finger is the Haddon Diamond. After breakfast, she will be taken in the carriage with the butter-soft leather seats to Oxford Street, where a small group of dear friends will be waiting to advise her upon morning robes and other items of female apparel.

She has everything a young society belle requires. And that is even without contemplating the latest pile of packages delivered to her door. But all this wonderfulness pales into insignificance, for she has not received the letter assuring her that the past will remain in the past.

Until she does, everything else in her life is dust and ashes. Juliana toys with her food. Sighs. Then rises from her place. She is lucky: a maid servant hurries forward and removes her plate before her Mama notices that she has not breakfasted.

A few hours later, dressed becomingly in a rose-pink morning dress, with a paisley shawl and a pink feather-trimmed bonnet that emphasises her dewy complexion, Juliana alights in front of the prestigious department store John Gould & Company, where her father has an account. She is bowed inside by the doorman.

A floor-walker shows her to one of the large private fitting rooms, where Fiona and Charlotte, seated side by side on a chintz sofa, eagerly await her arrival. The other three sofas are strewn with nightgowns, caps and pairs of stockings and stays. Rainbow-hued morning robes and gowns hang from wall-pegs.

Two showroom women in the sober black uniform of the store hurry in and out, replacing and rearranging. There are big looking-glasses in gilt frames, and a richly patterned Turkish carpet.

"There you are, Jules," Charlotte says cheerfully. "We have been waiting an age! Come and see these lovely things!"

And indeed, they are lovely. Such exquisitely fine silk. Such beautiful lace trims. Stockings and rosetted garters to die for. Stays and undergarments in bright exciting colours. The three young belles feast their eyes on the riches displayed.

The showroom women subtly point out this or that feature. How a bow, placed just so, will enhance the slenderness of the waist. That ribbon can be changed to match the colour of the eyes. These stays came in last week from France, where they are all the rage ~ see the cunning front fastenings.

The three observe and feel and coo. Juliana tries on a selection of morning robes, and twirls in front of the glass, basking in the praise and admiration of her friends. The showroom women comment discreetly upon how fine she looks.

Eventually, Juliana makes her choice of items. She orders them to be packed and dispatched straight away to Park Mansions, along with the bill, which her Papa will settle, in due course.

At which point, Charlotte rises, announces that she will meet the other two in the first-floor restaurant in a short while, as she has some errands to do for her Mama. She glides out, leaving Juliana, Fiona and the showroom women, who bustle in and out, taking garments to be boxed and folded.

"I have never owned silk morning robes like these," Fiona murmurs, looking thoughtfully at the lovely bright garments. "My Mama only allows me to wear plain cotton wrappers. They are very fine though. I should like to have one. Or two. I should like that very much."

Juliana laughs her tinkly little laugh. The idea of Fiona Blythe, plain, muddy-haired snub-nosed Fiona parading round in these beautiful bright morning robes is just too ridiculous. Fiona is barely five foot two, and so pale, she looks as if she has come from some icy planet where she is in a tribe of one. Besides, when would she have need of such garments? She has no fiancé, no male admirer, no marriage prospects.

"Have you had a letter from You Know Who?" Fiona suddenly asks.

Juliana's laugh dies in her throat. She shakes her head. "I cannot understand why he has not written. It has been days. I thought I made my instructions quite clear. Oh, it is worrying me so much. I hope I did the right thing. Do you think it was the right thing to do, dearest?"

There is a long pause, during which Fiona Blythe stares hard at her friend. Then she looks off into the distance and smiles. It is the sort of smile that contains concealed weaponry.

"Ah, secrets. How we love them," Fiona murmurs. "But sometimes, they can lead us into … perilous ways, can't they?"

Juliana nods her agreement.

"I have been thinking a lot about our little chat the other day," Fiona says slowly, not looking at Juliana at all now. "It brought back so many memories: midnight conversations over a box of marrons glacés. Do you recall them? Oh, those naughty confessions!"

Juliana swallows, her eyes widening. So Fiona has not forgotten. Oh, the horror!

"Perhaps you would care to treat me to a lovely silk robe too ~ for friendship's sake and in memory of all those midnight secrets we shared together," Fiona says, innocence hanging from her words like loops of toffee.

The meaning is crystal clear. It could not be clearer. Her silence on the subject of the past affair comes with a price tag. Juliana feels a cold shiver run down her spine.

"I think there might be other things you'd like to buy for me in the future. To say thank-you for being your dearest friend and confidante," Fiona says silkily. Her slanty eyes gleam. Her lips are so thin they could have been embroidered onto her face in stem-stitch.

"I … I …" stutters Juliana.

"Of course, you could refuse. But then, I could also refuse to keep silent about your Romeo. Oh, I don't *want* to tell, I really don't, but you see, I may have to. It is so hard keeping other people's secrets, isn't it? My little conscience is very troubled. I have barely slept a wink since we last met, thinking about what you made me promise to do."

A sudden urge to scream rises up in our fair heroine, coupled with the most unladylike desire to grab Fiona by her muddy ringlets and slap her across her thin pale spiteful little face. Hard and for a long time. But of course, she does none of these things. She cannot afford to.

"Please choose a robe. Of course, I shall be happy to treat you," she says stiffly, between gritted teeth.

Fiona immediately picks out one of the most expensive garments, the buttercup yellow robe with a bright Japanese print, that Juliana particularly liked, and had hoped to secure for herself, and passes it to one of the show room women. Juliana instructs her where to send the robe, agreeing that it will be added to her bill.

She can hardly bring herself to look her former friend in the eye, but politeness demands that not only must she do so, but she must accompany her up to the restaurant, where innocent Charlotte, who knows nothing of what has occurred, is waiting to order tea and cakes to celebrate her purchases.

Sometime later Juliana Silverton is dropped at her front door. She hurries into the house and heads straight for her bedroom. She has barely thrown herself into one of the rose-covered chairs when there is a knock at the door.

She jumps. The door opens and her Mama enters. She. Has. An. Open. Letter. In. Her. Hand. Juliana feels her blood run cold, the breath leaving her body. Surely he has not ... but a glance at her Mama's face brings reassurance.

"A letter from Lady Grantley, my sweet," Doria Silverton beams, rustling across the room to show her. "See ~ she is planning a supper party with a ball to celebrate your engagement to dear Harry. She writes that, after you met her older friends, she'd now like to meet all your young friends. It will be a wonderful occasion, I am sure."

"Oh. Yes. How delightful," Juliana stammers.

"Lady Grantley writes so prettily to ask for the names of your own particular friends, whom she intends to invite to share your triumph. Is that not generous of her? Now, who shall I suggest? Charlotte, Alicia and perhaps dear little Fiona ~ we must all try to find her a suitable man; her parents seem to have given up on her. What do you think?"

Juliana tries to smile but fails to do more than hoist her lips upwards at the sides. What she thinks is: if she never saw 'dear little' Fiona Blythe again, her life would be very much easier.

"I am sure that will be delightful, Mama," she murmurs dutifully.

"And this afternoon dear Harry's stepmother will be paying a morning call. We must not forget our obligations, must we? It has been nearly a week since we visited Haddon Hall. We should not want to be found in dereliction of our obligations."

Juliana's smile locks itself in place at the edges.

"She won't be bringing the little boy, will she?"

Doria laughs, "I do not think so. Did she not say he was being tutored privately? He will be at his lessons. I hardly think she will bring her child and his tutor to visit."

But she might, Juliana thinks desperately. Given what she is currently experiencing, anything is possible. Any aberration. Any divergence from the norm. Oh, how could she face *him* and make polite conversation over the teacups?

Doria Silverton pats her daughter upon her dainty shoulder and hurries away to compose a suitably gushing reply to Lady Grantley and then check on the kitchen preparations for the afternoon, leaving Juliana to stare gloomily at her hands and contemplate how difficult life becomes when one's youthful folly returns unexpectedly to bite one.

She spends the next few hours trying to cultivate a really bad headache, but to no avail. Three o'clock rolls around, and she is forced to put on a pretty sprigged dress and subject her hair to the ministrations of her maid.

Her heart pounding, Juliana hovers on the first-floor landing until the doorbell rings, and the parlour-maid opens the door. By squinting through the bannisters in a very unladylike fashion, Juliana sees Lady Marie, swathed in furs, even though the weather is not inclement. She is unaccompanied.

Oh joy! Relief surges through her. Juliana almost skips down the stairs. She slides into the drawing room, fielding a disapproving glance from her Mama, who expects her daughter to be *in situ* to receive guests.

Juliana greets Lady Marie, inwardly noting once again that although her dress is particularly *à la mode*, she wears it awkwardly, as if she is unused to such finery. There is a brief moment of embarrassment when she extends two fingers, just as the guest nervously extends three, (a major *faux pas* by Harry's stepmother, noted by both mother and daughter), but she lets it pass.

Juliana seats herself next to her Mama and folds her hands in her lap. The opening salvos are fired: the journey to their house, the state of the roads, the clement weather for the time of year. The parlour maid hands round teacups, cream and sugar.

There is a temporary lull in proceedings while some tiny freshly baked biscuits are passed round. Doria Silverton does not believe in stuffing her guests. She has not put on an inch round her waist since she was eighteen ~ well, she can still lace to twenty-three inches, with a bit of an effort.

Lady Marie nibbles listlessly at her biscuit, trying not to spill crumbs on her silk dress. Juliana observes her covertly from under her long lashes. Harry's stepmother really is a study. Her diction is impeccable, her clothes expensive, yet she stumbles over the most basic social conventions.

"So, now, tell me, how is your dear boy? Juliana is desperate to see the little chap," Doria Silverton says brightly, trying to push the conversation up the steep hill.

"Really? Is she?" Lady Marie turns quizzical eyes to Juliana. There is something in the way she speaks, combined with the expression on her face that Juliana can't quite put her finger on. It is almost as if this awkward woman is amused by the suggestion.

"Oh, she adores all small children," Doria continues. "Why, when my dear sister comes to visit ~ she has twin boys, you know, you can hardly hear yourself think for the noise they make together. Romping up and down the stairs all day!"

Juliana bites her lip. She wishes her Mama would not go on in this fashion. The boys in question are now thirteen. And she has not romped since she was in the nursery. It is not only untrue, it is embarrassing.

But if Lady Marie senses Juliana's finer feelings, she does not show it. Instead, she sits a little more upright, and leans forward as if she is preparing herself to say something. Doria Silverton leans forward in anticipation.

"I do not know whether Harry has made you aware, but it is Sir Nicholas' birthday on Sunday. I ~ no we," she corrects herself, "are holding a small family dinner to celebrate. Quite informal, of course. My husband does not like formal occasions. We would be delighted if you, your husband and Juliana would care to join us. Harry will be there, of course."

Doria claps her hands.

"But how lovely! A family gathering. Of course, we shall be delighted to accept. Dear Harry has told us so much about his beloved father. Juley, do you hear ~ a birthday dinner at Haddon Hall!"

She hears. She is not deaf. The smile dies from her face, suddenly, as though someone has blown out a light.

Lady Marie continues. "You will be able to meet my little boy ~ for he will dine with us, as it is a special occasion."

For a moment, she pauses, her lips slightly parted, as if she is about to say something more. She glances quickly at Juliana, who is turning her uneaten biscuit into a hundred tiny uneaten biscuits. Then Lady Marie seems to think better of it. She presses her lips together, hands her half-drunk teacup to the hovering parlour maid, and rises to her feet.

Formal farewells are exchanged. Lady Marie Haddon is conducted to the hallway, re-swathed in her furs, and shown out into the street, where the Haddon coachman awaits. He hands her in, mounts the box and flicks his whip. The high-stepping pair of bays break into a smart trot.

Inside the carriage, Lady Marie Haddon sits back, letting relief flood over her. The visit went well. And now it is over, and she has fulfilled her social duties. Only Sunday, and the birthday dinner to go. Usually, she dreads her husband's birthday dinner, for Sir Nicholas is at his most bitingly irascible when in the company of his oldest son, enumerating his faults and shortcomings at great length, all evening, to her intense discomfort.

She thinks about the upcoming celebration, thanking the God of Uncomfortable Events that her gentle suggestion of a few extra guests was accepted. A smile curves the corner of her lips. She was not looking forward to competing with the tutor for her little son's attention. However, given what she has accidentally discovered about him, she thinks that this year, she is going to enjoy the occasion after all.

****

It is Sunday in London, and it is raining. The shops are shuttered up. The streets are almost deserted. The rain is small, compact and pitiless. It gives the impression it might continue until the end of time. Water is everywhere, splashing underfoot, churning up the streets, filthy and impregnated with the smell of soot.

A brownish haze fills the air, sweeping down from the sky to the pavement. At thirty paces, all the houses and public buildings appear like spots upon blotting-paper, and the few passers-by, under their umbrellas, have the look of uneasy spirits who have risen from their graves, this impression accentuated by the bells from the city churches, summoning the faithful to worship.

Here in Richmond, the climate has been altered for the worse. As the tutor sets out to discover why his grandfather has not replied to his letter, and to explore the city he has read so much about, the distant hills before him are hidden by ugly mists.

Nevertheless, he trudges on. The rain soaks into his shabby shoes, and the bottom of his trousers are caked in thick clayey mud. *Che importa*! His face is set towards the streets of London. He has the whole day at his disposal, and he is glad to have left the frenetic atmosphere of Haddon Hall, where the birthday celebrations of his employer are being prepared.

Every time he leaves the confines of the big house, the tutor experiences this sense of breaking-free. His identity is not obliterated by his labour. The constraints and restrictions of his daily life are shucked off. He does not have to prove himself to anybody. He can be utterly and completely who he is.

The great city lies before him, the motley streets of the metropolis, the silver river snaking through its beating heart. All is his to possess. For a few hours. This is his day of rest from his labour, and his day of exploration.

The tutor makes swift progress and soon reaches the dingy rain-spattered street where his grandfather lives. He raps smartly upon the door. There is a pause. He raps again, calls out his grandfather's name.

Footsteps sound on the other side of the door. Running along the hallway. He frowns. Neither Nonno nor Ysabella are what he'd call fleet of foot. Then the door is flung open. Two men he has never met before stand staring at him, their eyes widening.

"*Dove Nonno?*" he asks. "*Dove Ysabella?*"

Instead of replying, the strangers pull him into the house and slam the door shut. The tutor removes his hat, makes a palms-up gesture. The men begin explaining what has happened to the old man. They speak very fast, and at the same time, so that the tutor is forced to turn from one to the other in quick succession.

A moment's pause to take in what he has been told. Then he claps his hat back on his head, wrenches open the door and takes off down the street as if he were being pursued by every fiend in Hell.

****

Meanwhile, the Silverton carriage, bearing Doria Silverton, her husband Maldon Silverton, her daughter Juliana and fiancé Harry Haddon, approaches the ornate wrought-iron gates of Haddon Hall. Doria and her husband are seated on one side, facing the coachmen. The two young people sit opposite.

Doria Silverton prides herself upon being a 'modern' Mama: none of the tiresome old-fashioned chaperoning rituals and restrictions that she had to undergo. Juliana has benefited from freedoms she never dreamed of:

finishing her education abroad, shopping trips in the West End, meeting her girlfriends unaccompanied, walks and tea-parties.

And it has paid off. Her daughter has the free and easy airs and graces that elicit admiration wherever she goes. She is welcomed not just for her face, but for her delightful personality and excellent manners.

The proof is seated directly opposite (awkwardly trying to stop his leg from touching hers). Harry Haddon was the catch of the Season. So many Mamas set their sights on him. But Juliana fished for him, hooked him and landed him safely.

Doria allows herself a small smile of satisfaction.

Juliana's reputation is spotless. Like fish, (her mind is taking a decidedly piscine turn), a young woman has always to be fresh and unspoilt. The slightest whiff of impropriety or the slimy taint of scandal, and she is finished at once, doomed to live on the margins of good society. Or grind out her days as a governess.

Doria pretends to chat to her husband, while keeping a watchful eye on Juliana and Harry. The seating plan has been deliberately engineered so that the two lovers can enjoy the proximity of each other, while murmuring sweet nothings.

How lovely her daughter is in her new peach-coloured day dress. The tiny seed-pearl necklace highlights her slender throat, and adds lustre to her complexion. A good choice. See how she lowers her eyes demurely whenever Harry addresses her.

Albeit she is a little pale, and some of her natural sparkle seems to be missing, but that could be put down to the gravity of the occasion, Doria thinks. The coach pulls up in front of the steps. Harry scrambles out and offers Juliana his hand.

What a pretty pair they make. So well-matched. She barely comes up to the top of his shoulder. See how she looks up at him, her expression apprehensive, as befits a young woman about to meet her future father-in-law.

Doria takes her husband's arm. "We are so lucky, Maldon," she murmurs as they follow the young people to the front door, where the Haddon butler is waiting to take their outdoor coats and announce them.

****

The old man dreams. It is spring. There is an orange grove. The sun is slanting through the dark green leaves, making silver-shimmer patterns on the ground. He is walking amongst the orange trees, the air rich with the scent of orange blossom. He can hear bees humming. He is happy.

Then someone is walking just behind him. He hears their soft breathing. It is a woman: he hears the sound of her long skirt brushing through the grass. She speaks:

"I am waiting for you, *amore*. I have been waiting a long time. My heart aches, Gio. Come to me soon, *caro*. Soon."

In his dream, the old man tries to turn his head, to look once again into the face of his long-dead wife, but he cannot. He knows she is there, but he cannot touch her. He feels tears running down his face. Anetta. Lover, wife, comrade.

He calls her name, but the word falls upon empty air. Mist swirls in, blocking the sun, hiding the trees. He tries desperately to peer through the grey curtain, reaching out to part it with his hands. It fades into darkness.

"Anetta! Anetta!" he calls, over and over.

A hand touches his shoulder, lightly, as if it were a butterfly landing on a flower. He hears a woman's voice speaking his name. The old man opens his eyes slowly, praying that he has finally passed from the weariness of this world to that place just beyond the horizon, where she is waiting to meet him.

But he is still here, in this strange bed in the whitewashed room. He has not passed. And the physical pain is so terrible it feels as if someone is cutting away portions of his flesh. He utters a long heartbroken sigh, "Aiyeee," and turns his face to the wall.

Sarah Lunt gently leans over him. "Mr Bellini, there is somebody here to see you."

He grunts, turns slowly, gasping as the pain tears into him with renewed force.

"*Nonno?*"

He stares up into the troubled eyes of his grandson. Opens his mouth, but can only croak his name. Words seem to have seeped out of his brain. He, who once wrote fiery revolutionary pamphlets, who could sway crowds of thousands with his rhetoric. Now he is reduced to a few muttered words.

"Sit by the bed," Sara Lunt says to the young tutor, bringing over a chair. "Take his hand. Talk to him. Maybe it will rally his spirits. He asks for you every time he comes back to us."

She does not say that these moments of consciousness are becoming fewer and happening at longer intervals, as the old man drifts towards that bourne from which no traveller returns. It cannot be more than a few days before he will slip away.

The grandson stifles a sob. "*Nonno*, oh, *nonno* ~ I did not know. I am so sorry, *scusa*! But I am here now, and I will never leave your side."

Sarah Lunt tiptoes to the door. On the threshold, she glances back. The young man has laid his head on the old man's pillow. He is gazing fixedly into the tortured pain-racked face. The expression of deep love and devotion in his eyes catches her throat. Wiping the tears from her eyes, she goes to attend to her next patient.

****

Sir Nicholas Haddon's birthday luncheon has been set out in the conservatory, the intention being to catch the warmth and rays of the afternoon sunshine. Alas, it continues to rain, so a grey gloomy sky and the sound of raindrops pattering off the glass roof is what greets the guests as they take their places at the festive table.

Nevertheless, this is a celebration, so a bad job must be made the best of. At least the food does not disappoint. A whole salmon, assorted salads, a raised fowl pie (with the legs of the unfortunate occupant sticking out of the top-crust) are laid out on platters ready to be served.

Wines, lemonade and a selection of fruit tarts, jugs of cream, bowls of late peaches and moulded jellies are waiting in line. A row of uniformed staff are also waiting.

Here comes the birthday celebrant, with Juliana on his arm. He is followed by her father and Lady Marie, with Harry and Doria Silverton bringing up the rear. They sit. There is a pause. Two places remain unfilled. Sir Nicholas beckons one of the staff.

"Tell Mr Bellini we are ready for him and Danny to join us."

Seated on his right, in the place of honour, his future daughter-in-law feels her face freeze. Her nails dig into her soft palms. She holds her breath. Here, finally, comes the moment that she has been dreading ever since she awoke this morning.

She flicks a glance across the table at Harry, who is eying the food hungrily. Please let him not notice anything amiss, she prays to the Goddess of Youthful Regret. The servant re-enters the conservatory holding the hand of a small boy in a Norfolk jacket.

He runs across the room and buries his head in Lady Marie's lap.

"Hey, hey, Daniel! What is all this!" his father commands sternly. "Make your bows to the company."

The boy lifts his curly head and peeps over the rim of the table, his blue eyes wide. His mother gently whispers in his ear. He stands up, places both hands behind his back, and in a piping treble, at great speed, he recites a short Latin verse. There is a silence when he finishes. Then Sir Nicholas smiles and applauds him.

"Well done, my boy! I don't recall your brother being able to recite Ovid at your age, eh, Harry? Now, where is that tutor? His place is empty and the food awaits."

The man servant steps up to the head of the table and murmurs something in the host's ear. Sir Nicholas' face falls as he registers his disapproval.

"I see," he says. "Well, it cannot be helped. We are not going to wait for him. You may begin to serve the food. Danny ~ you shall choose what you'd like to eat as a reward for your efforts."

Juliana bends her face over her plate. Of course, she will not eat any of the food; a young woman should never be seen to be eating in public, but as she moves it around her plate in a pretence of consuming it, she feels a warm glow of relief stealing over her.

She does not know where her former lover is, and frankly, she doesn't care. Alive or dead, it is of no concern. As long as he isn't here, that is all that matters. She turns to Sir Nicholas and favours him with a charming smile. Now she can get on with doing what she does best: being utterly delightful.

****

The tutor sits on the floor, his head resting on the pillow. Time has lost its meaning. It is meted out in the hoarse ragged breaths of the dying man that occasionally cease, making the young man's heart almost stop beating, until they resume again.

Every now and then, an orderly enters the room, observes the old man, checks on his breathing, makes a note on the chart at the end of his bed, and silently leaves. Once, a silver-haired man in a frock coat enters, lifts the limp wrist and stares at his fob watch.

At some point, a cup of tea and a plate of coarse bread and butter is placed on the floor next to the young man. He eats and drinks, tasting nothing. He falls asleep, though he doesn't remember doing so, but when he wakes, somebody has lit a candle and put it on the small table in the corner, and has placed a grey blanket round his shoulders. It smells of carbolic soap.

He watches the night shadows chasing each other across the far wall, and wonders which one heralds the arrival of the Angel of Death. He knows his grandfather no longer believes in God, having witnessed the slaughter of so many comrades, and the needless, agonising death of his grandmother, but he finds himself praying, nevertheless.

Eventually, pale-fingered dawn comes feeling for their faces. The young man opens his eyes, and stares directly into the eyes of his grandfather, which seem cloudy, as if somebody has forgotten to dust them.

The old man is watching him fixedly, with the desperate intensity that comes from knowing one will never again see the face of the other person in this life.

"*Nonno* ~ you are awake! You are better!" The young man sits up.

The old man smiles wearily, reaches out a trembling hand. He knows his time is very close. It is not possible to lie to himself. He feels the door to the world slowly swinging shut. Death polishes all truth and turns it into knife edges that cannot be hidden.

"Come closer, Angelo. It is hard for me to speak."

The young man leans towards him, his eyes bright and full of hope.

"You have been a source of joy all my life," the old man whispers. "For so many years there was no child to carry on the family name. Then you arrived. That is why you were given the name Angelo ~ for you were sent by the angels. A miracle from God."

He breaks off, gasping for air. The young man lifts the glass of water to his lips. The old man takes a minute sip and continues.

"When I am dead, the comrades will take my body back to Italy and bury it next to Anetta ~ you will find the money you need to pay them in a drawer in my study. There are letters in there too ~ burn them. All of them.

"In my Will there is money for you and Ysabella, enough for her to go back home to her family, and enough for you to live on for a while, if things go wrong for you here. My books must go to the Italian Workers' Library. My signet ring is yours ~ make sure you take it."

"*Nonno*, this is foolish talk. You should rest. Get back your strength."

The old man places his hand on his grandson's head and closes his eyes. His face suddenly loses all colour. His profile looks thinner, the nose more prominent, the cheeks hollowed out. He breathes in. A shallow breath. Then out. A long rattling breath. Then silence.

A cry breaks from the young man's throat. He grabs the motionless figure by the shoulders, attempts to raise it from the bed, tries to shake life back into it. An orderly hurries in. Takes one look, and pulls him firmly away.

"Let him be, young sir. He's gone. There is nothing more you can do."

"But I didn't say goodbye," The young man cries. "And I had things I needed to talk to him about."

The orderly's face is kind. "You tell him now, young sir, while I fetch the doctor and the nurses to wash and prepare him. He'll hear you, wherever he is."

He folds the old man's arms across his chest, closes his eyes, straightens his head, and is gone. The young man sits on, motionless. It feels as if he is waiting for his grandfather to open his eyes, laugh at him, say it was a good trick. A game they used to play when he was a child.

But this is not a game, and he is no longer a child. With a long, heartbroken sigh, he gently removes the finger ring from his grandfather's left finger and places it upon his own. Then, hearing footsteps approaching along the corridor, he bends down and kisses the old man's peaceful face. A final farewell.

"*Arrivederci, Nonno. Riposare in pace,*" he murmurs.

****

The rules for dealing with a debtor are quite clear and known to all who deal in such matters. Nobody can be arrested on a Sunday. A bailiff cannot enter a property except by invitation, or via an open door or window, and then in daylight only.

Harry Haddon wakes on Monday morning, still basking in his father's approval of his future marital partner, still seeing the warm blush on her cheek, still feeling the outline of her shapely leg pressed against his on that blissful carriage ride back.

He hauls himself out of bed, thinking what a lucky chap he is. His levitation coincides with the arrival of his man (who lives out) bearing his shaving water and the ominous announcement that: '*there is a gent from Swifte & Brewtal waiting on the landing.*'

At which pronouncement, all bliss evaporates like morning mist and Harry Haddon turns as pale as his flannel nightshirt. Throwing on an old dressing gown, he strides to the door and flings it open.

"What is the matter here?" he demands.

A solid unshaven man in a greasy suit is sitting on the top step. He hands Harry a document.

"Morning young sir. Morning. I have here a bill for one hundred and fifty-three pounds, seven and ninepence owed at the suit of Mr E. Smith at the Cremorne," comes the implacable reply. "And I ain't to budge a ninch until I gets it, sez he. In cash."

Harry scans the document. "But … but," he stutters, "What is all this? I do not recognise any of these sums."

"Business additions, sir. Obligations incurred, professional expertise employed, paperwork, shoe leather, ink and quills, penalty percentages, waiting time, wages of workers, heating, lighting, coals, future Christmas bonuses for the clerks. Soon mounts up."

Harry retreats into his living toom to consider his options. It is certainly not the first time he has found himself in the neighbourhood of Queer Street, heralded by a similar visitation from a process-server working for some collection agency operating in a semi-legal capacity out of a public house taproom off the Strand.

This is different, though. For a start, it has nothing to do with his personal exploits, being the bill originally racked up by Anthony Rice and his friends, on the evening he was deliberately sent packing with a flea in his ear. And the sums accrued in those former instances were paltry compared to this.

Harry scribbles an urgent note, instructs his man to take it straight round to Rice's apartment, with instructions not to return without the money. While he waits, he paces the rooms, too agitated to break his fast.

His brain whirls with a thousand thoughts. He cannot believe he has been treated thus. It must be some mistake. After all, he was at Eton with these chaps. The honour of the school, and all that. After an ominously short time, footsteps are heard on the stairs and his man enters.

"Mr Rice is not there. I have been told that he has gone to his parents' country estate. He is not expected back for some time."

A strong tremor passes through Harry Haddon. Just as his life was turning a corner, the stigma of dishonour and disgrace has crept in once again. He opens various drawers, scribbles figures on a piece of paper, and reaches the unfortunate conclusion that he has not enough disposable funds to honour the debt.

He knows his father will not meet the bill. He does not want to call upon the sympathy of his aunt, Lady Grantley. He has recently cast off all his former friends. There is nobody to stand up for him.

Harry suddenly envisages the sweet innocent face of Juliana. How will she bear it when she discovers that he, the man in whom she has put her trust, the man who will shortly stand by her side in a House of God and promise to love and cherish her as long as they both shall live, is in reality a miserable debtor?

He returns to the process-server, who, in the absence of any developments, has spread out a greasy packet of sandwiches on the landing floor and is tucking in with relish. An uncorked bottle protrudes from his jacket pocket.

"I can give you a note of hand."

The man repeats his original mantra that it is 'cash only'.

Harry suggests a cheque drawn on his bank.

Same response.

"Then I regret I cannot meet this bill at present."

The man wipes his mouth with the back of his hand.

"I am sorry to hear it. Wery sorry indeed. Well sir, that being the case as you tells it, I am instructed to accompany you to Mrs Twort's, where a room will be made available for you until sich time as you are able to avail yourself of the necessary readies. You may pack a bag. Take as long as you like. I ain't going nowhere, and there is a man waiting outside the house in case you tries to bolt."

Harry Haddon throws a few shirts, underclothes, his cut throat razor, (resisting the temptation to use it to guarantee his immediate exit from Queer Street) into a travelling bag. He is in a state of shock. That a former schoolfriend should play such an evil trick upon him is almost beyond his simple comprehension.

But he can bear it. He must bear it. For her sake. He tells himself this, over and over, as he hauls the bag down to the street and is borne away in a shabby hackney cab.

****

While Harry Haddon is being transferred, slack-jawed with horror, from his nice bachelor apartment to a down-at-heel spunging-house off Charing Cross, let us transfer our attention to another house, another breakfast table. Another absent breakfaster.

At Haddon Hall, mealtimes are adhered to strictly. Thus, when the young tutor fails to appear at the summoning of the breakfast bell, Sir Nicholas Haddon, suited and booted and ready for the City, commands a servant to fetch him forthwith.

The return of the servant with the information that Mr Bellini is not in his room and his bed has not been slept in, elicits a growl of annoyance.

"Where the devil is he then? He wasn't here yesterday either. I do not recall receiving any request to leave the house. Nor would I have granted it. The man's clearly done a flit, damn him!"

"Perhaps he has been involved in an accident?" Lady Marie suggests gently, as her husband beats an irritating tattoo on the side of his plate with his teaspoon.

"Accident? What accident? You think he is still here? Joseph," he calls loudly. "Tell the staff to check the traps immediately."

The manservant's exit coincides with the entrance of one of the housemaids, carrying a letter on a silver salver. She places it before Sir Nicholas, curtseys, and leaves the room.

"What is this, now?" he grumbles, slitting the envelope with his butter knife.

There is a pause while he reads the missive enclosed. Then he throws it down on the table.

"Ah. Now we know why Bellini is not favouring us with his presence."

"We do?" Lady Marie asks. She doesn't.

"He writes that his grandfather has just died in hospital. He apologises for the inconvenience, but informs us that he intends to accompany the body back to Italy for burial. Did you know he had a grandfather living in London?"

Lady Marie shakes her head.

"Well, he certainly never mentioned it to me. But see here ~ he 'informs' us, no 'may I, if you please'." Sir Nicholas Haddon rolls his eyes towards the ornate ceiling. "That's the younger generation for you. He will be gone for several days, so I shall have to find some sort of temporary tutor until he returns. I won't have Daniel's lessons interrupted."

"But I can easily teach him," Lady Marie says gently. "I know all the books Mr Bellini has been using. It would be much less troublesome for Danny to have somebody he knows instructing him, rather than a total stranger, do you not think dear?"

Silence. It feels to Lady Marie as if the whole room is suddenly holding its breath.

"We'll see," comes the reply. "Maybe for a day or so. It's not as if he'll fall behind if he misses a few days' professional tuition. But then we shall have to reconsider. And when that young man returns, if he returns, I shall be having a few words with him. This is not how I expect a member of my staff to behave."

Lady Marie bows her head over her plate. She hopes her irascible lord and master does not observe her sudden delight. She gobbles down the rest of her breakfast, willing Sir Nicholas to finish his bacon and eggs equally quickly, and be on his way.

As soon as he leaves the house, she knows she will be free to rush up to the schoolroom, where, for the first time in weeks, she can spend a whole long, uninterrupted day with her little son. What bliss awaits!

****

Many years ago, Detective Inspector Stride learned that one of the manifold virtues a police officer must possess is the ability to be patient. There are times when nothing happens. When an investigation gets bogged down, or grinds to a halt. There are days spent waiting for things to happen.

All one can do when that occurs, is to be patient and wait. Stride knows that his younger colleagues are desperate to hurry things along. They are wrong. Mistakes are made when you try to push through the invisible barricades that surround a difficult investigation.

Not that any investigation ever comes to a complete halt. Most of the time you work with a dark lantern in your hand, pointing it straight in front of you so you can see the way ahead. But sometimes it is a good idea to swing it to either side. So that you can see where you're not putting your feet.

Stride is engaged upon this process, which involves making marks on a map and creating a list on a piece of paper. Thus, after a few hours' intensive focus, he is able to determine the extent of the arson attacks and the areas in which they took place.

It is also clear that certain communities have suffered more than others. Since the start of the summer, the Jews have had more than their fair share of both personal abuse in the street, and vandalism of business premises, though other groups, Italian, Huguenot, German have suffered too.

The aggressive letters campaign being waged in the correspondence pages of various 'popular' newspapers continues unabated. Day after day, so-called respectable members of the community, largely writing under some pseudonym, rail against everything 'foreign' that is apparently diluting the character of the great city.

The few letters praising the contribution foreigners make to the life of the city are immediately countered by a tirade of negativity, with examples of the deleterious effect of their presence ~ most of which are so far-fetched that they are clearly made up.

He skims through the latest batch of faux outrage, noting the not-very-subtle suggestions that nefarious foreign practices are being carried on behind closed doors, or via secret foreign bank accounts. **Anarchy is on the March! Revolution is being Plotted! Conspiracies Abound! John Bull can no longer sleep safely in his bed!** (*The Inquirer* is at the frothy forefront of the disquiet, as usual.)

Stride has been a police officer long enough to remember previous uprisings of such hatred ~ the Irish community bore the brunt of it last time. However, he knows that it only takes a few sparks to set an inferno blazing, and London, after a hot sticky Summer, is ready to burn. Careful and judicious policing at street level is vital.

He is interrupted in his thinking by the appearance of Detective Inspector Lachlan Greig, his face grave.

"I have just come from the hospital: Mr Bellini is dead. That means we have a murder on our hands. I shall send new instructions round to all the police offices. Our man is no longer a person of interest, he is a wanted suspect in connection with a brutal murder."

Stride considers. "Are we looking for the same people?"

Greig spreads his hands, "I cannot see how one single group could be responsible for every attack, every act of vandalism or every letter. But it is like the plague: it seems to be spreading everywhere. I have frequently been told to 'go back where I came from' by people in the street.

"I think the newspapers are also much to blame. People tend to believe what they read in print, and they have been fed a rich diet of hatred for foreigners. You and I, and the likes of Richard Dandy know full well it is lies, printed only to sell copies, but this is the result. People are jumping to conclusions, and then acting out of their emotions rather than the facts. To stop the flow, we have to damn up the source. And that will be no easy task."

Stride sighs wearily. "There are times when I wonder where the world is going to, Lachlan. When I started out, you knew who the criminals were. They hid round corners or down dark alleyways. They ran away. You chased them. Now, they hide behind desks and defy you at every turn."

"But they cannot hide for ever. We always catch them, in the end," Greig says. "And we shall do so again."

Stride picks up a pencil and drums it against the side of his desk.

"The Bellini business. We must proceed with caution. If the public becomes aware that London was harbouring a notorious foreign revolutionary, we will have even more riot on the streets."

"Perhaps we should allow a few newspapers to publish the image we have, but without connecting it directly to Bellini's death?"

Stride agrees. "There are always so many questions, but in the end, it always comes down to a who and a why. We think we know why. We must now discover who, before they strike again."

****

Meanwhile, Harry Haddon has arrived at the well-known spunging-house of Mrs Beatrice Twort, where he is given a small room on the first floor, furnished with a rag rug of dubious provenance, a chair, a single bed, some much-darned sheets, and told by the ferocious Mrs Twort, whose false front of yellow curls are enough to strike fear into the heart of any debtor, to *'make yerself at 'ome, ducks. We don't stand on ceremony here.'*

Left to himself, Harry Haddon throws himself into the rickety basket-weave chair and gives way to despair, which is closely followed by the realisation that, much as he hopes to hide his disgrace from his father, his failure to turn up to work will lead eventually to the discovery of his current plight.

For a brief moment, he thinks again about employing the cut-throat razor in his bag. Then rejects the idea. There must be a way out of his situation that does not involve paternal wrath, or the shedding of his own blood. All he has to do is discover what it is.

But first, a letter with some sort of plausible explanation must be composed and dispatched to his place of work. Harry sets to with a will, and after a certain amount of head-scratching and quill-biting, manages four lines of reasonable mendacity that he hopes will head off the paternal wrath.

Time drags limp-footedly by. Three long hours pass in staring out of the cloudy window while trying to work out who, of his diminished circle of acquaintances, might be prevailed upon to bail him out.

Eventually, having missed both breakfast and luncheon, meals he enjoys and consumes lavishly, Harry's growling stomach forces him to venture from his small sparse first-floor room in search of something to eat.

He enters the parlour, hoping to buy a dinner with some of the loose change he has found in his trouser pocket, only to discover another occupant is already ensconced. A portly, grey-haired, lavishly side-whiskered gentleman stands with his back to the meagre fire. He is humming a ditty, while tapping a foot in time to his music.

To Harry's astonishment, the man is garbed in the striped motley of a medieval fool ~ down to the pointed shoes with bells on the toes and parti-coloured hat. Seeing Harry hesitate upon the threshold, eyes widening, the man sweeps off his hat and makes him a low bow.

"Prithee enter, young fellow-partaker in misfortune. Fear not the vision you see before you, for be it known unto you that I am William Horatio Falstaff Tregorran, a strolling player."

"Huh, strolling out of your lodgins without paying, more like," Mrs Twort puts in acidly from her seat by the window.

"As our good hostess has suggested, such was the sad reason for my being taken up, whilst in the middle of a performance of King Lear. I was playing the Fool, and as you see, fellow inmate, had not time to change from my stage costume into my street dress. Alack and woe!"

The man has a deep, sonorous voice that sounds as if it has been dipped in treacle, and marinaded in port wine before indulging itself in many fine cigars. But his pale blue eyes under the bushy brows twinkle, and his smile is infectious, so after an initial hesitation, Harry finds himself shaking the proffered hand and accepting a place by the miserable coal fire.

"I await the arrival of my good wife, bearing such sustenance as a man requires to hold body and soul together. I trust you will join me in my repast? Your face, like Cassius of old, hath a lean and hungry look."

Harry explains his current financial state, but his excuses are summarily waived aside.

"I will hear none of it. We are fellow travellers on life's rocky path, currently washed up on this bleak and barren shore. We have suffered a blow. A setback. What we have, we share. That is the code of the wayfarer."

There is a sniff from the chair by the window.

"Mrs T. will not begrudge us the use of two plates and some cutlery, for old times, eh, Margery?" William Tregorran booms, winking at Harry.

"Thruppence for the usage, and it is Beatrice, as you very well know."

"Her bark, young fellow-traveller, is not quite as bad as her bite. Though it runs it pretty close," the actor murmurs darkly, as Mrs Twort flounces out of the room to find plates and spoons.

When she returns, she brings with her a slight, pretty woman, with a pale anxious expression and soft fair curls peeping out of a faded straw bonnet. She carries a large basket over one arm, and in her hands is a china basin covered by a cloth.

At the sight of her, Tregorran instantly brightens, and she is greeted rapturously with a smacking kiss on each cheek. He leads her over to Harry.

"This is Affy, young sir. The light of my life and joy of my declining years. For who shall find a virtuous wife, as the Good Book says, her price is far above rubies. Tell me, dear wife, how is the Small Incumberance today?"

Affy replies that he is still happily ensconced with Mrs Harris and was chasing chickens around her back yard when she left him to come here. She sets down the basin, announces that it is 'stew', then opens up the basket, from which she produces a pair of woollen trousers, a rolled-up jacket and a creased collarless shirt.

"You see," Tregorran booms, gesturing towards the clothes. "I have everything I need: victuals, raiment and the love of a good woman. What more could any man want?"

"Rent money?" comes the laconic suggestion from the passageway.

Tregorran completely ignores the interruption.

"Come, young man, tonight you dine with me. The victuals may be simple, but I hope the company will make up for it. I shall tell you tales of Araby, of Malfi and of Rome. Just a brief pause, while I garb myself for the feast."

And ten minutes later, Harry Haddon finds himself seated at the bare parlour table, a bent spoon in his hand, tucking hungrily into mutton stew with dumplings, while listening entranced as Tregorran describes his various theatrical performances, accompanying himself with loud declamations and expansive spoonish gestures. Affy looks on affectionately from the far side of the room.

Just as the meal has reached the final plate-scraping stage, there is a loud knocking on the street door. All three pause, their eyes swivelling towards the origin of the sound. Mrs Twort frowns.

"More customers? At this time of the evenin'? One of you'll have to share a bed tonight then."

She goes to answer the door. Words are exchanged. Then Mrs Twort returns, her face even sourer than before.

"Young person for you, Mr Tregorran. Says she's come about the rent money you owe."

She stands aside as a slim dark-haired woman strides confidently into the room. Tregorran takes one look, gasps, places his hand upon his bosom in a theatrical gesture, then leaps to his feet, holding out both arms.

"Mimi! Mimi Casabianca! It is you! What in the name of all the Gods of Theatre and Thespians are you doing here?"

Essie Marks (for indeed, it is she) grins mischievously as she unfolds herself from his bearhug of an embrace.

"I could say I was just passing by, and my mystical powers sensed you had been taken up again," she says, looking innocent. "Truth is, I was talking to the new costume manager at the Queen's about a bit of business, and he mentioned it. So I came over to see what I could do."

"Ah. I see. Good man, that Thomas. But Mimi ~ sit, sit, child. I heard you had quitted the profession."

"You heard correctly: I have indeed," the young woman says. "But the stage never quits you, does it? Once it gets into your blood, it's always there, like the veins that run through your body, just under the surface of your life."

William Tregorran throws back his head and roars with laughter.

"A typical Mimi Casabianca answer! My dear, I have not introduced you to my dinner companion ~ this is young Mr Harry Haddon, a fellow prisoner in misfortune. Mr Haddon, I give you the great, the miraculous, the unique, Miss Mimi Casabianca, the Masked Medium.

"We have trod many a board together, though Miss Casabianca was always much higher up the bill than yours truly. Rightly so. Rightly. So. What this young lady could effect through the mysterious arts of hypnotism and divination have to be witnessed to be believed. You have not seen ectoplasm until you have seen Mimi in action. Her decision to quit the profession was a great loss indeed. She has no replacement."

Essie makes him a mock bow.

"That is very kind of you to say. However, it is not why I am here. Though in a way, maybe it is ..." Essie's face takes on a thoughtful expression. "I remember a kind friend who helped me when I was on my uppers. A kind friend who gave me a bed for the night when I had nowhere to sleep. A kind friend who fed me when I had no money to buy food. A kind friend who got me a stage booking when I had nowhere to work."

Tregorran makes a dismissive gesture and opens his mouth to speak, but Essie waves him away.

"You and Affy saved my life. If it was not for you, who knows what would have become of me? And it was because you helped me to get back on my feet that I was finally reunited with my real mother, and found my true family.

"My happiness is laid at your door, both of you. And now, I am here to repay that kindness ~ though pounds, shillings and pence is a poor recompense for all you meant to me."

And with that, Effie opens her purse and pours a fistful of silver coins on the table. Tregorran stares at them mesmerised.

"But Mimi, this must be your life savings! I cannot ~"

"Yes, you can and you will," Essie breaks in firmly. "And it is not my money. Since I returned to London, I have discovered my true identity: I am a Jewess. The money you see has been given by members of my new-found family. When I explained the role you played in bringing me back to London, everyone wished to show their gratitude. Please take it. Use it to pay off your landlord and any other creditors. It is what we call a *mitzvah* in my community."

There is a long silence when she has finished speaking. Harry Haddon sees tears gathering in Tregorran's eyes.

"So shines a good deed in a naughty world," he murmurs. With great dignity, he picks up the money. He places some coins back upon the table, saying: "Dame, I believe this is what I owe you for three nights' board and lodging. Now, wife of my bosom, let me first gather up my scattered goods and chattels. Then we will shake the dust of this place from our feet and be on our way."

"Oi, I keep a clean house, I'll have you know," Mrs Twort snaps, her long bony fingers reaching out greedily to scoop up the coins.

Tregorran ignores her. He makes a low bow to Essie and to Harry, then offers his arm to Affy, and leads her out of the poky back parlour. Mrs Twort follows them, jingling the coins in her apron pocket.

"That was indeed a generous thing to do, Miss Casabianca," Harry says, when they are alone.

"My name is Essie Marks," she replies. "And that is what you do for your friends. Don't you have any friends to bail you out of this vile place?"

To his shame, Harry feels his cheeks reddening. He thought he had friends, but they turned out to be no better than enemies. Their faces suddenly rise up before him, taunting, sneering, mocking him. Exactly as it was when they made his life a living hell at Eton.

"I shall manage," he says stiffly.

Essie looks up at him from lowered eyes. She prides herself on being a good reader of character, not that she needs to be in this case. Abject misery surrounds this young man like a grey shroud. But she has no money to give him. She points instead to his jacket.

"I see you have a pocket come unstitched. May I repair it for you? I carry my work tools with me wherever I go."

Harry looks down, then takes off his jacket. Essie sidles into the seat next to him, opens her workbasket and gets out threads, a packet of needles, a silver thimble. Harry watches her thread up the needle. As Essie bends over the jacket, he notices an unusual chain about her slender neck. She catches his glance.

"You are looking at my strange necklace? Let me take it off so you can view it better. There ~ what do you see?"

He glances down. In his hand Harry now holds a thin strip of grey leather, threaded through a brass button which itself is attached to a piece of cloth by the shank. A strange jewel for a pretty young woman.

Harry stares at it, mesmerised, not noticing that Essie has quietly set down her work and is regarding him with totally focussed attention. Her eyes seem to have got larger, the pupils like black holes. It is almost as if she has gone into a trance and is reading his thoughts.

"There is a story to my necklace, if you care to hear it," she says softly.

"I should like to hear it, very much."

So Essie tells him about her little business, the fire that destroyed it, and the piece of paper with its vile slur that was left at the scene. She describes finding the button, and her suspicion that the owner of it was the person who started the fire and left the racial abuse.

"We are slowly rebuilding Nathan & Marks now. We have new premises, sewing machines and new fabric. We have new clients. But something has been lost that can never be replaced. Nor will it be until the person who set the fire and wrote those hateful words is made to pay for what he said and what he did. That is why I wear the button. It is a reminder. My mother has a saying: *the heart has no bones, so it cannot be broken*. She is wrong."

Essie bites off her thread, and hands the mended jacket back to its owner. She gives him another hard and searching look. Then, seeming satisfied with what she has discovered, she takes back her necklace, packs up her basket and rises from her seat.

"I will bid you goodnight, Mr Haddon," she says. "I hope you find a way out of your predicament. Perhaps we will meet again some day. May I leave you my card?" she continues, handing him a tiny pasteboard square. "This is where I work. *Nathan & Marks, Theatrical and Private Costumier.* We are always gratified to receive the patronage of new clients."

Essie slips out of the room, leaving Harry biting down upon his thoughts as upon an aching tooth. He puts the little card carefully in the newly mended pocket, and, having experienced the kindness of strangers, returns to his own room. There, he composes a suitably supplicant letter to his Aunt Grantley, upon whose mercy he has decided to throw himself, once again.

Luckily for Harry, his aunt will be in a good mood when she receives his penitent missive and will send money to release him into the world again.

****

Alas, no mercy of any kind has been extended to the fair and exceedingly anxious Juliana. Days and days and days have now passed without Romeo replying to her letter, and she is no longer able to put it down to bashfulness or embarrassment. The meaning cannot be explained away. It is a clear cut. He does not consider her *worthy* of a reply.

That a mere tutor ~ as she has taken to thinking of him, should treat her with such casual indifference is almost more than she can stand. And her casual lurking on the first-floor landing whenever the post is due, has not gone unnoticed by her Mama.

Juliana has had to lie, pretending she is waiting for a letter from Harry, which seems to have diverted suspicion from her real reason for hanging about like a seagull in an updraft. Here she is now, mid-morning, hovering by the upstairs bannisters.

The letterbox clangs. There is the dull thud of something dropping onto the floor. Juliana hurries down the stairs, almost getting a foot caught in her dress in her eagerness to reach the letters first.

A parlour maid appears from the sitting room, where she has been dusting the furniture. The two of them edge across the gleaming black and white square marble tiles towards the front door. Their joint reflections in the numerous gilt mirrors give the impression they are moving about on a chess board.

Juliana just beats the servant by a hairsbreadth. Check maid. She flicks through the pile of correspondence: a clothes bill addressed to papa, another clothes bill for papa, a bonnet bill for papa.

Oops. But she reminds herself: she is engaged, and an engaged young woman needs a lot of clothes, because

168

she has to entertain a lot of friends to tea and cakes to celebrate her good fortune and admire her ring and congratulate her upon her choice of husband.

No letter from her former lothario. But at the bottom of the pile is an envelope whose large curly writing is all too familiar. Her heart sinks. She has tried to shake off Fiona Blythe, but like a burr, she persists in clinging on. Juliana pockets the letter from her erstwhile best friend, hands the rest of the letters to the waiting maid, and returns to her own room.

Please let this not be another demand for money, Juliana thinks despairingly, as she opens the envelope. She has spent all her allowance. She is running out of viable excuses to borrow from her mother.

If this ruthless blackmailing continues, she might have to start selling some of her jewellery. Whatever her Italian dalliance was worth, it is not now worth what she has paid in money and anxiety and sleepless nights of worry.

But to her surprise, the letter is not another request for more frills or fripperies, bonnets or bon-bons. Instead, Fiona is proposing a 'truce' as she calls it. She would like to call upon her 'dearest Jules' at three o'clock to discuss 'certain matters'.

Now, what on earth is she to make of this? Juliana reads the letter several times, trying to work out whether to bar the door or get out the best china. In the end, she decides upon neither course of action. She sends Fiona a polite reply saying she will be at home between two and four, and looks forward to receiving her then.

Time absolutely flies when you are not looking forward to something. Almost before she has tidied her drawers and re-arranged the bottles and boxes on her dressing table, and brushed her little dog, the tiny quartz clock on Juliana's mantelpiece chimes three.

And almost before she can arrange her features into a suitable expression of fake amicability, the doorbell rings, followed by the sound of two sets of footsteps on the stairs, then a discreet knock at her door, and the maid's announcement that: 'Miss Blythe is here for you, Miss Juliana.'

Juliana folds her hands determinedly in her lap and arranges her features into as composed an expression as she can manage, given the trying nature of the prospective meeting. Meanwhile Fiona Blythe swishes into the room, all smiles, and in a dress of a viciously bright arsenical green colour, with matching bonnet ribbons, and a small green reticule.

The two former friends greet each other with feigned warmth. Fiona inquires after Juliana's health with an air of anxious solicitude which implies that if she was quite well, it was what she ought not to be.

Juliana waves languidly at a small chintz chair. Fiona lowers herself gracefully onto it. Juliana bids the hovering maid to leave them. No refreshments have been requested. It is not going to be *that* sort of a visit.

A silence descends. Juliana sits a little more upright in her chair and regards Fiona thoughtfully. That particular shade of green does nothing for her sallow complexion, she thinks. And her hair is still the same mousy colour, her eyes are too slanty and cat-like, and her mouth too small and mean.

She cannot now recall why they ever became such good friends in the first place. As if she is reading her mind, Fiona Blythe's face flushes and her eyes darken.

"So you have heard nothing from Romeo? How tragic. Maybe he does not regard your former acquaintance as being of any account, eh? I know I should be mortified if any man treated me so disrespectfully."

Juliana regards her steadily. She deliberately rearranges her hands so that her engagement ring is in plain sight.

"Please tell me what you came here to say, Fiona. Mama will be back from her charitable committee very soon, and we have so much to plan before my marriage."

Fiona Blythe sucks in her lower lip. Then she begins to speak. As she outlines what she wants, Juliana feels herself drifting away, as if what is happening is not happening to her, but to some other person, and she is hovering overhead, watching and listening to the little drama being played out below, but not participating in it.

"And that is your final demand?" she says, when the other has talked herself to a halt.

"It is. And frankly, I do not think, in the circumstances, I am being unreasonable. You have everything you desire. You always have had. I, on the other hand, have nothing."

Juliana regards her.

"And how on earth am I supposed to bring it about?"

"Oh, I am sure you will find a way," Fiona purrs, smiling like a cat in a creamery. "Given the probable outcomes of *not* managing to achieve it. Besides, I *trust* you, Julie. I really do. I know that if you set your mind to a thing, that thing is as good as done."

She gestures towards the Haddon Diamond glinting on Juliana's finger. "I clearly remember the first time you saw Harry Haddon: we were attending the Buckland's ball, and you said: *'I think I have just seen the handsomest young man in London. I wonder if I could get him to fall in love with me'*. And you did, Julie, didn't you?"

Juliana bows her head. She cannot deny it.

"Besides, what I am asking you to do is so little. Any good friend would not think twice about it."

Juliana bites her lower lip and stares off. Silence descends. Then, Fiona rises, smoothing down her dress with a gloved hand.

"So, it is agreed then? Good. I shall wait to hear from you. I am happy to play my part in the business. And I will do so to the best of my ability. Till we meet again, dear schoolfriend …"

Another feline smile. Fiona glides from the room, not waiting for Juliana to ring for the maid to show her out. Juliana goes to the window and watches as Fiona leaves the house, strides down the steps and disappears around the nearest corner.

She is still standing there, seeing nothing, hearing nothing, deep in thought when Doria Silverton enters, breaking the spell. Doria stands on the threshold, glancing round the room.

"I believe I just saw little Fiona Blythe leave the house. Why did you not offer her a cup of tea? Did she tell you the news? Arethusa St Edwardes has got engaged to that dreadful artist! Apparently, he is a member of the Pre-Raphaelite Brotherhood, whatever that means. I was hearing all about it from someone in my committee. Her parents are furious, but Arethusa is quite determined. I gather she has threatened to *elope* if her parents do not give way. Can you imagine it! Elope!"

White-faced, Juliana turns to face her.

"I see from your expression that you are as shocked as I am," Doria continues, mis-reading her daughter with her customary lack of intuition. "I always thought young Arethusa was a pillar of propriety, just like you, dearest. I never supposed for one moment that she was capable of forming such a wildly unsuitable attachment, did you?"

Juliana mumbles something.

"Her poor, poor parents ~ their good name is about to be dragged down into the dust," Doria continues. "I do feel such sympathy for them. I was only saying to your father the other day: we have been so lucky in our daughter. Not a single whiff of scandal or impropriety ever. And now an engagement to a young man of impeccable breeding and background."

Each word seems to enter Juliana's sub-conscious with the piercing sharpness of a knife. She feels herself wincing. Nevertheless she forces herself to smile wanly at her mother, who hurries over to her, enfolding her to the ample bosom in a maternal embrace.

"There, there, my brave girl: I know you are upset. These things happen, and we must just deal with it as best we can. Arethusa will regret bitterly what she has done, I am sure, given time. Meanwhile the Edwardes will never be invited into good society again. Such a shame for Athena and Raglan ~ their chances have gone now.

"But we must put this unpleasantness aside. I have bought a copy of Madame Fifi's Finest French Fashions and there are some lovely patterns in it for day dresses ~ let us look over them together with a nice cup of refreshing tea and perhaps a piece of sponge cake. Come, Juliana, come. There is still so much to plan before your wedding day."

Reluctantly, Juliana allows herself to be taken by the arm and led out of her room and down to the sitting-room. Thereafter, she sips her tea, crumbles her cake and expresses delight at everything she is shown. The dutiful daughter.

But it is all a front. Behind the front, her mind is in turmoil as she tries to think of a way to enact Fiona Blythe's final demand. And tries not to think of the consequences if she does not succeed.

****

173

There are consequences to every action we carry out in this world. We cannot know what they will be, so, in a way, we cannot structure our life around what might, or might not happen. It is better to do what seems right at the time, regardless of what could develop as a result.

Such are the thoughts running through Angelo Bellini's mind as he stands on a hillside in Italy, watching as four men reverently lower the simple wooden coffin of his grandfather into the newly-dug grave.

He hears birdsong, the high trill of skylarks, the sound of women weeping, of men trying not to weep, of curious questioning children who have been brought to see the burial because this man, this great leader, whose name is only whispered, was part of their parents' history.

The coffin touches the bottom of the grave. There is a communal sigh. The men pull the cloths free. The tutor picks up a handful of yellow earth and stones, and lets it rattle onto the lid of the coffin.

Later, in his parents' house, he listens as old men with weather-beaten faces and twisted, arthritic hands recount stories of former campaigns, reciting stirring speeches and proudly showing their battle-scars. Their eyes are misty with recollection, their voices low and reverent as they speak his grandfather's name.

Meanwhile, black-clothed women carry platters of food to and fro, children run in and out and neighbourhood dogs lie prone in the hot sunshine, occasionally raising a tired head to snap at a passing fly.

He chooses not to see the silent appeals, to notice the significant nudges, the pursed mouth of his mother as he checks his watch. He will not accede to her unspoken want, to the barely concealed demands of the comrades ~ old men with both minds and feet in the past.

There is no mantle to inherit. The fight is over. They lost. The country is united. People have chosen peace over conflict. His sights are set on the future, and it is not going to happen here. He stays for one more night. Then he embraces his parents, shoulders his travelling bag and sets off on foot for the local station.

His journey passes uneventfully, and soon, the tutor finds himself stepping out of a railway carriage and hauling his bag along a platform. He breathes in acrid smoke, sees the soot-blackened walls and iron girders, and hears the cries of newsboys and hackney cab drivers.

He hails a cab, (he has some money left from his trip) and is soon standing at the gates of Haddon Hall. As his footsteps crunch up the gravel drive, the front door ahead of him opens and a young man hurries down the steps, his shoulders hunched, his expression tense.

The tutor pauses. He has never met him, but he knows instinctively who the young man is: Harry Haddon, the eldest son. The Disappointment. Engaged to the fair Juliet, whose letter is still the cause of much head-scratching and indecision on his part.

Harry Haddon comes to a halt. The two young men face each other. The tutor makes a low bow.

"Good day to you," he says politely.

Harry Haddon returns the greeting, pulling a face.

"If you're that tutor fellow, I'd watch out. The Pater is in a right temper. As I know to my cost," he says ruefully.

"Ah. I see."

The information does not come as much of a surprise. The irascibility of his employer has been witnessed on a daily basis. Anything from the freshness of his breakfast egg, to the state of the nation, can provoke an angry outburst. Only his small pupil and, to a limited extent, the wife, are relieved of the verbal scourging.

"You are Signor Harry Haddon? May I congratulate you upon your forthcoming marriage," he says.

Harry Haddon's features relax into a smile.

"Thank you. She is a wonderful girl, and I am a lucky man. Still don't know why she agreed to marry a reprobate like me." He gives a short laugh, and nods towards the house. "Even the Pater likes her, which must say something, eh?"

"Indeed, it must."

The tutor picks up his travelling bag once more.

"I shall take your advice and enter judiciously by the rear door," he says.

Harry consults his watch.

"Give him an hour or so," he advises. "Should have calmed down by then. Good luck to you."

The two young men nod cordially to each other. Then the tutor heads towards the door to the back kitchen, and Harry goes to catch the next river boat to Chelsea. Once inside Haddon Hall, the tutor goes up to his room and unpacks his belongings.

When he is finished, he descends the stairs and enters the drawing room, where Sir Nicholas sits fuming behind a newspaper, while Lady Marie fiddles with her needle and a piece of embroidery.

He makes his bows to his stern-faced employer and his silent watchful wife, uttering his humble apologies for his absence. Luckily for him, his small pupil enters the room and runs straight up to him, shouting with delight and clinging to his legs.

"Papa! Papa ~ look who is here! Mr Bellini is back!"

The tutor detaches himself gently from the child's grip, and greets him formally in Latin. The boy thinks for a second, then responds in kind.

"Ah, you see, Bellini: the lad remembers," Sir Nicholas says, his features softening as he looks upon his youngest son.

"He is a dutiful student," the tutor says, because the primary duty of a good tutor is always to praise the intelligence, ability and wit of the pupil. Regardless.

Sir Nicholas nods his agreement, then snaps his fingers to summon the maid. He orders tea and cakes to be brought.

"You will take tea with us, Bellini? I'm sure Daniel will be interested in your descriptions of your native land. I want the lad to realise there is a world out there, waiting for him to conquer."

The tutor clamps his mouth shut. The British and their desire to subdue and conquer everything was a topic frequently brought up by his university friends. The British think Britain bestrides the world like some Colossus. It is an opinion not shared by the rest of the world. He positions himself a discreet distance from the fire and the family, sipping his tea and observing.

He notes how Lady Marie never takes her eyes off the child, and how her features fall whenever the little boy flashes a grin of delight in his direction. He lets Sir Nicholas' complaints about the folly and foolishness of his oldest son wash over him.

Later, when he is alone in his room, he takes the letter from Juliana out of a drawer and re-reads it. Then he sits and thinks for a while. Finally, he tears the letter into several pieces, places the pieces in the empty grate and strikes a match.

He has only met Harry for a few minutes, but he'd instantly felt they were *sympatico*. In a different life, they might even have become friends. Besides, *Nonna* Anetta always used to say something about not relighting a flame under an old pot ~ though admittedly it sounded better in Italian.

****

There is no finer public place in London to see and be seen in than Hyde Park. Here, at four o'clock, on a fine afternoon such as this, you might lean on the railings and watch the parade of open carriages pass by, each one bearing some exquisite beauty and her handsome escort.

You could marvel as a regiment of horse-guards trot by on their magnificent mounts, their bright red uniforms catching the light, the horses' harness jingling. For this is society displaying itself to itself, and for its own satisfaction. It is as much a part of the London scene as the balls held in the great Mayfair houses.

Mixed in with the cream of fashionable society as they ride, drive or promenade, are the 'pretty horse-breakers' in their tight riding-habits, saucy bonnets and tiny polished boots. They too are mounted upon expensive hacks, loaned by the owners of livery stables.

Look more closely: here come two familiar faces.

Juliana Silverton and Harry Haddon, seated side by side in a shiny carriage drawn by a fine pair of bays. She holds a blush-rose parasol over her curls, shading her delicate porcelain skin from the Autumn sunshine. He wears a dark cloth frockcoat and a silk top hat, and looks every inch the handsome young buck about town.

Juliana is keeping half an eye upon the crowds thronging the railings, and half a brain upon what she is about to suggest to her future husband. Harry is just relieved that he has been sprung from Mrs Twort's by his generous aunt, who has somehow squared it with the Pater so that he has not been sacked from his job. Never has a small cupboard, a little grey clerk and a ledger of figures seemed so welcoming!

They trot past one of the relics of ancient days, a bulky older carriage driven by a venerable retainer. Juliana steals a sideways glance into the deep interior. Her glance is met by a haughty old lady with a steely expression, who lifts a lorgnette to her eyes to observe her more closely.

Blushing under the critical gaze, she turns to Harry and places her little gloved hand on his sleeve.

"I am so excited about the ball," she murmurs.

For a split second, Harry honestly hasn't a clue what she is talking about. Then he remembers: Aunt Grantley is holding a ball in his and Juliana's honour. His heart sinks.

"Ah. The ball. Yers."

"I am sure it will be a memorable occasion."

So is Harry sure, but not for the same reason. He gathers from his Aunt Grantley that all his former group of friends, including Anthony Rice, have sent acceptance letters. Juliana pauses for a heartbeat, then squeezes his arm gently.

"There is something I want to ask you, Harry, dear. Just a little, little thing, but it would give me so much happiness."

He glances down at the gloved hand, so small, so trusting, the half-moon of delicate cheek, the curved lips. How could he deny anything to this beautiful bewitching creature, who has, by some miracle, agreed to share his life?

He bends his head closer to the rosy lips. Juliana speaks in a low, urgent voice. Over the past few days she has rehearsed what she is now asking him, trying different approaches to see which sounds the most likely to get the answer she wants.

When she has finished, she sits back, folding her hands in her lap and waits for his reply. She hopes Harry cannot sense how fiercely her heart is beating, how hard her teeth are biting into her lower lip, so hard she fears she might draw blood. She stares straight ahead, not daring to look at him.

"Are you sure?" he says, frowning.

She nods. Oh yes. She is. Quite, quite sure.

"And it will make you happy?"

Oh, so, so very happy, she assures him.

Harry shrugs. He has been brought up without a mother, without sisters; he has been educated in a world consisting wholly of boys and men. His experience of women has been limited, and usually paid for. He is a stranger in this female land. He has no compass or route map.

"Ah. I see. Well …"

"So, you can bring it about? Really?"

Her eyes search his face. Her expression is so sweetly anxious that something inside him just melts. He feels a lump in his throat. Nobody in his life has ever looked at him in such an endearing way. Harry clears his throat, and agrees. Of course. He will. Exactly as requested.

Her smile in response is as wide as Africa. She snuggles against him, looking up at him, bright-eyed and joyous, like a child who has just been given the keys to a sweetshop. Harry is utterly enchanted. So this is love, this warm glow, this contentment. Who knew?

The carriage bearing the two lovers swings out of the park and into Kensington, where Harry has booked a table for two at a nice little restaurant he knows. It is the sort of place a chap can take a young lady of good breeding without a chaperone and without eyebrows being raised, plus it is not too expensive. Funds are a little straitened right now.

Also, the food is plentiful and good. Not that Juliana will eat any of it. Harry is baffled by the little she seems to consume. How can anyone keep body and soul together on such tiny portions? He is a formidable trencherman, three square meals a day barely satisfying his appetite.

The carriage turns down a side street. They sit side by side. Neither of them speaks. Harry glances sideways at

Juliana's delicate profile and wishes he better understood how the female mind worked.

But in the end, what does it matter? His Juliana is the sweetest, kindest girl on earth. The glow from her beautiful eyes lights the way to a better life. As for what she has asked him, he vows to try and do his best for her. She deserves no less.

****

The detective division of the Metropolitan Police, based at Scotland Yard, ought to bask in the gratitude of the population of the city for its unstinting pursuit of nefarious characters and heinous crimes.

Chance would be a fine thing. Not to say that they, the general public, do not try to help out where they can. Thus, Detective Inspector Stride arrives for work on Monday morning to find the outer office besieged by tall, saturnine-complexioned men in top hats eager to assist the police in their current inquiries by informing them that the person they are seeking, as depicted on various Wanted Posters distributed around the city, is very definitely not them.

Many also carry copies of certain daily publications, folded to the story and drawing of the suspect. They are accompanied by various females, all equally keen to reinforce their man's upstanding character, because when it comes to loudly protesting one's innocence, you cannot beat the love of a good woman, or acceptable equivalent.

Stride takes one despairing look at the protesting mêlée, then elbows his way through, shouting for Cully, who emerges down the back stairs. He has been playing cards in the upstairs rest room with some of the day constables.

"I see we have had quite a response to Lachlan's appeal for information," he remarks.

Stride regards him gloomily. "I swear I actually recognise some of them. They turn up to every appeal for information. It's as if they can't help themselves. What is it about these people and their need for constant public recognition?"

Cully shrugs. He, too, has spotted a few familiar faces on his way in ~ faces now augmented by dark whiskers and the judicious application of burned cork to the eyebrows to make them appear more like the drawing supplied by one of the Italian victims.

"Shall I get a few constables to take down the details?"

"Please do," Stride says crisply. "The sooner we can clear that riff-raff off the premises, the sooner we can get down to what we are paid to do: find and apprehend the real people behind Mr Bellini's brutal murder ~ oh, and if one of that riff-raff is Mr Horatio Ignaz Grinder, I'd like to have a word with him. In private, and he knows what it is about."

Stride heads briskly for his office, leaving Cully to deal with the regiment of totally innocent lookalikes. Cully goes to summon up the troops, and within a surprisingly short space of time, the outer office is clear again.

He is just closing the door after the final innocent suspect has gone, when it is abruptly thrust open again. An officer he does not recognise enters. Cully greets him politely, but his greeting is cut short.

"Where's the Scotchman?" the man demands.

"If you mean Detective Inspector Greig, I believe he is somewhere hereabouts," Cully says coldly.

"*Detective* Inspector is it now? Well, go find him, there's a good man. Tell him it's Will Atherton from

Bow Street Police Office ~ he knows who I am right enough."

"And your business with him?"

"We have got his wanted man. One of our constables recognised him from the poster. Picked him up on the street last night. He's in the cells waiting for you, all nice and snug."

Cully goes to locate Greig and tells him there is a former colleague waiting to see him. When Cully says the officer's name, Greig winces. Inspector William 'Ally' Atherton is not a man he cares to meet again.

Since leaving Bow Street, Lachlan Greig has studiously avoided mixing with his former colleagues, who subjected him to much teasing and mimicry while he was a member of 'A' Division. It was not a pleasant time, and he was glad to move on.

As he recalls, the fair-haired, moustached inspector, who instigated much of the unpleasantness personally, fancies himself as a bit of a ladies' man, and is not above accepting a bribe to turn a blind eye. Bracing himself, Greig follows Cully back along the corridor.

"Well, Lachlan my old friend and colleague, we meet again," Atherton greets him affably. "And so, you are a detective ~ going up in the world, eh?"

"What is it you have come to say, Atherton?" Greig inquires.

"Not William now? Well, well. How promotion changes a man. Don't recall you being so high and mighty when you were a Bow Streeter. What I have come to say, *detective inspector*, is that we at Bow Street may not be as clever as you detectives, but we know our patch, and we know our criminals."

He waves a hand towards the 'Wanted' posters on the wall.

"We have m'laddo over there locked up in our cells. Caught him red-handed last night trying to set fire to a

German butcher's shop. Now, I've got a cab waiting outside if you can lower yourself enough to pay us a visit, or we can just charge him and take all the credit for what you lot didn't manage to do. What's it to be?"

Greig restrains himself with an effort, merely tightening his hands into fists. Atherton's insolence can wait. There is a bigger picture here, and a criminal right at the forefront of it.

"I'll away and fetch my hat and coat," he says.

On the way over to Bow Street, Atherton lights up one of his foul-smelling cigars, and proceeds to describe the circumstances surrounding the arrest of the subject. His men were patrolling their usual area. They saw the suspect walking ahead of them 'in a suspicious manner'. He then stopped outside a German shop and pressed his face to the glass.

Next thing, he drew a weapon from his back pocket (here the story wanders into the theoretical), and started hitting the shutters vehemently. When he was restrained, he kept on trying to hit the shutters with equal force. A box of lucifer matches was also discovered in his coat pocket.

Given the suspicious nature of his actions, his refusal to account for them and the startling resemblance to the face on the Wanted poster, the man was instantly hauled down to Bow Street and put in a cell to await developments.

****

Detective Inspector Greig has not set foot inside the Bow Street Police Office since he departed several years ago. It has not changed at all ~ same dingy interior and old-fashioned wood and brass fittings. This is both dispiriting and reassuring. The young constable on the front desk, whom he does not recognise, jumps to attention and rips off a smart salute as he enters the outer office with Atherton.

"See, that's the way to train 'em up," Atherton murmurs. "Start how you mean to go on. None of your lounging around reading the Police Gazette under the counter. We run a tight ship here. And we get results."

Greig follows him to the long row of holding cells. Atherton unlocks a door and flings it open with a dramatic gesture.

"Rouse yourself, matey," he shouts at the occupant, who is lying on a wooden slab, and covered in a grey blanket. "You have company. Look lively now!"

The suspect groans, then sits up, rubbing his eyes. Greig notices some dark bruises on his face and across the backs of his hands. His shirt is torn in several places. Greig makes no comment.

The young man stares, bleary-eyed at the intruders. He does, indeed, bear a striking resemblance to the drawing that has been circulated. Dark, feral eyes, like a cat waiting to pounce. Thin face and a high-bridged nose. Dark hair. Atherton advances upon the prisoner and grabs him by the shoulder, hauling him roughly to his feet.

"Stand up when two police officers enter your cell, you verminous scum!" he exclaims, slapping him hard round the side of the head.

"Is that really necessary?" Greig says.

Atherton turns furiously on his former colleague.

"This is my prisoner and these are my rules, detective inspector," he snarls. "We don't go in soft, like you do over at Scotland Yard. Now then, are you going to question him? Or shall I do the job for you?"

Fearing that Atherton's 'questioning' will involve more punishment beatings, Greig motions the man to sit back down on the wooden plank that suffices for his bed.

"I am Detective Inspector Greig of Scotland Yard," he informs him. "Can you tell me your name?"

"No, he can't," Atherton interrupts. "Or rather, he won't. We've been asking him for hours. He won't answer." He aims a kick at the prisoner, who flinches. Atherton follows this with an unverifiable remark about the man's mother.

Greig shoots him an exasperated glance.

"He just won't talk. We've been trying all ways to get him to speak. Oi, tell the detective your name, scum," Atherton shouts, bringing his face to within an inch of the prisoner, who turns his face away in response. He stares hard at the wall, lips clamped firmly shut.

"What. Is. Your. Name?" Atherton hisses.

Again, there is no response. It is as if the young man has retreated into himself. He cannot hear, so he cannot respond. Or will not respond. Greig stares hard at him, sensing a darkened mind, but he is not sure whether it is an absence of light or the presence of evil.

Not sure enough to charge the man with murder, at any rate. But, on the other hand, he is not confident enough to request him to be released back into society. He is pretty sure that Atherton would be reluctant to release his prize without very clear proof that he has captured the wrong prey. He frowns, pondering the best course of action.

Meanwhile Atherton continues striding round the tiny cell, stopping every now and then to tower over the prisoner and verbally belabour him.

All at once, Greig knows what he must do.

"I shall send for the young artist who drew the original portrait," he says. "He will be able to identify whether this is the man we are looking for. Or not."

"Oh, it is him alright," Atherton sneers. "But you go through the motions, detective inspector. Meanwhile, we'll look after your prisoner for you. Here to help."

"Has he had any food?" Greig inquires, noting the lack of plate and cup. His question is greeted by a roar of laughter.

"Food? We aren't running a bleedin' coffee stall. This is a place of serious business. He can have something to eat when he has been charged. And hurry it along would you; we have other things to do."

Biting his lower lip, Greig spins on his heel and walks away. He returns to Scotland Yard, where he has left the folder containing all the information on Mr Bellini's attack. In it, he has also left the name and address of the young artist.

But Greig is going to be out of luck. The young man, along with his companions are no longer in the city. They have not yet returned from their own country, whence they have gone to bury and mourn their hero and mentor, Giovanni Bellini.

****

It is one thing to detain a man in a police cell. It is another to keep him there. A few hours after Greig has walked out of Bow Street Police Office, a small crowd walks in. They are led by a formidable middle-aged woman with a red face, and an embonpoint of massive size. She wears a rusty-black coat that strains across the chest area, and a black hat with enough featherage to start its own exotic avian collection.

The woman marches up to the desk and halts. The crowd piles in behind her, falling automatically into innocent bystander mode. She bestows a proportion of bosom and both elbows on the desk and bends forward slowly, causing the young constable behind the desk to lean back and grip the sides of his seat nervously.

"Oi," she yells by way of greeting.

The young constable swallows and pages mentally through the Police Handbook to see if there is anything that might be useful to apply to an occasion like this. There isn't.

"How may I assist you, my good woman," he says.

"Werl, for a start, I ain't your good woman. And I ain't here to be pateronised and demuned to neither. I know my rights, I does. You got my boy locked up in your cells. Wot you accusing him of? Eh? Coz he ain't done nuffink, so you got no right to keep him."

The support club goes into sympathetic murmuring with a side-order of implied belligerence.

"Can you tell me his name?" the constable asks. "Only we have quite a few criminals in the cells at the moment."

The woman bridles.

"Her ain't a criminal! He's just a lad who wanted 'is sausage dinner wot he was promised. Only when he got to the shop, it were closed. You fetch him out here quick sharp, or you'll see what happens."

Ah. Now the constable remembers page 22 of the Police Handbook.

"Are you threatening an officer of the law, madam?" he inquires coldly.

"I ain't threatening nobody; I'm *telling* you. And I ain't a Madam, never was, never will be. Respek't'ble married woman for thirty years and proud of it."

The young constable slides off his seat. If in doubt, fetch reinforcements.

"Wait over there," he says, waving towards a bench in the far corner, "I shall go and find out whether your son is on the premises."

Leaving the woman and her entourage to grumble their way across the front office, the constable goes to find Inspector Atherton, who is reading *The Inquirer*, with his feet on his desk and a lighted cigar in his hand.

After carefully explaining what the problem is, twice, because the inspector had a fit of coughing and missed the salient bits, he persuades Atherton to quit his desk, newspaper and cigar, and proceed to the front desk to deal with it.

The sight of the sneering moustachioed inspector seems to rouse an extra degree of ire in the small crowd, who rise up and advance menacingly.

"Now then, now then, good people," Atherton says, holding up a well-manicured hand. "Let us have none of this, eh? You say we have a prisoner on the premises who is innocent. I say, can you prove it?"

"You show me my boy, and I'll show you an innercent. Innercent as the day he was born," the woman exclaims. She goes over to the Wanted poster pinned to the wall and rips it down.

"This ain't nothink like him," she says, thrusting the poster under Atherton's nose. "You bring him outer them cells, or so help me, I'll do summat I might regret. Only I prob'bly won't."

Despite being a bully of some reputation, Inspector Atherton has a secret fear of women like this, having been brought up by a battler of a mother, who was free with her fists both in drink and not. He takes a cautious step back.

"If, as you say, madam, your son is not that person, how come he refuses to tell me his name, his abode and what he was doing attacking a foreign shop with a weapon?"

The woman gives him a withering look of contempt.

"I told that officer already, I ain't a Madam. And he don't talk. He's dumb. And he don't hear. Been that way since he had the fever when he was two. Addled his poor brain as well. He's like a small child; he don't know any better, and for you to keep him locked up in this place ~ well, it's plain cruelty an' that's all there is to say about it! His name is Dolloby Tuggs, and I'm his mother and I ain't budging until I sees him. So there."

A small face-off takes place, after which Atherton caves, and orders the constable to fetch the prisoner. After a few tense minutes, he returns, hauling a filthy, red-eyed, shambling wreck whose boots lack laces, and whose trousers are soiled. He takes one look at his mother, and breaks into a howl of anguish, like an animal caught in the jaws of a steel trap.

"Oh, my Gawd, Dolloby, what 'ave they done to you, my preshus boy?" she screams, rushing over to him and enfolding him to her chest.

The crowd mutters to itself about shocking treatment, police brutality and reporting this to various authorities. Atherton gives them all a venomous stare. Then he fetches the log- book from behind the desk.

"Now then Mrs … Tuggs," he says, "Am I to understand that you identify this lad as your son?"

"'Course he is my son. And wot you done to him is a disgrace! You should be ashamed of yourself. Call yourself a hooman being? I wouldn't treat a rat the way you've treated my boy. Come on son, mum's going to take you back home and get some nice stoo into you. Looks like they ain't fed you in days."

She takes the youth by the arm and steers him towards the exit. Atherton holds up a cautionary hand.

"Wait a bit, madam. Not so fast. We still haven't got to the bottom of why he was seen attacking a butcher's shop. And then there's the small matter of the box of matches in his jacket pocket."

"He was bringing them home from the chandler's. As for the other, I'd promised him a plate of sausage and gravy for his supper. Only summat must've distracted him and by the time he got to Fritz's, it was shut.

"He gets into a temper when he's promised summat and then it don't happen. That was why he started hittin' the shop. I bin nearly out of my mind with worry these past nights wondering where he was. Bin to all the orpsitals, an' then went to Marylebone P'lice.

"The p'liceman on the desk there said he thort he'd heard a boy answering Dolloby's description 'ad bin taken up by the Runners for murdering some old man in the street. As if my poor boy would do a thing like that!

"So I come straight here, and now you know the truth on it, I'll thank you to get outer my way. Me and my son is going home. Shame on you! Every one of you! You're not fit to wear that uniform! And you ain't heard the last of this, I can tell yer! Not by a long chalk."

Still sparking fury, she hauls the hapless and wimpering Dolloby towards the street door, where one of the Bow Street officers is blocking the doorway, arms folded, waiting for further instructions. Mrs Tuggs advances upon him like a galleon in full sail.

"Get outer my way young man, or so 'elp me Gawd, I'll swing for you and you'll be picking yer teef up from the floor. And no judge in the land will find me guilty after I tells him how you treated my boy!"

The officer, who only came out from the back office to see what the shouting was about, shoots a helpless glance at Atherton over the head of the redoubtable matron.

"Oh, let her go," he says, waving a dismissive hand. "We don't have any more time to waste on this sort of thing."

Inspector Atherton turns his back and fumbles in his pocket for his cigar case. The officer steps aside to let Mrs Tuggs and Dolloby stumble out into the street, followed by the crowd of supporters.

By the time Atherton has lit another cigar, the station is empty, except for a knot of police officers clustered round the desk, staring at each other in amazement. Atherton glares at them.

"Why are you all standing round idling?" he shouts. "Get back to work, all of you. This is a place of business, not a circus."

He returns to his office, feigning deafness to the chorus of '*Here we are again*!' and a whistled refrain of '*Hot Codlins*'. Atherton may pride himself upon running a tight ship, but the crew are not above a bit of subversive mutiny from time to time.

Inspector Atherton will spend the next few hours composing a blustering missive to Detective Inspector Greig, exonerating both himself and his men from any blame for their 'honest mistake' and blaming the hapless artist for his lack of portraiture skills.

****

A ball, as everybody knows, is like a marriage. It should never be entered into lightly or frivolously, but soberly and reverently, considering the purposes for which a ball is intended.

Firstly, it is intended to show off the finery and figures of single young women, thus indicating that they are available for suitable alliances with single young men. Secondly, it is for the mutual encouragement of the Mamas of the single young women, whose one desire is their happily married future.

And thirdly, it is to ensure the Papas of the single young women dispense as much money as is necessary to show off the finery and figures, and secure the happy marriage.

Lady Grantley, of course, is far too old to organise a whole evening's entertainment involving supper and dancing. She has therefore made a list of all the most important things: Refreshments, supper menu, musicians, table decorations, flowers, waiting staff, and parcelled out bits of the list to various friends.

It is clearly understood by all concerned that when the ball is a resounding success, she will take all the credit. More so as the guests will marvel at a woman of her great age planning and hosting such a magnificent event.

Here is Lady Grantley now, seated in her high-backed red velvet chair, like a queen on a throne. Here, on a smaller less upholstered chair, as befits his status, is her favourite nephew and godson Harry Haddon.

In front of them is the guest list, which they are going through carefully to make sure that an equal amount of young men and young women have been invited, and that all the men are 'dancing' ones. To attend a ball without intending to dance with a partner is a heinous crime.

Similarly, to have nobody to take one in to supper, or to wander in to the supper room solo, and then stand around like leftover mutton while the rest of the guests dance the night away, is something else that neither wishes to see happen.

"I have asked a recommended confectioner to provide the ices and supper refreshments," Lady Grantley says. "I cannot rely on the current cook: she will only do roasts and cold joints, which are too solid for a supper table. I trust that is acceptable to the young guests?"

Harry is so unused to being consulted by anyone about anything, that it is a minute before he realises a response is required. He voices his agreement. And adds that, as most of the guests are under thirty, a set supper might be unsuitable, and in preference, a twelve o'clock supper could be served with such viands as might suit a more grazing sort of consumption.

"It shall be as you wish, Harry," is the gratifying response. "My house is at your and Juliana's disposal. I shall arrange for the doors upstairs to be taken off their hinges and muslin hangings to be suspended. It will be jolly to have the house filled with young things once more."

Harry reaches out a hand and places it upon his aunt's lace-gloved one. For a moment their eyes meet. There is a wealth of sympathy in the older glance, a deep gratitude in the younger one. Many envelopes containing money, many hampers of pies and cakes are in the glances and have brought the two to where they are now.

Aunt Grantley picks up the guest list and hands it to Harry with the suggestion that he might like to think about who would pair well with whom ~ for of course no young man will dance with his wife, nor can Harry and Juliana dance together too often.

Looking down the list, Harry's eye is caught by one name. He feels a familiar comet's tail of dread run down his spine. He has vivid memories of Miss Fiona Blythe. Before Juliana burst upon his existence like a heavenly vision, Fiona Blythe had made his life a living hell by her open and blatant pursuit of him.

Wherever he went, the Opera, the Park, Burlington Arcade, Regent Street, any party or ball, sooner or later, he'd bump into Fiona Blythe. It was hard not to think she was deliberately following him around.

Harry began to understand exactly how a hunted animal must feel. He also recollected that female cats (and there was something very feline about Miss Blythe) were said to be much better hunters than males and seemed to take more delight in torturing their prey.

At one point, he even found himself checking the doorway opposite his rooms every morning, in case she was lurking there in disguise.

Her methodology was always the same: a little too much surprise at seeing him, a little too enthusiastic delight that they had met, and a tendency to cling, leechlike, to his arm in such a helpless fashion that politeness forced him to squire her around.

It was to escape her clutches that he'd retreated to the Arundel's conservatory the night of the fateful ball, where moonlight, rather too much punch and a desire to rid himself of Miss Blythe and her unwelcome overtures once and for all, had thrown him at Juliana's feet.

Of all the things Harry is grateful for (and admittedly there are not many), escaping from Fiona's clutches comes pretty well top of the list. Yet here she is again, like the proverbial bad penny, her letter of acceptance gracefully penned.

Personally, he would not wish Miss Blythe upon his worst enemy, Harry thinks. Then he pauses as an idea steals into his mind. It is such a naughty idea that for a moment, he cannot believe he has just thought it.

But having done so, he decides to make the thought father to the deed. So, Harry turns his attention to the guest list, and mentally draws a line between two of the names. If nothing else, it will give him a great deal of satisfaction. And what's wrong with that?

****

Oh, the excitement at the prospect of a ball! The anticipation, that begins with the arrival of the gold-leaf, deckle-edged card, which is placed upon the mantelpiece, to be secretly gloated over as the weeks pull the actual event closer.

Then there is the flurry of letters to fellow invitees to make sure nobody is going to wear the same colour gown, or have similar jewels, or headdress, or hair ornaments, or carry the same bouquet, or fan, for each belle must appear completely original and new.

This is followed by the bewitching selection of lace, feather, trinket, spangle and ribbon. Haberdashery shops are scoured, dressmakers sought and the gay girlish chatter is all about the thrilling rapture and delight that awaits an event, which, if not quite up to the mark of Elysium, will be as near an approach as to answer every purpose.

Juliana Silverton, in whose honour the ball is being held, is the recipient of most of the letters, of course, for nobody wishes to upstage the guest of honour. It is in pursuit of this very objective that she is even now awaiting the delivery of her ballgown from one of the exclusive court dressmakers patronised by those with cachet and sufficient funds.

A discreet knock at the door heralds the Handing Over of the New Dress. The protocol runs thus: the door opens. The smart delivery boy bows. The maid nods. He hands over the big cream cardboard box, embellished with its yellow satin ribbon bow.

The maid receives it. The delivery boy bows again. The maid inclines her head graciously to acknowledge the end of the transaction. The door closes. The maid carries the ceremonial item to the dining room, where it is placed upon the dining table, now covered by a red chenille tablecloth with bobbles.

It is the same table under which the infant Juliana used to hide (oh, it seems like a lifetime ago) with her dolls, and make up fairy stories in which she featured as a princess. But this is no fairy story, although it does have a hero and a heroine, and a ball.

The heroine is currently up in her room looking over her jewellery with her Mama. Together, they are tracking a careful course, because as an engaged person, Juliana does not want to appear too ostentatiously showy, yet she does need to sparkle and shine over and above her contemporaries.

"How about this, Mama?" Juliana holds up a filigree silver chain with a tiny diamond hanging off it, like a teardrop. She purchased it in Mentone, whilst broadening her youthful horizons. Now she fastens it round her white swan neck and waits to see whether her Mama approves.

Doria considers the suggestion. Her daughter's new tulle dress is that particular shade of robin's egg blue that only a true blonde can wear with confidence. The hair ornaments are tiny dyed white and blue feathers on a silver arrow clip. Her white gloves are embroidered with little pearls, and she has white satin slippers and a white cashmere shawl.

"I think that would be just right. What an excellent choice, my love," she nods. "Perhaps with the silver bangle? Yes, I think so."

The maid then knocks with the information that 'a parcel has just come from Mrs Swain', causing mother and daughter to rise from their seats in great excitement.

"I shall follow you down, Mama," Juliana says, unfastening the little chain from her neck in preparation for laying it temporarily upon its velvet bed.

As she closes the lid, she thinks about who was with her when she visited the small jeweller's shop and bought it; whose was the first hand to help fasten the pretty jewel round her slender throat.

She has still received no letter from Romeo, but she has now decided in her own mind, that her letter went astray. It is the only logical reason for his lack of response. Plus, she is also beginning to doubt that he really *was* the same young man with whom she enjoyed her clandestine relationship. Time embellishes memories, but can also paint them in a deceptive light.

Of course, that still leaves the problem of Fiona Blythe and her demands (one arrived yesterday for the money to buy some Honiton lace for her ballgown), but after the ball is over, Juliana hopes, oh, she so hopes, that will end as well.

****

Detective Inspector Stride sits behind his desk, staring down at the slew of morning papers that have been hurriedly placed there by one of the newest Scotland Yard recruits. ('Knock, go in, put the papers down quick, then scarper.')

Unbelievable. Every front page features some variant on the treatment of Dolloby Tuggs at the hands of the Bow Street Police. On the one hand, it makes a change from the pasting Scotland Yard usually gets at the hands of the fourth estate.

On the other hand, the lad in question, ('**Boy Brutally Beaten Black and Blue by Bow Street Bullies**!' *The Inquirer*) was their only suspect in a brutal murder and possibly a couple of cases of arson. Now, they are back to square one.

Stride passes a stupid hour. Then another one. Then Cully knocks at his door. When he enters, one glance at Stride's face tells him what is amiss.

"Ah. You have read about it, then," Cully says.

"We do not seem to be making any progress," Stride says gloomily. He peers into the mug of cold black coffee that has been sitting on his desk since yesterday. It does not elicit any inspiration.

"At least there haven't been any more attacks," Cully says.

"Just a lot of writing on walls," Stride replies. "And more letters in the newspapers complaining about foreigners living in the city. Frankly, I don't understand people, Jack. They are happy to buy their food, their wine, their clothes ~ new or old, from foreigners.

"Damn it ~ they even go abroad to see the sights in foreign countries. Yet the presence of these people in London is treated as if it were a crime. Someone ought to point out that our beloved Queen is actually a German. So is the Prince Consort."

Jack Cully shrugs. The mind of the average Londoner is as much of a mystery as the small kitten his older daughter has recently found and adopted.

Stride jabs a finger at the newspapers.

"It says here the youth was in a terrible state when his mother got him released. What on earth was Atherton thinking? This isn't the 1830s. You can't expect to get away with that sort of treatment today. Not now the newspapers are all just waiting to cry 'foul'."

"Good thing his mother was on hand, then."

Stride pulls a face. Then shudders. "Never underestimate the power of a mother, Jack," he says somewhat elliptically.

Cully shoots him a curious look. Stride rarely mentions his private life. His wife, a formidable Scotswoman, is known for her boots-off-at-the-door policy, but he's never gone any further back into his past.

Thinking about it, Cully finds it almost impossible to imagine his grumpy, slightly overweight colleague ever having *had* a mother, let alone being a small child in rompers. It just doesn't seem possible.

"Two deaths," Stride reflects. "One of them definitely murder, and we are back where we started: not a clue as to who carried them out. We only know the reason why, that is all."

"A murder and an attempted murder," Cully says. "You are forgetting Miss Essie Marks and her business. It was only by chance that she was not killed in the blaze that gutted her premises."

"Yes, you are right, Jack. I had forgotten all about her."

But Cully has not forgotten. How could he? Essie's life is inextricably woven into his own, ever since the day he first saw her, alone on that empty theatre stage in Cardiff, metaphorically alone in the wide world.

Cully had successfully appealed to her to forsake the vagabondage of her previous existence and return to London to be reunited with her real mother, Lilith Marks, who'd always believed her baby daughter had died.

Throughout his career in the Metropolitan Police, Detective Sergeant Jack Cully had rarely allowed himself to become personally involved in any investigation. This case was one of those rare exceptions. Essie could have burned to death. The person who fired her shop certainly intended her to die. And Cully was damned if he'd let that person get away with it.

****

Of course, Essie Marks is unaware of Jack Cully's determination, though it accords with her own. But she has something more at her disposal than the man who rescued her from her past: she has her psychic powers.

Essie has rarely had to fall back on her gift ~ as she likes to call it. Now safely housed, fed and loved, her life has fallen into pleasant lines. Or rather, it had done so until the night of the fateful fire.

The destruction of her little business suddenly pitched her mentally back into that rootless hand-to-mouth time, when her life see-sawed between security and desperation, and only her gift of seeing what nobody else was capable of seeing, and being able to foretell the future, had saved her from becoming a street whore, selling herself to any stranger for food and drink.

Essie knows the horrors of that life only too well. She'd encountered enough victims of it in the course of her wanderings from town to town. Had helped a few where she could. Life back then was hard and unpredictable. Up and down it went, like the see-saw. Highs and lows.

Now, Essie sits by her window, the sky outside gently slipping into twilight. Her candle flickers as her needle flashes busily along the seam she is sewing. A costume for a masked ball. As she sews, she is thinking about the young man she met at Mrs Twort's spunging-house.

Essie's mind throws up a clear image of him. She focuses on the part where he asked about the button she wears about her neck. She focuses further, onto his face as she related the circumstances surrounding it.

She identifies what it was she saw there: recognition. He *knew* where the button came from. But it was not his, of that she is sure. Someone else. Known to him. Essie sends out thoughts across the darkening sky. She plants the memory of their meeting into his mind. He will be the one to bring that man to her. She does not know when, but she has summoned him. Now all she has to do is wait.

****

Night falls, but the heart of the great city does not stop beating. Down the many-branching slums that lead off St Giles as it winds towards to the Strand, the shops are still lit and still clamorous with clients.

Here, women pick over coarse scraps of meat in cheap butchers' shops. Here are haberdashers, patronised by dressmakers and home-workers demanding a ha'pporth of shirt buttons, or a farthings-worth of thread.

Here are dimly lit shops selling sausages of dubious provenance, mutton pies, fried fish and baked potatoes, their frontages full of wizened semi-naked children who peer through the glass, their faces pinched with want.

Here are low coffee shops where, if you have the time or the inclination, you can read newspapers a fortnight old decorated with coffee cup rings. Everything is squalid, sordid and low, except for the gin shops, ghastly in their newness and richness of decoration, their doors temptingly ajar to lure in the men in cloth caps and out-at-the-elbow jackets.

Here are oyster-stalls, costermonger barrows full of bruised fruit; here are orange-women, match-sellers, crossing-boys, tinkers, tailors, poor men, beggar-men, and thieves. Here are second-hand clothes sellers, ballad-singers, kicked dogs, howling children and bare-foot flower-girls, all elbowing and jostling their way along the crowded thoroughfares.

All forms of want are here, in the great gulf stream of this human ocean that flows to and fro in an incessant tide, carrying its flotsam and jetsam with it.

The rich dine in fine restaurants on salmon with lobster sauce, or partridge with mushrooms and truffles at five shillings a dish. The poor dine on scraps of ham, yesterday's stale bread and fragments of Dutch cheese, or maybe for a penny, trotters bought from the old woman of unappetising appearance who stands outside the local tavern with a flat basket lined with a cloth.

As the poet says: *'Hell is a city much like London.'*

Time passes. The pale moon meanders across the star-studded sky until something akin to a deep sleep falls over the city. Not all are sleeping though. The homeless and hungry wander the gas-lit streets seeking somewhere to lay their heads. Small vagrant children huddle under tarpaulins. Gin-befuddled men and women stagger and weave their erratic way home.

A young dressmaker in an attic bites off her thread, sets the bodice and sleeves she has been sewing on the table, then blows out her candle and throws herself, exhausted, onto a mattress on the floor. She has not eaten since the morning. She has not changed her clothes for two days. Her eyes are red-rimmed, her head throbs.

In a couple of hours, her day will begin again, when she will take the pieces to her employer, who will check it for fleas and bugs, before passing it to the next young women to attach to the voluminous skirt.

The dress, a beautiful pale-yellow ballgown, trimmed with handmade Honiton lace, will then be delivered to the customer's house and hung up by the ladies' maid, ready to be put on that evening by the new owner, (who is the same age as the dressmaker, but has never done a day's sewing in her life).

As *Madame la Modiste* is wont to remark: "We will never disappoint our esteemed clients, your ladyship. Any sacrifice, *any sacrifice whatsoever* will always be made."

****

Lilith Marks and her team of bakers and confectioners know all about making sacrifices. While the city has been shaking itself awake, they have sacrificed a full night's sleep and are now out and about buying the ingredients needed for the day's business.

Lilith owns the restaurant concessions for three department stores, as well as her own tearoom, the Lily Lounge. She has also started supplying food for parties, wedding celebrations, musical evenings and balls.

This has meant taking on some cooks, new premises, a delivery man, and a lot more pots and pans. Today, Lilith and her team are catering for a ball to be held at a fine house in Bruton Street. It is a ball for young people, so a sit-down meal or a set supper will definitely not suit.

Lilith has devised an appetising menu, which includes: French chicken cutlets, lobster patties, partridge pie, fish and oyster pie, salmon in caper sauce, various salads, and French beans. For dessert, there are to be moulded jellies, chocolate souffle, Italian and ginger creams and lemon blancmanges.

Some of the dishes and shapes have already been made, and are cooling on various larder shelves. Lilith and two assistants will collect them later, and transport them to the location, ready to set out on the long tables.

Meanwhile, preparations are also well underway at Bruton Street. The broad veranda is being turned into a conservatory. A covered way is being erected from the road to the front door, to maintain the privacy of the guests, and in case of rain.

Inside, the lobby is rich with ferns: it is like walking into one of the tropical houses at Kew Gardens. The hallway is a paradise; the staircase is fairyland. Candelabra have been added to all the chandeliers, and cane rout seats placed strategically around the two rooms on the first floor ~ now being transformed for dancing by the addition of a linen drugget covering.

By nine o'clock in the evening, the house is ablaze, and carriages are lining up outside, watched by the inevitable crowd of gawping onlookers who always turn up to watch the rich enjoy their pleasures. They are, in turn, being watched by a couple of constables.

Given the grandness of the occasion and the setting, there are bound to be thieves, pickpockets, muggers and ladies of negotiable affection. Possibly even some journalists. It is not a good idea to allow the event to proceed unscrutinised. Especially with the current bad press.

Lilith Marks, carrying a list and a supper-table plan, threads her way through the crowd. Then, as befits her non-guest status, she steps down the area stairs and knocks at the kitchen door, where one of the house staff lets her in.

Lilith mounts the back stairs and makes her way to the rooms set aside for supper, relishing the chance to enter the beautifully appointed house. She is always struck by the paradox of her life now, a successful caterer with entrée to the finest establishments in London, and her former life as a *horizontale*, when the tastes she was catering for were very different, and her client list was exclusively male, and usually married.

Lord William Grantley (deceased) was one of 'hers'. Twice a month at a considerable outlay for half an hour. At various times Lilith has encountered former clients entertaining their wife or latest mistress to afternoon tea in her Hampstead restaurant.

The men never recognise the attractive middle-aged woman dressed in discreet black who takes their order, and writes out their bill. Horizontal and naked, they might, but Lilith has come a long way since those days, as tonight clearly indicates.

First Lilith checks off the supper dishes from her list. She inspects the serving layout, re-arranges some of the decorations and makes sure all the plates are unchipped, the silverware uncloudy, and the wine glasses are shining and soldier-straight.

Her staff and the waiters hired for the evening watch her walk up and down, pausing every now and then. Finally, she nods her approval. There is an almost palpable sigh of relief all round.

Music filters through the ceiling. Footsteps go up the stairs, the happy laughter of young men and women fills the air. Lilith is tempted to sneak a look at the gay scene, but restrains herself.

She must snatch a few hours' sleep, before returning in the small hours to supervise the clearing up and re-packing of the hired crockery and glasses. A final look round, a few last-minute instructions, then she glides from the room, leaving the house once more by the area steps.

****

Meanwhile, on the first floor of Lady Grantley's palatial mansion, the guests are arriving. Harry and his beautiful Juliana stand at the door to receive, together with Lady Grantley's butler, a man of impeccably haughty demeanour.

They are there to meet and greet. He is there to take instructions upon which belle should be introduced to which beau, and to hand out small dance cards and red-tasselled pencils, for what is a ball without the souvenir of a full dance-card to take home and pore over in the wee small hours?

Once appraised of the names, the butler conducts the individuals or couples to where Lady Grantley is seated, and effects the formal introduction of guest to hostess, before leading them to a group or a seat.

Harry Haddon is as handsome as ever, in his black evening suit and an embroidered waistcoat. His gloves are lavender, his cravat white, and he has a small flower in his buttonhole.

He is trying to mask his impatience as the precious minutes slip by. An annoying feature of Anthony Rice is his deliberate tendency to arrive late, thus making his arrival an occasion for drawing attention to himself.

But at last he hears the familiar voice ascending from the hall. Harry steels himself as the tall figure slopes into view, accompanied by Giles Cooper. Setting eyes upon the host of the evening, Anthony's dark eyes light up with malicious pleasure.

"Evenin' Haddon. Haven't seen you around town for a while. Been busy, have you? Lookin' forward to tonight, my friend. Hope to catch a word with you at some point in the proceedings. We have much to talk about, eh?"

Before Harry can reply, Rice bows to Juliana, sweeps his companion into the receiving room and saunters over to Lady Grantley, whom he greets with an even lower bow.

Harry ungrits his teeth, and murmurs a few words to the butler, who follows the young men. He takes Rice over to a small group of gauzily-dressed girls, and as Harry and Juliana watch, introduces him to one of them. She is dressed in a lemon-yellow dance dress, her hair elaborately arranged in a series of cascading curls and fastened with a pearl clip.

Fiona Blythe (for it is she) drops a curtsey, flutters her fan, simpers, and places a hand lightly upon Rice's sleeve as he leads her onto the dance floor. She has come with her older sister Venetia, who has only agreed to chaperone on the understanding that her duties will be no more onerous than sitting in a corner all evening.

Venetia is in the early stages of her third pregnancy, and views the evening as a chance to escape her maternal duties and her uxorious husband. She has also been instructed by their mother to get the name, occupation and address of any unattached young man who shows a scintilla of interest in Fiona.

The Season has ended with no profitable outcome and every member of the Blythe family are as determined as their youngest member to ensure that the next Season will not see her trotted out again.

And so, the music swells, inviting the happy young people to '*chase the glowing hours with flying feet*', until eventually, the last dance before supper is reached. Once again, Harry Haddon signals to the Grantley butler, who fetches Fiona Blythe from her rout seat, and takes her over to Anthony Rice, now lounging against the window, and staring in a bored fashion down into the street.

Fiona shows him her dance card, and twinkles up at him, winningly. Of course, etiquette demands that, having signed up for the pleasure of her company, he must now squire the fair and very eligible Fiona round the dance floor once again, and then take her in to supper.

As Anthony Rice spins her round the room, Fiona catches Juliana's eye and flashes her a triumphant smile. Juliana feels her shoulders beginning to untense. She does not know the tall dark-haired young man with the long aquiline face and unpleasantly supercilious expression, but she cannot deny that Harry has carried out her wishes to the letter.

Now all she has to do is cross her fingers and pray that whoever he is, he will become the focus of Fiona's attention. And will reciprocate it. Juliana sends up a quick arrow prayer to the Goddess of Sudden Attraction & Short Engagements, before the music swirls to a close, and supper is announced.

****

It is a few hours later. The food has been eaten. The punch drunk. The chaperones have tactfully retired. Harry Haddon, as befits a good host, has remained in the supper room to make sure all the guests have had their fill of the good things on display.

Now, he has secured a plate of bits and pieces of broken victuals and a glass of hock, and retired to a table. All around him, the hired staff and the caterers are clearing plates and packing baskets.

Harry is so exhausted that he barely notices their presence. Nor the entrance of Anthony Rice, who glides

208

over to his table and pulls out a chair. Harry looks across at him with indifference.

"What do you want, Rice?" he asks wearily.

Anthony Rice pretends to fiddle with the buttons on his gloves.

"I thought we might have a chat, Haddon my old friend. Catch up on things, as it were."

"Are you going to honour your debt to me? One hundred and fifty-three pounds, seven shillings and ninepence I had to pay to Mr Smith at the Cremorne. For an evening I did not attend."

Rice bats the suggestion away as if it were an annoying insect. "Oh really, Haddon, have you nothing better to talk about? A gentleman does not discuss money on an occasion like this ~ surely you must know it? Or has your menial status driven away all your manners and good breeding? I gather your father is employing you as some sort of dogsbody in his office. The chaps say they haven't seen you at White's or the Rat's Castle for weeks."

"I'm afraid I do not choose to spend my evenings drinking and betting upon dog-fights any longer," Harry replies stiffly.

Rice throws back his head and laughs. "More fool you then. What a prig you have become. I expect that's the influence of the little woman, isn't it? Pretty thing, ain't she. Shame about her provenance."

Harry stares at him. "I do not know what you mean, Rice."

Anthony Rice leans in. "Something a bit 'Jewy' about her."

"Dewy?" Harry frowns, visualising Juliana's porcelain complexion.

"No, *Jewy*," Rice replies. He taps the side of his nose with a finger. "Bit of the Hebrew connection there. Oh ~ did you not know? Dear me! Y'see, while I was out of town, I did a bit of detecting, and it appears that all is not as it seems. Your future father-in-law was not christened Morton Silverton. Quite the opposite. He was born Mordechai Silverburg, youngest son of Jakob Silverburg, a German Jew moneylender. They changed the family name when they came here from Europe.

"That's what they do, these Jews, to fit in. They change their name, join a church, take the Sacrament, and then, hey presto: there they are, British Christians. Only of course, they aren't. Not in the real sense of the word. They can never be. They are filthy Jews. Christ killers. Making their money on the backs of honest Englishmen."

Rice's dark eyes burn with a fanatical hatred. His gloved hands are balled into fists. Harry stares at him, open-mouthed, stunned into silence. Rice leans forward until his face is an inch from Harry's.

"Understand this, Haddon, if you go ahead with the marriage, I shall cut you. We will all cut you. And I'll make sure everybody in our set and beyond knows exactly why."

Harry finds his voice. "Why are you doing this, Rice? What harm have I ever done to you that you should bear me so much hatred?"

Rice sits back, folding his arms. "I don't hate you, Haddon. I despise you. You're weak and pathetic. You were always weak and pathetic ~ snivelling because your father hadn't sent you a letter. Whining because I ask you to do me the least little favour. And I'm doing it because I can. Because it gives me infinite pleasure to squash people like you and your little Jewess under my foot."

He pushes back his chair. "Now, if you'll excuse me, I must make my farewells to dear Lady Grantley. I wonder how she will react when she discovers what your fiancée really is. Doubt if she'll be quite so forthcoming with the ready cash in future, eh."

Rice stalks off. Harry sits motionless. His plate of broken viands remains untouched on the table in front of him. He stares straight ahead. His face is set and deathly pale.

Meanwhile Lilith Marks, who has overheard every word, covers the last of the cutlery baskets, then pauses, as if committing what she has just heard to memory, before picking up the basket and quietly leaving the supper room.

****

In the days following a ball, it is usual for the guests to call on the host and hostess. It is less usual for the host to call on somebody who wasn't even a guest. Although there is a connection to the evening, albeit unknown to this particular host.

The host in question is Harry Haddon, and he is carrying a business card, which he consults at regular intervals, while methodically checking the small shops and factories he walks past. This is not a part of London he frequents, nor even knew existed.

Small shops, many just the ground floor front of a lodging house, are crowded together higgledy-piggledy, as if some giant hand had carelessly thrown them down. Butcher, baker, candlestick maker, the three golden balls of the pawnbroker, its windows packed with tarnished spoons, trays of bracelets, watches, signet rings and chains. Sunlight filters dustily down from patches of pale sky, barely visible above the crooked chimney tops.

Women wearing head-shawls stare curiously at him from doorways. Washing hangs from poles above his head. Small corkscrew-haired children shout and spin wooden tops along the paving stones. The air smells of baking and exotic spices.

Eventually, after asking directions off a couple of locals, he reaches his destination. Harry opens the unpainted front door and enters a world of dazzling colour. The contrast with the grey ashy street on the other side could not be greater.

Here is a veritable Aladdin's cave: bales of brightly coloured silks and satins are stacked against the whitewashed walls. There are rolls of sequins, bolts of coloured lace, trimmings, beads, feathers and buckles. A riot of colour, sparkle and shimmer, meet the eye in every direction.

Various costumes hang from nails. Venetian carnival masks leer down from the low wooden beam. In a back room, he can hear sewing machines whirring. Behind the counter, a young man wearing a black jacket and traditional Jewish headgear regards Harry's entrance with polite interest.

"Good day, sir," he says. "May I assist you in any way?"

Harry remembers Miss Marks telling him that she was in partnership with her cousin. This, he decides, must be that cousin, though for the life of him, he cannot remember his name (if he ever knew it in the first place).

"I am looking for Miss Marks," he says, placing the card Essie gave him onto the wooden counter.

"Is it about purchasing a costume?"

Harry shakes his head.

"A design for a costume, perhaps?"

Harry indicates that it is not.

The young man's expression slides from polite interest to indifference. "She ain't here," he says shortly.

This is an unexpected blow. But Harry is not going to be deflected by the absence of the person he has come to seek. The young man folds his arms and waits for Harry to make the next move. Harry clears his throat.

"Perhaps I should explain."

"Please do, sir."

Haltingly, because it is not something he is actually proud of, Harry describes the circumstances in which he met Essie. When he has finished, the young man nods thoughtfully a couple of times. Then he says,

"But, as I said, I am afraid Essie is not here today. She is working at her mother's house. Can I take a message?"

Harry bites his lip. "I would rather speak to her in person, if you don't mind. It is a personal matter. And rather important."

Another pause.

"I see. I can give you the address, if you wish?"

Harry certainly does wish, and a few minutes later, armed with a piece of paper, and feeling much relieved in spirit, he hails a cab, and is borne away through the morning traffic to his father's office.

He has decided that he will forgo his luncheon, and thus finish work in time to call upon Miss Marks. Sometimes, dire situations call for drastic measures to be taken. This is one of those times.

****

Detective Inspector Stride is doing something most unseasonal: Spring is a long way off, yet here he is, clearing the pile of folders on his desk with the zeal and commitment of a housewife on the first day of Spring.

Admittedly, he is only moving them from the left side of the desk to the right side, and to the floor, but it is a start. Rome was not burned in a day. And a few folders have actually been consigned to the wastepaper basket, including the green one.

Stride has given up expecting the stolen animals to be found and returned to their original owners. By now, he reasons, they have ended up as so many tasty Sunday dinners. Many of the folders that remain could probably be junked also.

Stride pauses and thinks about 'probably'. How many times has an investigation prospered or foundered upon that single word? The lawyers called it 'hearsay evidence' ~ a kind of linguistic alchemy that tried to transmute gossip and rumour into something more credible.

He sighs. Another letter from the Home Secretary has been passed his way. The Italian Ambassador is unhappy that the unfortunate death of Mr Bellini is not being fully and speedily investigated. Nor was it given any prominence in the British papers.

Politics. Stride hates politicians almost as much as he hates journalists. One minute, you are told to hush everything up, the next, to proclaim it from the rooftops. He clearly recalls reading an officially signed letter stating in unequivocal terms that Mr Bellini's murder was to be kept out of the public arena at all costs, as he was a former anarchist, a revolutionary and a wanted man in his own country, and should his demise leak out, it might start an uprising amongst the Italian community, with questions asked in the House.

Stride wonders how quickly the newspapers will now seize upon the story and emblazon it on all the front pages. At which point, there will probably be some sort of outcry from the usual suspects saying there are far too many foreigners in the city, and if you let them come flooding in, then this is exactly what you can expect to happen.

However it plays out, the finger will quickly point to the Metropolitan Police and its perceived inadequacy to keep the peace and prevent violent attacks on law abiding members of the public.

Stride feels his spirits sink even further. There is no probability here. On the contrary, it is all completely predictable.

****

Essie Marks stands at a table, sketching designs for pantomime costumes ~ admittedly, it is some way to the arrival of the Panto Season, but always good to keep ahead of the game. The table and most of the surrounding floor area are spread with sheets of paper covered with pastel chalk drawings.

Essie is so focused on her work that for a split second she is unaware that she is not alone, and the parlour maid has to announce Harry Haddon's name again before his presence registers, and she looks up.

"Ah. It is Mr Haddon. I was expecting you to visit today."

Harry's eyes open wide. "You were? I forgot that you had mystic powers, Miss Marks."

"My cousin wrote me a note," Essie says drily, waving him to a chair. "He says you wish to see me upon a personal matter?"

She sets down her pencil and pulls out another chair. Harry hesitates, begins to speak, stops. So many conflicting thoughts crowd into his mind. The honour of the school. Never betraying a friend.

Then he remembers a small boy running down a school corridor. It is his second day at Eton, and the imposition of the no-running rules had not kicked in. A slightly older boy lounges on a low windowsill, watching him intently.

As the little chap comes closer, he opens the window inwards. It is cruel, and it is deliberate. The boy crashes straight into the frame and falls, stunned, to the ground. Blood pours from a deep cut on his forehead.

As other boys gather, roused by his cries of pain and shock, the perpetrator slides casually off the sill, stands over his victim, and laughs. Then he saunters off, still chuckling. That was Harry's first introduction to Anthony Rice. He carries the scar to this day.

"When we last met, you showed me the button you wear," he says, finding his voice and his fluency. "You told me the story behind it. I am now come to beg you to let me take the button ~ just for a short while."

"You recognised it, didn't you?" Essie says. "You know who it belongs to, don't you?"

Harry nods briefly.

"Why now? Why not then?"

"I have ... personal reasons. I did not have them at that time."

Ah, Essie thinks. The upper classes. A wrong is only a wrong when it is done to them. How well she remembers that world.

"And shall I know the name?"

"I promise I will let you know his name when I return the button to you."

Essie regards him narrowly. Summing him up. Then she slides her thumbs into the top of her overall and lifts out the little button necklace.

"The person who owns this button destroyed my livelihood. They did not regard my life as worth a speck of dust under their shoe. The person who owns this button was quite happy for me to burn to death. I want you to remember this, when you show it to them."

She takes off the necklace and places it in Harry's palm.

"If I do not hear from you by the end of this week, I shall go to the police myself. I will tell Detective Sergeant Jack Cully of this conversation, and that you know the man who tried to kill me because I am a 'filthy foreigner'. If you are trying to protect your friend, it will go badly for you both."

Harry stands. "Upon my honour, Miss Marks, I shall not let you down. I will return your necklace. You have my solemn word upon it."

He makes her a low bow, then turns and leaves the room. Essie goes to the window. As she stands watching him through the glass, her fingers lightly brush her breast bone, where the button hung.

It feels as if a part of her soul has left her. But it will return, she tells herself. And when it does, she will exact her revenge. It has taken some time, but as her mother has always told her, it is a dish best served cold.

A few hours later, Harry Haddon arrives at the block of bachelor apartments where Anthony Rice rents a first floor flat. He rings the bell. The door is answered by Rice's manservant, who informs him that his master is dining in town.

Harry expresses regret. Then, casually, he produces Essie's button and shows it to Beasley.

"Ah sir, where did you find that? The master was most put out when he discovered his favourite jacket had lost a button. He is particular about his clothes, as I'm sure you know. I searched high and low to find a replacement. In the end, I had to give the jacket away."

Harry pockets the button without comment. "Thank you, Beasley. Perhaps you can tell me where your master dines tonight?"

Beasley's expression softens.

"Well I could sir, but I don't think I ought to. You see, he is entertaining a young lady ~ they met at a ball a few nights ago, and I do not think he'd thank me if his dinner was interrupted just for a button, would he now?"

"No indeed," Harry says, deliberately misinterpreting. "Never mind. I shall no doubt see him shortly. I bid you good evening, Beasley."

The door closes and Harry makes his way down to the communal lobby. Of course, he could end it here. Beasley has supplied him with the proof that Miss Marks asked for. All he needs to do is return the button in an envelope to her workshop, with a note saying what he has discovered, and let her inform the police.

But he won't let it end there. Because this is more than a missing button. This is years of abuse, years of bullying and being taken for granted. Years of biting his tongue for the sake of a friendship that never really existed, except in his mind.

It has taken a long time, but the iron has finally entered his soul, and Harry is not going to let Anthony Rice get away with his actions any longer. He is a man and he must do what a man has to do. Even if it doesn't involve a brace of pistols, a trusty second, and a dawn encounter at Parliament Hill Fields.

Plotting his next move, Harry makes his way to his club, where a tasty dinner and the evening newspapers await his attention.

****

It is the morning after Harry's discovery, and here is his future bride in a becoming morning wrapper, sipping a tiny cup of hot chocolate, while at the other end of the dining table, her parents tuck into a hearty cooked breakfast.

Juliana prefers not to breakfast. She doesn't lunch much either, and her dinner tends to involve a lot of moving meat and vegetables around her plate and very little eating.

A girl doesn't maintain a sixteen-inch waist by stuffing food. Juliana is famous amongst her circle for her tiny waist. She doesn't have to tight-lace, like some. She gathers that after marriage, one's waist increases alarmingly. Thus, she is making the best of what she has, while she still has it.

A clang at the door heralds the morning post shooting through the newly-fitted letterbox. There is a short pause while the housemaid collects it, places it on a silver tray, and brings the tray into the breakfast room.

"Three catalogues for you, Mrs Silverton," she says. "And a letter for Miss Juliana," she adds, laying it down by Juliana's plate.

Juliana glances down at the envelope. She recognises Fiona Blythe's round cursive. Is there to be no end to this torture, she wonders gloomily? She slits open the letter with her unused butter knife and reads:

Dearest friend

I cannot wait to tell you how happy I am. Since the night of the Ball (for which, many congratulations), my heart has been captivated and held prisoner by Mr Anthony Rice, the delightful young man Harry introduced to me.

I know it has only been a very short while since we met, but I feel as if I have known him for ever. Our thoughts and ideas are so similar. Our tastes and inclinations match so perfectly.

I shall forever remember your kindness in this matter. Any past awkwardness between us must be put aside, as I am sure you will want to do. L'amour conquers all, as the poet says.

I remain,
Your constant friend,
Fiona

Well! Goodness gracious! Juliana's eyebrows, which have almost disappeared into her hairline, such is her astonishment, slowly descend. She remembers Anthony Rice as a tall black pillar with a scowl.

She certainly did not notice any special preference for Fiona in his demeanour. Far from it. During supper, he stared over the top of her head, his expression blank. Juliana feared her request to Harry to introduce Fiona to one of his unattached friends had misfired badly.

Indeed, she was so sure of it, that she was steeling herself for a resumption of the threats and blackmailing. However it appears, from the gushing missive she holds in her hand, she has misjudged the situation.

"Good news?" her Mama asks.

"Oh, yes. In a way. Just a thank-you from Fiona for the ball."

Juliana re-reads the letter, feeling the burden of dread suddenly lifting from her shoulders. No more Fiona. No more blackmail. No more raiding her funds to satisfy her former friend's importunate and never-ending demands.

She eyes the breakfast fare on display with new interest. She might, just possibly, treat herself to half a slice of dry toast, as a reward.

****

Meanwhile, in a doorway outside a tall apartment block, a shadowy figure lurks. It is waiting for one of the occupants within to finish their breakfast and emerge into the gloomy morning street.

Harry Haddon is taking time by the fetlock. As he stands across the road from Rice's place of abode, he runs through various scenarios in his head. They always end up with Rice, humbled and contrite, promising faithfully that he will never interfere with Harry or his future wife ever again.

So confident is he, that he almost misses his quarry slipping out of the building and heading towards Regent

Street. Gathering his wits, Harry hurries after him, catching him at the corner, where Rice is looking around for a cab.

Harry taps him on the shoulder. "Rice," he says "Stop. I want a word, if you please."

Anthony Rice turns to face him, his expression one of cold contempt.

"Ah, Haddon. I know what this is about. A button. Beasley told me all about your unexpected visit last night. Kind of you to take such an interest in my wardrobe, old chap, but as he also told you, I no longer have the jacket from whence it came. I have to say, I fail utterly to understand why you are bothering me about a button."

Harry proceeds to enlightens him. Rice listens, tapping an impatient foot. When Harry has explained the circumstances, he smiles. It is not a pretty sight.

"Ah, I see. Can you prove it though, Haddon? More to the point, can your little Jewess? Because neither of you saw what happened, did you? You weren't there. And if the police should come knocking at my door, both I and Beasley will deny any knowledge of the button, the jacket and the events of that night.

"You are wasting your time. Both of you. If this is an attempt to smear me and ruin my standing in town, consider it failed. If it is an attempt to stop me revealing the origins of the Silverton family, consider it failed also. And now, I have better things to do than stand here listening to a clodpoll like you. Get out of my way!"

Rice tries to push past him. Harry grabs him by the arm and holds him. Rice tries to pull free. Harry hangs on. A few passers-by stop and eye them curiously. Rice twists round until his face is so close to Harry's that he can smell the morning coffee on his breath.

"Take great care, Haddon," Rice hisses. "I have powerful friends in high places. If you want to spend time in prison for assault, you are going the right way about it. Now, you release me at once, or I shall have no hesitation in summoning up a constable and having you taken down to the nearest police office and charged. And then what would your precious little sweetheart think, eh?"

The two men lock eyes. Harry stares into the black depths of his adversary, and sees nothing there he recognises. No flicker of humanity. Nothing redemptive. Nothing that is worth sacrificing his future for.

He lifts his hand away from Rice's arm and releases him. Rice tips his hat mockingly and strides off. As he walks away, swinging his cane jauntily, Harry can hear him laughing.

****

Detective Sergeant Jack Cully is having problems with teeth. Not his own, which are perfectly sound, but those of the latest addition to the Cully family. A teething child is a sleepless child, and a sleepless child means a sleep-deprived parent.

Cully had forgotten the awful greyness of a day without proper sleep. It doesn't help that Violet Cully is going through an interrogative phase, where 'because that's just how it is,' does not satisfy her need to find out.

Cully always thought he was a reasonably intelligent man. Now, he realises how little he knows of the world around him. He doesn't know why stars shine, why water is wet, where the moon goes during the day, and how horses turn hay into … well, best not to think about that one.

On and on it goes, from the moment his feet cross the threshold, to the moment Violet's eyes close in sleep and Cully sinks gratefully into his armchair by the hearth, where his attempts to regale Emily his wife with highlights from whatever newspaper Stride has thrown into the waste-paper basket in disgust, are interrupted by the baby grizzling and demanding attention.

Cully is so exhausted that sometimes, he falls asleep at his desk. In future times, this will be called a power-nap. In 1866, it is a reason for demotion. Cully is fortunate that he is a popular detective, and the men know what he is going through.

A cautious knock at his door wakes him from one of those deep, black-hole dreams. It takes him a few seconds to remember where he is. Cully rises and goes to the door. One of the impossibly young fresh-faced constables is standing there.

"Two ladies are here to see you, sir."

Cully notes the lack of air-quotation marks around the word 'ladies', meaning that whoever these ladies are, they do not belong to the usual euphemistic meaning of the word. He follows the constable to the outer office.

Lilith Marks and her daughter Essie are sitting on the Anxious Bench. Cully greets them warmly and invites them into his office. When they are seated, he leans against the front of the desk, "I am afraid we are no further in our investigations," he says apologetically.

Paradoxically, Essie's face is alive with excitement. "But I know who he is!" she exclaims. She digs in her pocket and produces the button necklace, which she hands to the detective sergeant.

"I found this button caught in the windowsill of my workshop. It was clear that it came from the jacket of the person who'd broken the window. It must've got caught as he reached in to set the fire. I have kept it, hoping to discover who this man was. And now I know!"

Essie tells Cully about her first, and subsequent meeting with Harry Haddon.

"Mr Haddon kindly sent the button back, with the man's name. Mr Anthony Rice. I have his address also." She places a piece of paper onto his desk. " So you see, all you have to do is go round to his apartment and arrest him!"

Jack Cully breathes in sharply. "Did you actually see him set the fire, Essie?"

Essie shakes her head.

"Did this Mr Haddon see him?"

Another shake.

"Then we cannot arrest him. I know this isn't what you want to hear, Essie, but consider the facts: you have a button ~ but what if this man says it is not his, that you or your friend, or his own servant made a mistake? Or he could say he was passing your business and lost it trying to put out the fire? Do you see what I mean?"

"But it was him," Essie persists.

"How can you be sure?"

"I sense it. I have held that button in my hand ever since I found it, and when I read his name, then I knew."

Cully pulls a face. He is hating this. Essie's expression is so full of passionate conviction, and he now has to pour cold water all over her bright hopes.

"Essie, you must believe me: no judge in the land would convict a man on the hearsay of what you have told me. There needs to be a witness. Someone who actually saw him break the window and set the fire. Someone who is prepared to stand up in court and accuse him. Your friend was not there. You were not there. Therefore, there is nothing we can do. I am so very sorry."

Essie stares at him in disbelief. "But how can this be?" she exclaims. "What use is the law of the land when someone is allowed to break it and get away unpunished? How is that fair? It isn't fair! I cannot accept it! I won't accept it!"

Cully closes his eyes to better focus his mind. Essie's impetuous outpouring reminds him, on a different level altogether, of his own small daughter. Everything has to be black or white, right or wrong. There can be nothing in the middle.

"Life isn't fair, Essie, you and I both know that," he says patiently. "Sometimes we just have to accept that things aren't going to go the way we want them to. You have created a new life for yourself. You have found your loving mother, and a whole new community to support you.

"Now you have also managed to pick yourself up from a disaster and start again. Isn't that something to be proud of? I wish I could arrest this man for you, Essie, I really do. Believe me, it would give me no greater pleasure, but without sufficient proof, I would be wasting my time, and yours."

Essie's eyes flash sparks. She opens her mouth ~ but before she can launch into another outburst, Lilith puts a hand on her arm.

"Enough. Let us go home, Essie. There is nothing more we can do here. Mr Cully is right: we don't have enough proof. I know how hard this is for you, but we must just accept it."

Essie's face flushes, and she looks as if she is about to make another protest, but Lilith puts a hand under her elbow and levers her to her feet. Not making eye contact with either of them, Essie shakes herself free and stalks to the door.

"Thank Mr Cully for doing his best to help you," Lilith says, in the tone of voice Emily uses when she is chastising Violet over some breach of etiquette. But Essie ignores her mother's request and continues walking. Lilith meets Cully's gaze and spreads her hands in the time-honoured gesture of parental helplessness.

The two women enter the outer office, heading for the street door. And then Lilith's eye is suddenly caught by one of the Wanted notices pinned on the board. She stops. She stares hard. She screws up her eyes in an effort to concentrate better. After which, she walks over to the board and unpins the notice.

Telling Essie crisply to sit on the bench and wait for her, Lilith goes to find Jack Cully.

****

Night-time London is all twinkle and shine. It is gaiety, glitter and trickery. Secrets and fantasy elide. A slippage between real and unreal, the familiar and the strange. A condition of the partially illuminated darkness of gaslit thoroughfares.

Here, at Granthams Club, off Bow Street, the dining-room is full of swaggering rakish young swells, enjoying their dinner before venturing on to whatever swaggering rakish entertainments await their patronage.

All except for one diner. Harry Haddon sits on his own, toying with a plate of roast beef. He is not feeling twinkly or shiny. Nor does he have a destination. The reason for his discontent is seated at an adjoining table: Anthony Rice, with his familiars, Giles Cooper and David (Duke) Stuchberry.

From the raucous laughter, and almost constant sideways glances in his direction, it is clear that he is both subject and butt of their discourse. It is a hard and bitter pill, but he dares not show by any flicker of expression that he knows what they are saying, nor cares if he does.

Eventually, Rice snaps his fingers to summon one of the hovering waiters.

"A bottle of your finest champagne, Edwards. I wish to treat my good, loyal and true friends here!" he exclaims in a loud voice.

The waiter glides away, shortly returning with a silver tray, an ice bucket, three champagne flutes and two members of the Scotland Yard detective division, who position themselves either side of Rice's chair.

"Hey! What is all this?" he demands angrily.

The taller of the two detectives, a handsome moustached individual with broad shoulders and an expression that says he does not care at all for posturing young men, whatever class they might come from, introduces himself as Detective Inspector Lachlan Greig.

"I believe I am addressing Mr Anthony Rice?" he says in a Scottish accent.

"What of it?"

"Ah, so I am correct, then. Mr Rice ~ your man told me I might find you here. I must request that you accompany myself and Detective Sergeant Cully down to Scotland Yard."

Rice's face encrimsons with anger.

"What the blazes? I shall not! Indeed, I shall not! The very idea! Oh, I know what this is about. He ~" he shouts, pointing at Harry, "that weasel Harry Haddon over there, that snivelling sneak has been telling you some cock and bull tale about a lost button, which he thinks is mine and was found at some Hebrew woman's shop that got burned out.

"He is lying! If anybody should be arrested, it is him, for persecuting me and wasting your time. I suggest you ignore what he says, and be on your way, my good man. I shall say no more about this ~ I could make it very hot for you if I chose, believe me, but I will let it go. This time."

Greig's expression during this outburst is that of a crouching tiger. Focused, intent upon its prey and waiting to spring at exactly the right moment.

The moment arrives.

"I'm afraid I am not your good man, nor do I have any knowledge of this matter," he says smoothly. "I am investigating the brutal murder of Mr Giovanni Bellini, an elderly Italian citizen, formerly resident in London. You have been identified as the assailant, and I have a witness who was there on the night in question and who can prove it. He is a fellow compatriot of the dead man, and is waiting at Scotland Yard to identify you. If he does, he is prepared to swear under oath to seeing you attack the defenceless elderly man.

"I believe the Italian Ambassador is also eager to question you, as Mr Bellini was a highly regarded citizen in his own country. Now, you can come quietly, Mr Rice, or I can summon my men, who are waiting just outside, and remove you by force. It is your choice."

Greig takes a whistle out of his top pocket. The dining room, which is normally so loud one has to shout to make oneself heard, instantly falls completely silent. Everybody's eyes are fixed, like the Roman audience at a gladiatorial contest, upon the two men.

As Greig raises the whistle to his lips, Rice abruptly thrusts back his chair with such force that it crashes to the ground.

"Alright! Hang it! No need for that. I am coming," he blusters.

Greig calmly replaces the whistle. "And your two friends as well," he adds, his eyes raking Cooper and Stuchberry, who are desperately trying to pretend they are not present. "I gather the group of men who set upon the Italians was three in number. I should like my witness to take a wee look at them too," and he bestows upon the two bucks the sort of smile that lurks on sandbanks awaiting unwary swimmers.

The three young men are escorted from the dining room. There is a long pause after they have gone. Then the conversations resume, as if they were never there in the first place. The waiter still stands by the empty table, balancing his tray. Harry beckons him over.

"I shall take a glass of champagne," he says. "Just put it on Mr Rice's bill, if you would."

The waiter pours the frothing liquid into a glass and hands it over. Harry Haddon sips the ice-cold champagne and thinks about the strange and unexpected turn of events. There is so much to think about, that it takes him some time and several glasses of champagne.

At the end of his cogitations, Harry has pretty well worked things out, except for one curious thing: as the group passed by his table, he could have sworn the second detective glanced in his direction, then deliberately closed one eye in a wink.

But that would have been totally unprofessional, and as he is now on his sixth glass of champagne, he assumes he must have imagined it.

****

The village of Richmond might be only a few miles outside London, but it could be in another country altogether. In the green lanes and small hamlets, time seems to move at a different pace to the frenetic city.

At Haddon Hall, time barely moves at all. Or so it seems to Lady Marie Haddon. One day follows another. The Summer sun blazes in cloudless radiance, followed by the breezes of Autumn, that send the leaves of the trees skittering and dancing.

Lady Marie's hands lie idle in her silken lap, which is surprising, given the diverse choices available to her.

Her pianoforte is open and covered with sheets of music. Her easel stands by the window, bearing witness to her artistic talents in the shape of a water-colour sketch of the trees in the park.

Her delicate embroideries and workbox with rainbow-hued silks and wools await her nimble fingers. Nothing is lacking. Yet instead of filling her time usefully with one of the many ladylike occupations available to her, she is staring pensively out of the window, her large clear eyes focussed upon nothing in particular, feeling as wretched in this elegant room as any half-starved seamstress in a dreary garret.

The reason for her misery can be traced back to earlier in the day. Breakfast was over and Lady Marie, having given orders to the cook for the evening meal, was walking through the house, checking that all the surfaces were shiny.

Sir Nicholas set great store by shiny surfaces, clean linen and well-brushed carpets. Having inspected the ground floor and the first floor, and found it satisfactory, she decided to venture up a flight and visit the school room. It had surfaces, after all.

Lady Marie had sidled into the room with an apologetic cough. Her small son and Mr Bellini were engaged in turning a globe, the tutor pointing to countries, the boy naming them and their capital cities. It was a perfect picture.

But as soon as he saw his mother standing in the doorway, her son's face darkened. He folded his little arms, stuck out his bottom lip and glared at her.

"Go away, Mama!" he exclaimed petulantly. "I don't want you here!"

Shocked to the core, Lady Marie had advanced a few steps into the room, holding out her arms to him. Alas, instead of running into them, the little boy had retreated to the far side of the room and defiantly turned his back on her.

"Danny!" she'd gasped, a sob in her voice.

The small boy did not turn his head. "I am a man now, father says. I must learn my lessons so that I can make my way in the world."

The tutor, who had watched the little exchange without comment, went over to the boy. He bent down and said something in Italian. Immediately, the boy lifted his head, smiled, and took his hand.

"We must finish our work, Danielo. Then you will spend some time with your Mama. Playtime is as important as learning."

"Aww, must I?" the boy pouted. "I'd rather play up here with you."

The tutor shook his head. "Mama and Papa are your family. You must always obey and love them."

He made Lady Marie a low bow. "I shall bring Danielo down for his luncheon as usual, signora," he said.

Not waiting to hear the wailed protest, she had slipped away, tears sliding down her cheeks. To have her relationship with her beloved son mediated by a stranger was unbearable. Before the tutor arrived, Danny was hers. His love for her was absolute. She was his entire world, as he was hers. She cannot bear it if she is to lose that precious bond between them.

Luncheon was eaten in sulky silence, her son picking at his food and shooting her dark glances from under lowered brows. Lady Marie barely touched her food. Her mind was in uproar. Little by little, day by day, the young Italian has stolen her son from her!

And her husband is in his power as well. How often did Sir Nicholas turn to Bellini to discuss matters of the day or talk about some Italian painter or philosopher that she knew nothing about.

This is the cause of her current distress. But as the long afternoon drags its weary way towards the return of her husband, and the ringing of the dinner gong, Lady Marie's secret anguish turns to something more focused: she must win back the love of her boy. But how?

Various stratagems come to mind, though it takes a while before the memory of the incriminating letter that the tutor left so carelessly by his plate surfaces. Surely something can be made of it? Lady Marie's thoughts circle and settle. She sits on, thinking it through.

If she tells her husband, she might destroy Harry's forthcoming marriage. Lady Marie has no quarrel with her stepson. He always arrives at Haddon Hall laden with treats and sweetmeats for his small stepbrother.

But can she just discard her strongest weapon? No, she cannot and she will not. A mother's love overrules all else. She has only a short time in which to bind her boy to her with strong cords of maternal love before he is sent away to some preparatory school.

The plan slowly forms. She will wait until tomorrow, when her husband is out of the house. Then she will confront the tutor with what she knows about his secret affair. She will point out the untenability of his position, in the light of Juliana's engagement to her step-son. She will advise him to pack his bags and leave Haddon Hall, before Sir Nicholas discovers his secret.

Lady Marie spends some time rehearsing what she intends to say, and the tone of voice in which she will say it, until the sound of the front door slamming heralds the arrival of Sir Nicholas Haddon. Home early, for a change. He enters the sitting room. In his hand is a copy of *The Times*. He greets his wife in a distracted manner.

"See here," he says, handing Lady Marie the paper. It is folded back to an article headlined: **The secret life and tragic death of Mr G. Bellini, Italian Anarchist & Revolutionary**

"This man was the grandfather of our tutor. That is where he was when he skipped off without a 'by your leave'. We have been sheltering a revolutionary's offspring. Our boy is being tutored by the grandson of an anarchist! An *anarchist*! Good God! I blame myself entirely. Heaven knows what ideas he might have put into the boy's mind."

Scarcely believing her luck, Lady Marie skim-reads the article.

"Danny's behaviour has certainly … changed since the tutor has arrived," she says carefully, trying to be truthful.

Sir Nicholas pulls at his chin with his thumb and forefinger, always a sign he is thinking hard.

"I want the boy to have all the opportunities his poor brother never lived to enjoy," he says slowly. "But I think, my dear, we will have to find somebody else after all. If it got out that we were employing the grandson of a known revolutionary as a private tutor, it might spoil his chances of getting into a top public school. It is a shame ~ I warmed to the young man: there was something about him I very much liked, and I know the boy likes him too. But it cannot be helped."

Lady Marie gathers herself. Unexpected and un-looked for, her moment has arrived.

"I am perfectly happy to take charge of Danny's lessons. I was thinking only the other day that I'd like to take him to the British Museum ~ there is a lot that he could learn about ancient civilizations."

Sir Nicholas eyes her speculatively.

"And then there is the Zoological Gardens and the National Gallery. So much of London that he has never experienced," she continues. "He is quite old enough to accompany me, and it would be a joy to instruct him. Truthfully, I am not sure being stuck in the schoolroom all day is good for his health. He has looked rather peaky of late. Children are so precious and fragile."

There ~ the link between the two boys, one living, one dead, has been made. Lady Marie smiles brightly and confidently at her husband. A way out of her trouble has presented itself, and she has not had to do a single thing at all.

Now all that remains is for her to reinforce the tutor's departure, without seeming to want it too much. It must be her husband's decision. Then, once the young man who captured her son's heart and all his love is sent packing, she can regain her position again.

"I shall speak to Mr Bellini after dinner," Sir Nicholas says, frowning. "He does not have to leave at once ~ after all, it is not as if he has committed any crime. I shall explain the situation ~ I'll tell him we require a tutor more familiar with the English style of teaching, and give him until the month's end to pack his things. Does that suit you, my dear?"

"Whatever you think is best, Nicholas. I am always guided by you." Lady Marie says evenly. And she stares down into her silken lap so that her husband cannot see the joy and triumph in her eyes.

****

A damp rain-soaked morning, the streets slushy with mud and animal excrement. Gutter overflow and drip. Carriage wheels throw up a noxious brown spray that coats unfortunate passers-by. Umbrellas spin out of control and courtesy has gone out of the window as people jostle and complain their way to work.

Jack Cully crosses the Covent Garden piazza, warily picking his way over rotten fruit and peelings. He has finally mastered the skill of walking while half-asleep. Reaching his destination, he pushes open the door and stands in the front office, gathering his thoughts for the day ahead. Slowly, he realises that something feels different. The atmosphere is loud with the silence of calamity.

Cully glances interrogatively at the desk constable, who jerks his thumb towards Stride's office. Cully hurries in that direction, finding his colleague Lachlan Greig and a couple of constables lurking outside the door.

"What's up?" he inquires.

Greig shakes his head. "You'll not have heard the news then? Those three young men, the ones we arrested on suspicion of murder and arson, have been released overnight. Orders from on high came in last thing yesterday, and he," he jerks his thumb in the direction of the closed door, "is not a happy man."

Indeed, the sounds of profane language, and items being thrown round the room can clearly be heard.

"What orders?"

"It would appear that Mr Anthony Rice's mother is a close relative of Lord Derby and petitioned to have her son and his friends released from our custody and sent straight back to their families. A letter was hand-delivered from the Home Secretary. We are not to pursue the matter any further. The higher-ups cannot allow their sons to be made the subject of a court case, possibly leading to their deaths by hanging. After all, what are the lives of a few 'filthy foreigners' in comparison to the lives of the English aristocracy, eh? No contest."

Greig makes no attempt to keep the withering scorn out of his voice. Cully stands in silence for a few minutes, taking in the news. The sounds emanating from the other side of the door continue. The two constables look as if they are mentally taking notes.

"Well, there's no help for it, we'd better go in," Cully says. He gives the door a gentle knock, then pushes it open.

Stride is standing by the begrimed window. The two detectives edge cautiously round the piles of paperwork strewn all over the floor. They try not to notice the ink splatter on the far wall.

"You'll have both heard the glad tidings, I presume?" Stride growls.

They nod.

"Justice has not been done."

"Ah well, we are not concerned with justice," Greig says drily. "We are functionaries. Thief-takers. We are mere enforcers of the law of the land."

Stride's face flushes. "You think like a policeman."

"Maybe because that is what I am," Greig says calmly.

Stride slams his fist against the wall. "There is a limit, Lachlan. A line in the sand. And it has been crossed. Two innocent men have died in horrific circumstances. A young woman has had her livelihood destroyed, and nearly lost her life also.

"Given time, I am quite sure we could link those men to each of the three cases. Maybe more. But we aren't going to be allowed to. Instead, they can walk free, because their upper-class families don't want a public scandal.

"You should have seen their smirking faces when we unlocked the cells and told them they could leave. I expect they now think that they are protected from the forces of law and order for ever, and can do exactly what they want. Well, they aren't, and they can't. Not on my watch. Gentlemen, the time has finally come: I am going outside; I may be some time."

"Where are you off to?" Cully asks.

"I am going to do something I have never ever done before," Stride replies. "I am about to give various members of the press an 'anonymous' tip-off. If you do not wish me to do this, for whatever reason, you can always try to stop me."

Stride lifts his coat and hat from the peg and walks towards the door of his office. Neither man tries to stop him.

****

Ten days after Stride's announcement, two young belles meet in the conservatory of the Pantheon. With the aviary and its warbling occupants, and the gentle plashing of the fountain in the background, it is a pleasant and safe place for young ladies to gather.

There is a pot of tea, three cups, a plate of cakes and an air of expectation, for Charlotte Rockingham and Juliana Silverton have both received the same brief little note from Alicia Downe-Edwards urgently summoning them to attend her in this place, at this hour.

Naturally, she is late. Alicia's lack of punctuality is notorious. That she arrived on time for her own wedding was greeted with universal surprise at the time. But her absence is allowing various lurid and unlikely scenarios to be dreamed up by the other two. They are thoroughly enjoying themselves.

Eventually, Alicia breezes in, greeting her friends as if they are the tardy ones, before sinking into one of the plump armchairs with a sigh. Charlotte and Juliana watch her remove her gloves, carefully puffing into the fingers. Then she looks up at them and smiles triumphantly in an I-know-something-you-do-not manner. They lean forward, their eyes bright with expectation.

"Well," Alicia drawls. "I bring amazing news. You will never guess what has happened."

"Are you to be congratulated, dearest?" Charlotte asks.

"What? No, no indeed, it is not *that*, thank goodness. Something far worse! Fiona Blythe has gone."

"Gone? Where has she gone?" Juliana gasps.

"My dears, she has *eloped*," Alicia pauses dramatically, tossing her raven curls for added emphasis. Then she continues, "My Mama had it from Mrs Teagarden, whose maid heard it from the Blythe's house-keeper. Apparently that young man she met at your ball, Jules, the one none of us liked, got into some terrible scrape ~ it was in all the newspapers, and his parents decided to send him abroad.

"His father is a high-up in the Colonial Office, so they arranged for him to go out to a hill station in India, and Fiona has gone with him! She only found out he was going at the last minute, and when she received his letter, she just packed her things ~ not a word to her parents, mind, crept out of the house in the middle of the night, found a cab and followed him to the docks."

"Oh, my goodness me!" Charlotte says, clasping her hands in delight. "How very like her. She always reminded me of a cat we used to have. Once it spotted a mouse, it would never give up until it had caught the poor creature and killed it."

"Well, she has caught her mouse now, and I wish her joy of him," Alicia says.

"Are they not married then?" Juliana asks.

Alicia shrugs. "Who knows. They weren't when they left London. I gather they could be married by the ship's captain. Such things are possible. But the scandal! To go off like that! Her parents are mortified: her Mama has taken to her bed, and her sister is beside herself with fury."

She picks up one of the little sponge cakes and eats it in two bites. Meanwhile her two companions sit in silence, absorbing what they have just been told.

"It must be very hot in India," Charlotte remarks eventually.

"Oh, appallingly hot. I looked up the place where she has gone in an atlas and there is nothing there but jungle. Miles and miles of jungle. No nice shops, or little places to eat. None of her friends or family are out there. And there are snakes!"

Juliana tries to imagine Fiona's future with Anthony Rice (Harry has enlightened her a little about the sort of person he is), plus snakes and heat.

"Do you think she will ever come back?" she asks thoughtfully.

Alicia shrugs. "I don't think so," she says, reaching for another cake. "Not for years and years, at least. But at least she has got a man at last, so we need not waste any more time feeling sorry for her. Now, I suggest after we've drunk our delicious tea, we go and look at winter bonnets ~ I have seen a display of the most darling ones in a little milliner's shop off Regent Street."

Juliana claps her hands together, and beams at her two companions. In her mind's eye, she pictures the church, a balmy spring day, an arch of white roses and herself, the beautiful blushing bride walking down the aisle on her father's arm, followed by her bridesmaids, one of whom, thankfully, will not now be in attendance, spoiling the sweetness of the occasion with her sour face.

"Oh yes, please let us do exactly that!" she agrees happily.

****

The month turns. Autumn surrenders to the web of Winter, which is already spinning itself round the crowded city. The first London fog has settled in, and the newly lit gas-lamps hiss and flicker.

Look more closely.

The sound of solitary footsteps echo along a street, heralding the figure of a young man wrapped in a greatcoat and carrying a travelling bag. It is Angelo Bellini. He has quit his job as a private tutor and left Haddon Hall with its chilly occupants. He still recalls the sobs of his young pupil, the small arms flung round his waist, and the triumphant smile on the face of his mother, as she prised the boy away and carried him off to her own sitting-room.

Now, he is about to depart the foggy grey city as well. He steps out boldly, for he is heading towards London Bridge Station, where the train to Dover is soon to arrive. His pocket contains a single ticket for the night packet to Calais.

The young man's thoughts are already travelling ahead of him to his native land. In his mind's eye, he sees clear blue skies, warm sunshine, lemon trees blowing in the soft breeze, and the dear faces of his parents, who'd discovered him when he was just a small child in a sailor suit, lying unconscious and abandoned on one of the thousands of small beaches that dot the Italian coastline.

In time, he had regained consciousness, unable to remember his name, but able to recite several pieces of Latin verse, and when his real parents couldn't be traced, they had adopted him and brought him up as their own son.

The tutor reaches the outskirts of the busy station. For a moment he hesitates, as if recalling something liminal, on the edge of a memory. The tail end of a sad dream. Then he shakes his head dismissively and crosses the road. Angelo Bellini enters the brightly-lit station and disappears.

He will not come back.

Finis

Thank you for reading this book. If you have enjoyed it, why not leave a review on Amazon and recommend it to other readers. All reviews, however long or short, help me to continue doing what I do.